TRIAL BY FIRE

Jake saw Carl come crashing through the underbrush into his field of vision, shoving over a pair of saplings as he charged directly forward. Jake held his ground and drew careful aim, bracing for Carl's laser attack, which impacted directly on Jake's chest, melting armor and digging down to the myomer beneath. He could feel the scorching heat of the attack, but painkillers automatically administered by the suit cleared his mind for the counterattack.

Triggering all his weapons, the machine gun scored a line of bullet-holes across Carl's left leg and torso, while both SRMs found their target and hit directly in the chest, the twin explosions momentarily blinding Jake to their effects on the target.

Jake walked casually toward the fallen battle armor, the spent SRM pack falling from his suit's back automatically to reduce encumbrance, not that that advantage would be required in this battle. As the smoke cleared, Jake could clearly see that Carl was beaten.

Carl raised his suit's left-arm claw in salute. "You have won this trial, and my respect, Jake Kabrinski. I honestly hope that is enough to keep you alive on the front lines."

Jake raised his own suit's claw, returning the salute. "More than enough, old man. More than enough. . . ."

TEST OF
VENGEANCE

Bryan Nystul

A ROC BOOK

ROC
Published by New American Library, a division of
Penguin Putnam Inc., 375 Hudson Street,
New York, New York 10014, U.S.A.
Penguin Books Ltd, 80 Strand,
London WC2R 0RL, England
Penguin Books Australia Ltd, 250 Camberwell Road,
Camberwell, Victoria 3124, Australia
Penguin Books Canada Ltd, 10 Alcorn Avenue,
Toronto, Ontario, Canada M4V 3B2
Penguin Books (N.Z.) Ltd, 182–190 Wairau Road,
Auckland 10, New Zealand

Penguin Books Ltd, Registered Offices:
Harmondsworth, Middlesex, England

First published by Roc, an imprint of New American Library,
a division of Penguin Putnam Inc.

First Printing, June 2001
10 9 8 7 6 5 4

Series Editor: Donna Ippolito
Mechanical Drawings: Duane Loose and the FASA art department
Cover art by Dough Chaffee

 REGISTERED TRADEMARK—MARCA REGISTRADA

Printed in the United States of America

PUBLISHER'S NOTE
This is a work of fiction. Names, characters, places, and incidents either
are the product of the author's imagination or are used fictitiously,
and any resemblance to actual persons, living or dead, events, business
establishments, or locales is entirely coincidental.

ACKNOWLEDGMENTS

I could never have pulled this off without the help and inspiration of many, many people. I have to start by thanking FASA for giving me a shot at this, especially my editor for juggling my deadlines and BattleTech protégé Randall Bills for being there to lend a hand (which turned out to be needed more often than I had planned) and pushing to finish his own first novel so I could finally convince myself I could do it. Thanks to Herb Beas for the loan of the Hell's Horses (you can have them back now). To Jill, Jim, Sharon, Fred, Diane, Sam and all the others at FASA who have helped me over the years, I can never thank you enough. I want you all to know it was a great ride. Especially that unforgettable night in Frankfurt (you know what I'm talking about, Mike . . .)

Speaking of inspiration, there is none more powerful for me than music. Without great tunes flowing through my head, I doubt I would have ever been able to start this book, let alone finish it. I literally cannot imagine a world without music, so even though the artists will most likely never see this themselves, I offer humble thanks to the following, in no particular order, for giving color and intensity to an often drab world: Metallica, John Williams, XTC, Danny Elfman (with and without Oingo Boingo), They Might Be Giants, Barenaked Ladies, Pop Will Eat Itself, Rob Zombie (with and without White Zombie), U2, Wolfgang Amadeus Mozart, R.E.M., Talking Heads, Pink Floyd (with and without Roger Waters), Duran Duran, Beastie Boys, Pet Shop Boys, INXS, Ozzy Osbourne, Nine Inch Nails, "Weird" Al Yankovic, Tears for Fears, Stan Ridgeway (with and without Wall of Voodoo), Mighty Mighty Bosstones, DEVO, and the countless others that slipped my mind.

Of course, I wouldn't be here today if not for my parents (quite literally), so thanks to Brad and Genny for not forcing me to play football and letting me putter around with role-playing games and read a bunch of books (even comic books!) instead. Finally, while I'm on the subject of family, there's no one more important to me than my big brother who led the way for me in so many ways. How can I begin to thank a guy who pulls double duty as closest relative and best friend, with occasional stints as psychiatrist and land-lord on the side? Thanks. And please, never stop reminding me that it's all worth it.

This book is dedicated to Genevieve Louise Nystul. More than any one other person, she was directly responsible for nurturing my love of reading and writing (not to mention music). During my grade school years, my brother and I were fortunate to be able to go home for lunch, where she would read "grown-up books" to us every day while we ate. I didn't realize it back then, but the books she chose comprised a veritable laundry list of science fiction and fantasy classics, including such series as *Foundation, The Chronicles of Narnia, Dune*, and *The Lord of the Rings*. Although I never actually planned to be a writer, looking back on those formative years, it is no surprise to me now that I find myself penning a novel.

I miss you, Mom. Thanks for everything.

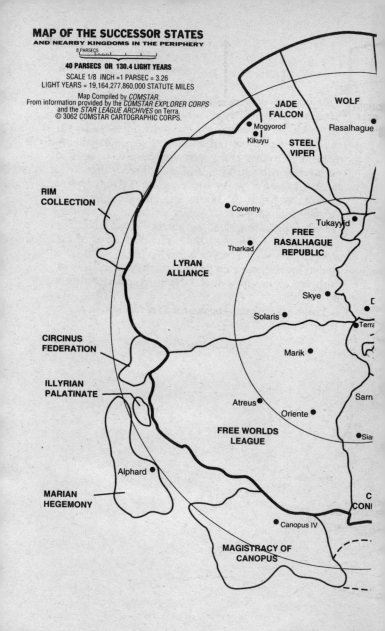

MAP OF THE SUCCESSOR STATES
AND NEARBY KINGDOMS IN THE PERIPHERY

8 PARSECS

40 PARSECS OR 130.4 LIGHT YEARS

SCALE 1/8 INCH = 1 PARSEC = 3.26
LIGHT YEARS = 19,164,277,860,000 STATUTE MILES

Map Compiled by COMSTAR.
From information provided by the COMSTAR EXPLORER CORPS
and the STAR LEAGUE ARCHIVES on Terra.
© 3062 COMSTAR CARTOGRAPHIC CORPS.

JADE
FALCON

WOLF

Mogyorod

Rasalhague

Kikuyu

STEEL
VIPER

RIM
COLLECTION

Coventry

Tukayyid

FREE
RASALHAGUE
REPUBLIC

Tharkad

LYRAN
ALLIANCE

Skye

D

Solaris

Terra

CIRCINUS
FEDERATION

Marik

ILLYRIAN
PALATINATE

Sarn

Atreus

Oriente

FREE WORLDS
LEAGUE

Sia

MARIAN
HEGEMONY

Alphard

C
CONI

Canopus IV

MAGISTRACY OF
CANOPUS

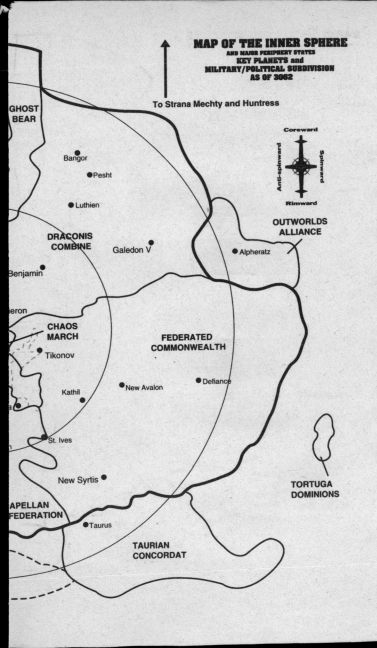

MAP OF THE INNER SPHERE
AND MAJOR PERIPHERY STATES
KEY PLANETS and
MILITARY/POLITICAL SUBDIVISION
AS OF 3062

To Strana Mechty and Huntress

Coreward

Anti-spinward

Spinward

Rimward

GHOST BEAR

Bangor

Pesht

Luthien

DRACONIS COMBINE

Galedon V

OUTWORLDS ALLIANCE

Alpheratz

Benjamin

CHAOS MARCH

ieron

Tikonov

FEDERATED COMMONWEALTH

New Avalon

Defiance

Kathil

St. Ives

New Syrtis

TORTUGA DOMINIONS

APELLAN FEDERATION

Taurus

TAURIAN CONCORDAT

Prologue

Hell's Horses Field Command Center
Talon Ridge, Bearclaw
Kerensky Cluster, Clan Space
5 December 3061

The force of a distant explosion rumbled through the floor of the field command center, but Malavai Fletcher, Khan of Clan Hell's Horses, barely noticed. Hunched over the glow of a portable holographic projector, he studied the terrain features of Talon Ridge and the variously colored icons representing his forces arrayed against those of Clans Ghost Bear and Snow Raven.

It had all looked so good on paper.

Fletcher and his force had already won away a good portion of the Bearclaw holdings the Bears had gifted to the Snow Ravens. Then came Talon Ridge.

A strategic choke point, it overlooked the valley that constituted the only land route between the mines and factories in the hills to the south and the nearest spaceport some thirty kilometers to the north. Fletcher had moved the bulk of his forces here to cut off Snow Raven access to the factories—a maneuver he'd expected to accomplish easily. Instead, he found himself sandwiched between the Ravens and a horde of Ghost Bear Elementals that had turned up yesterday. Unknown to Fletcher, some Ghost Bear troops had yet to abandon the planet and had been guarding the factory complex and surrounding hills for their Raven allies. Fletcher's DropShips, intended to carry off the spoils of war, were now being prepped for the unthinkable: retreat.

He had been poring over the tactical data for what seemed like hours, desperately searching for a way to snatch victory from the jaws of defeat.

The jaws of the Ghost Bear, he thought, the Clan that had brutally attacked the Horses on Niles fifteen years ago, leaving him the mutilated Khan of a mutilated Clan. What in the name of Kerensky were they doing here, blocking his progress? He was anxious to begin his journey to the Inner Sphere, and he did not intend to be delayed by these *stravags*.

"Those damn Bears were supposed to be in the Inner Sphere by now!" he roared, slamming his massive, battle-armored claw against the steel table, denting it and raising a shower of sparks.

Star Colonel Alicia Ravenwater, his second in command, glanced up from her handputer.

"My Khan," she said, "Alpha Keshik is prepared for our final push. We will make those meddling Bears pay for this as we pull back to—"

"We will *not* retreat from *them!*" Fletcher bellowed as he spun to face her, raising his armored claw in defiance. "We will *never* retreat from the accursed Ghost Bears. Not so long as I draw breath, so help me, Kerensky!"

Malavai Fletcher—with his ruined face and head—looked fearsome at the best of times. Dressed in his battle armor, a head-to-toe suit of high-tech metal weighing more than a ton, he transformed from a merely imposing Elemental into a raging monster. The right side of his shaved head consisted almost entirely of steel plates and ropelike myomer bundles. The gleaming metal contrasted with the scant bit of flesh that showed under his armor, and sweat dripped from his protruding brow into his good eye. He had lost the other eye in the battle on Niles, and Clan scientists had replaced it with an efficient cybernetic device that glowed a menacing red in the dim light of the holodisplay.

"I have no desire to retreat, my Khan. You know me well enough for that. I have been at your side for more than ten years. Have I not proven my tactical abilities time and again?"

Fletcher nodded silently, but he glowered even more in frustration.

"We have already claimed nearly a third of Bearclaw," she went on, "which gives us many other bases from which to regroup for another strike. Our position here has been compromised. The Ravens will have regained air superiority within the hour, blocking our DropShips from liftoff. We have no choice. We must withdraw now or face the loss of both our Khan and his Keshik."

As she spoke, Fletcher absent-mindedly flexed the endo-steel fingers of his battle claw. He glanced again at the holomap and realized that he was looking in the wrong place for the wrong thing. The situation did not allow for a winning plan, but it *did* allow for a course of action fit for a warrior.

"Once again, you are correct, Alicia Ravenwater. Have your star captains begin loading their OmniMechs onto the DropShips." He spoke from deep in his chest, soft but threatening, like a distant thunderstorm.

She offered him a crisp salute. "What of the rest of the Keshik's forces, my Khan?"

Fletcher reached up with his claw and lowered his faceplate into position. The seals hissed as they enclosed him fully in his Gnome battle armor, the Hell's Horse heavy-duty variation on the standard version. The suit's external speakers amplified his already resonant voice. "We may be withdrawing this day, but we will not surrender Talon Ridge to the Ghost Bears without a fight.

"They are honorless cowards who did not dare declare their units during the bidding for this battle. And now they expect us to turn and run with our tails between our legs. This is what we will do, Alicia.

"My Elementals and I will hold off the Claws of the Ghost, and that will give your 'Mechs enough time to board the transports. It will also give *me* enough time to teach those upstarts from Zeta Galaxy a thing or two about battle-armor combat."

The advanced sensors in the heads up display of Point Commander Jake's helmet gave him an excellent view of the terrain below. His point of five Ghost Bear Elementals were arrayed along the southern end of Talon Ridge. They were guarding the narrow pass between the hills to the south and the plains to the north, the direction from which the Snow Raven 'Mech forces were approaching.

The voice of Paul, his star commander, boomed through his battle armor's internal radio. "Status report, Delta Point. What is your situation?"

"All clear, Star Commander," Jake said. "My troops are in position. Nothing will get through this pass."

Paul gave a soft chuckle. "You are right, Jake, but not for the reason you think. Nothing will be coming through the pass, because we have learned that the Horses are withdrawing from Talon Ridge. Orbital surveillance picked up the heat signatures of their DropShips warming up. They will be long gone by the time the Ravens get here with their 'Mechs."

"Withdrawing, sir? But I thought Malavai Fletcher was with that unit—"

Paul cut him off. "I know what you thought, Jake. I have been listening to your wild suggestions all day. The fact is that *all* of their DropShips are prepping for lift-off."

"There is no way Fletcher would just abandon the field to Ghost Bear troops, Paul. His temper is legendary, and—"

"Enough, Jake!" Paul snapped. "If you were not such a valuable warrior, I would call you out for insubordination. Just keep your theories to yourself and hold your position until the Snow Ravens arrive."

Jake fumed, but remained silent. He knew there was a limit to how far he could push his commander, and he had exceeded it today.

"Relax, Jake. This battle is over. We can let the Ravens have the ridge and be damned. The sooner we board our own DropShips and get out of here, the sooner we will all be breathing Inner Sphere air."

The Inner Sphere. The place was almost mythical in Jake's mind: the birthplace of humanity, lost to the Clans since their founders had left it three centuries ago. "Why have we been kept back from joining the rest of the Ghost Bears?"

"Not that it is any of your business, *Point Commander*, but our cluster was simply not able to pull up stakes as quickly as the other Claws of the Bear. We had commitments to our allies here on Bearclaw to make sure the transfer of ownership was complete. And, as you know, the Horses invaded in the middle of the whole process so we . . . intervened."

Jake's irritation got the better of him. "And is that what justifies our using unClan-like tactics such as this ambush—" He broke off sharply when his peripheral vision caught something. He checked his heads up display. Was that a faint signal on his passive radar?

"Hold on, Star Commander. I think I spotted something at the edge of my radar range. It may be advancing on your position."

"My scanners show nothing, Jake. Don't let your paranoia ruin my good mood. Let's enjoy our victory while we can."

Jake winced at Paul's blatant use of contractions. He checked his sensors again. The signal appeared to be advancing on Paul's position on the other side of the pass. He checked the scanners for malfunction, but found everything seemed in order.

"Star Commander, there is definitely—"

"Enough," Paul said sharply. "I'm weary of these word games."

Jake looked once more at the advancing signal. Given the signal's position relative to Paul's, somebody had to do something. If Paul would not act, Jake decided he would have to, with or without orders. Paul's stubbornness could result in death for them all. Jake would prove his point where it really counted: on the field of battle.

"Delta Point," he called over his unit's frequency. "We are moving northeast. Dispersion pattern Beta."

"But Jake, our orders are to hold this pass." Valerie, his second-in-command, spoke over their private channel.

"Check your radar, Val. I am sure I saw a signal advancing on Paul's position. We cannot wait for him to come to his senses. If we move fast enough, we can flank them just as they hit."

Val hesitated for a moment. "I suppose there could be something there; the rocks are creating so much interference. I will take your word for it, Jake. I just hope you are right."

Jake laughed. "I am always right, *quiaff*?"

"Aff, so far. "

Jake engaged his jump jets, releasing plumes of super-heated plasma from the backs of his suit's calves and lifting his thousand-kilogram bulk up and over the pass to the opposite cliff face. "Do not worry, Val. Whoever is launching this surprise attack is in for a surprise of his own."

Malavai Fletcher opened a channel to his troops. "Their commander has no idea we are here. He thinks we are cowards, running from battle. Well, my Keshik, we will show him how wrong he is."

With the help of his suit's myomer musculature, Fletcher held his suit's right arm absolutely still until his HUD registered a positive target lock. In his sights was the Ghost Bear star commander, standing about two hundred meters ahead, with his back to Fletcher and his Elementals.

The Khan smiled at the thought of making the Ghost Bears pay for their meddling. "Their standard lasers cannot reach us at this range, which will give us the field for at least fifteen seconds. All Gnomes open fire on my mark."

"Sir, I have a signal coming in behind us!" It was Point Commander Harland on the open channel. Harland had only recently joined Fletcher's personal unit.

"You idiot, that was the open channel! Alpha Keshik, open fire!" Even as he spoke, Fletcher mashed his thumb down on the trigger inside his suit's right hand, firing both his extended-range support laser and a pair of Streak short-range missiles from his backpack launcher. A veteran of hundreds of battles, his aim was true, and his weapons hit their marks flawlessly. In an instant, the Ghost Bear commander's battle armor was reduced to tatters, and he was knocked from his feet, barely alive.

Fletcher's people were not so accurate. They were firing dozens of ruby laser beams toward their targets, but most of them missed. The Ghost Bears, looking like pheasants flushed from hiding by a hunter's dog, had evaded by jumping into the air with their jets. Though an excellent warrior, Harland's one and only career error had cost Alpha Keshik the full element of surprise.

The Khan was not pleased. "Point Three, about-face and contain whatever is behind us. The rest of you, find your targets before we lose our range advantage. Do not forget that they are lighter—and faster—than us."

Jake exchanged laser fire with the Gnome heading for him as he jumped backward toward cover. "Delta Point, keep moving, but stay close to them."

He saw Val close in on his right flank, unleashing her short-range missiles at the nearest Gnome. Jake keyed their private channel. "Thanks for the assist, Val. Our briefings made it sound like these lumbering hulks were some kind of doomsday weapon. More like shooting diamond sharks in a barrel, I would say."

"Do not get too cocky, Jake. Once the main body turns around, we will have more ER lasers coming at us than we can handle. And each one of these guys takes an extra shot to finish off."

As if to punctuate her last statement, Val let loose a bright red laser blast at a retreating Gnome, tearing its lumpy armor to shreds and surely killing the Elemental inside.

Jake grunted agreement. "I know how tough they are, but they were not expecting us. That advantage, plus our maneuverability, will cost them this battle."

An audible beep told Jake he had an incoming radio message from Beta Point. "Delta Point?" a voice said. "Glad you made it. This is Gerald. My point commander is down, as is Star Commander Paul. Chain of command puts you in the hot seat, Jake. What is our next move?"

Jake was elated. Finally, command! Too bad Paul did not live long enough to give Jake his due. He opened the star's frequency. "Attention, troops. This is Point Commander Jake. I am in command of this star, effective immediately. We will teach these Horses that it takes more than fancy new battle armor to stop Zeta Galaxy! Alpha and Beta Points, regroup to the west. Gamma and Epsilon, take the east flank. My point will hold the center. Hit them where it hurts, Ghost Bears!"

Malavai Fletcher braced against his latest victim with the gun muzzle of his right arm, and pulled his clawed arm from the open chest of his victim, his talons dripping red blood and black HarJel in equal measure. "Sorry, Ghost Bear. No amount of HarJel will seal *that* wound."

The radio interrupted his enjoyment of the kill. It was Harland again. "Khan Malavai, the Trinary is scattered! Where are you?"

"Close enough to snap your neck, Harland. I suggest you do more fighting and less whining. Let me worry about the big picture." Fletcher reminded himself to kill Harland in a Circle of Equals, provided the idiot survived the day's fighting.

Harland's message served as an important reminder, however. Fletcher had gotten caught up in the thick of battle, wanting to personally heap revenge on these Ghost Bears. As Khan, it was his place to stay back and command the operation. Sometimes he regretted his position.

It was time to finish this, before his DropShips left without him. "Star Commander Elsa, which Ghost Bear is leading them now?"

The Hell's Horses officer was quick to respond. "From what I have been able to detect of their radio chatter, it is a Point Commander named Jake. I believe it was his point that flanked us, sir."

Then, he is as much to blame for this debacle as Harland, Fletcher thought.

"Well done, Elsa," he said. "Their radio encryption is as incompetent as they are, *quiaff*? Take command. I am going to find this Jake and *congratulate* him on his fine tactical maneuver."

Jake was pleased, both with himself and his troops. Not a single member of his point had yet fallen, while they had made twice their number in Gnome kills, thanks to the fact that the enemy troops continued to dribble into range one or two at a time.

"This is almost too easy, Jake," said Val. "Have they no commander?"

Before he could reply, a static-laden transmission broke in on his commline. "Oh, *they* have a commander all right. Look behind you, Point Commander Jake."

Jake spun around as quickly as he could, firing a blast with his laser and diving to the right even before he saw whom he was firing at. The Gnome that had sneaked up behind him must have expected such a move. Firing his jump jets, he lifted easily over the shot. Fortunately for Jake, the counterattack was off-target; had he moved left instead of right, he would have been branded.

"We will dispose of the formalities of *zellbrigen*, then?" Jake asked, only half-serious. He squeezed off another shot before engaging his jump jets again, flying up and over his opponent before he could return fire.

The Gnome answered in a loud, angry voice over the open channel. "You Bears voided the ritual of the duel when you crept up behind my force like a gang of assassins. Besides, you are not worthy to clean my armor, let alone call me out, Point Commander Jake."

"And who do I have the honor of facing this day?" Jake asked sarcastically. When the enemy Elemental turned to face him, he noticed the black band and gold horse head emblazoned on the shoulder of his armor: the rank insignia of a khan.

"No such honor is yours, boy. I am Khan Malavai Fletcher of Clan Hell's Horses, and I am not your warrior opponent this day. I am your executioner!"

With that, he unleashed a full barrage, emptying his missile launcher and firing his laser at Jake, who dropped to the ground rather than jumping up again. His quick thinking saved his life.

Fletcher's missiles had locked on, dipping down and impacting against Jake's back, ruining his own missile pack. But the laser, being a beam of coherent light, had no internal guidance. It missed Jake by a wide margin, blasting a chunk of rock into rubble and starting a chain-reaction of small explosions across the ridge.

Jake and Fletcher both froze, momentarily stunned by the strange explosions. More blasts echoed up from the canyon as Val's voice came over Jake's commline. "It is the Snow Raven aerofighters!" she gloated.

"Excellent," Jake said. "Now we have you beat on the ground and in the sky, Malavai Fletcher. I will gladly accept you as bondsman." Jake's heart raced at the possibility of taking a Khan prisoner.

The explosions had stopped; the fighters were turning around for another strafing run. Fletcher engaged his jump jets to take higher ground, while firing another laser shot to keep Jake's head down. "Never! You overestimate yourself, cub. Better men than you have tried to defeat me, and better men have died!"

As Jake stood up, he had to jump back quickly to avoid another shot. "Have it your way. Regardless, this day belongs to the Snow Ravens . . . and the Ghost Bears."

Fletcher's voice came over the radio with a roar that sounded more animal than human. His anger and outrage had completely taken over.

Oddly, the roar increased in intensity, until Jake could hardly hear himself think. Before he could puzzle out what was occurring, the answer was revealed. The deafening sound he was hearing came from a DropShip's engines. The massive vessel rose slowly over the ridge where Fletcher stood, an enormous Hell's Horses logo emblazoned on its spherical bulk. A door slid open on the ship's underside, between two massive engines spewing nuclear fire. A ramp extended out from the opening to within easy reach of the Khan.

Jake was so frustrated he pounded his armored fist against the ground. It was obvious that the DropShip would get away before the Raven fighters could circle around. He could see his enemy disappearing into the bowels of the DropShip as it lifted into the darkening sky on four pillars of exhaust.

Jake could barely make out the transmission over the thunder of the DropShip's acceleration. Then he heard Malavai Fletcher's voice once more over his radio.

"This is not over, *Point Commander* Jake," the Khan said. "Mark my words: we *will* meet again on the field of battle. And next time, there will be no Snow Ravens to save you from my wrath!"

1

It was a good day to die.

"*Ichi* company, you are cleared for drop. May the Dragon guide your actions."

"*Hai*, drop command," confirmed *Tai-i* Shiro Kanazawa. "Acknowledging clearance. Combat drop to commence on my mark."

The opening of the DropShip's exterior doors sent a shudder through Kanazawa's 'Mech as he gripped the control sticks reflexively.

"Mark."

His *Atlas*, one hundred tons of humanoid war machine, was suspended directly over the bay door by a massive pair of clamps. As the door opened, he could see the clouds below him through his 'Mech's external cameras. Wind whipped up through the 'Mech bay, and the DropShip's roaring filled his ears.

Then the clamps snapped open, dropping the four assault-class 'Mechs of Kanazawa's command lance toward the spaceport below. The hub of all flights to and from the planet, Silverdale Spaceport was the most important target on Alshain. In thirty seconds, the second lance of his company would be in position to join them in the drop, followed by the third.

Looking up, the 'Mech's head tracking with his own head movement, Kanazawa saw the DropShip falling away quickly. A *Union* Class, it was designed to carry twelve BattleMechs into combat, and could travel from deep space to a planet's surface in a matter of days. The ship's 3,500-ton spherical bulk was held aloft by four plumes of nuclear fire, its fusion engines delivering millions of pounds of thrust to keep the vessel hovering stationary while delivering its deadly cargo. On the underside of the ship, for the enemy below to see, was painted the rearing red dragon, proud symbol of House Kurita and the Draconis Combine, Kanazawa's home.

Home, in fact, was what this battle was all about. Only eleven years ago, Alshain had still belonged to the Draconis Combine, and Kanazawa had called it home. All that changed when the Clans invaded. With their genetically engineered warriors and superior array of advanced weaponry, they had arrived in the Inner Sphere in 3050, attacking world after world in a blitzkrieg campaign. Their intention was to push through all the way to Terra, birthplace of humanity, and to conquer the people of the Inner Sphere in order to impose the Clan way on them.

One of the first worlds in their path was Alshain, an important Combine strategic and industrial center. The Ghost Bear Clan had invaded the world, and they had fought with the ferocity of their alien totem. Despite the hard battle fought by the Combine's most elite MechWarriors, Alshain fell to the Bears. Six months later, the Clan offensive came to a halt when a truce was achieved, leaving Clan Ghost Bear and the others stalled in their drive toward Terra for the next fifteen years.

Kanazawa was but a child when the Ghost Bears took Alshain, and he was one of the lucky ones to make it offworld with the retreating Second Sword of Light regiment. In the years since the truce, the Ghost Bears had permanently settled their conquered territory, renaming it the Ghost Bear Dominion. As their capital, they had chosen Kanazawa's beloved Alshain. Resist as they might, the people of this world were being slowly indoctrinated into the way of the Clan. If this continued, it might be impossible to ever bring them back into the Combine.

Which was what had brought about this battle. After eleven years of exile, he was returning to his homeworld as a MechWarrior member of the Alshain Avengers, sworn to return the worlds of the lost Alshain Prefecture to the Combine at all costs. After many months of planning, the moment had come to penetrate the heart of the Ghost Bear Dominion and take back Alshain for the glory of the Dragon. Kanazawa had heard rumors that there had been some initial setbacks, but his unit was part of the main assault force, the sledge-hammer that would wrest the planet's capitol and main spaceport from Clan control and turn the tide of battle.

As the DropShip faded from view, he looked down at the ground, which was growing nearer by the second. A warning light and a klaxon prompted him to reach for the ignition. Bracing himself, he flipped the red switch labeled External Boosters.

Immediately, he felt the kick of the temporary thrusters mounted on his 'Mech's back and legs fighting with gravity to slow his descent. His head ached as his neurohelmet struggled with the BattleMech's gyroscope to maintain balance in this wild free-fall. If not for the connection provided by his neurohelmet, the 'Mech would spin out of control and his only kill would be his *Atlas* smashing into some unsuspecting Clanner below.

BattleMechs were amazing machines. The pinnacle of ground-based warfare, each 'Mech was a virtual army unto itself, forged of nearly impenetrable alloys and carrying enough weapons to destroy a village. Adding to its flexibility was the 'Mech's humanoid shape. Towering more than ten meters tall and brandishing weapons in its arms rather than in turrets, the BattleMech projected an image of the warrior personified in a way no mere tank ever could.

This effect reached its ultimate extension in Kanazawa's chosen BattleMech, the AS7-K *Atlas*. Not only the tallest, broadest, and heaviest 'Mech ever made, its hulking body was carefully crafted to inspire fear in one's enemies. The grinning, skull-like head of the *Atlas* would surely haunt the afterlife of every warrior killed by one.

As the ground neared and he braced for impact, Kanazawa allowed himself a grim smile. The Ghost Bears' time on this world is over, he thought. My *Atlas* is going to tear it from their grasp and hand it back to Lord Kurita.

An incoming transmission caught him dreaming.

"*Tai-i*, my sensors detect no BattleMechs on the tarmac below. Please confirm."

It was his second-in-command, *Chu-i* Davison. The company's electronics expert, she often acted as the unit's eyes and ears on the battlefield.

Quickly checking visual and magnetic resonance scans, Kanazawa confirmed her findings. It was inexplicable.

"*Hai*, Davison-*san*. My sensors also report no enemies on the ground." Kanazawa did not let on his sense of foreboding, for the sake of his troops.

"Sir, this must be a trap," said MechWarrior Ito.

"Cut the chatter, Ito," snapped Davison.

Kanazawa knew it might be a trap, but there was no way to significantly alter a dropping 'Mech's trajectory. One way or another, he and his company would land on this apparently undefended spaceport. Soon enough, they would know the score.

"*Ichi* Company, prepare for impact. Assault pattern Delta," he said.

Although the Inner Sphere's knowledge of the Clans suggested that they disdained ambush tactics, Kanazawa had instructed his company to spread out quickly after landing to search for hiding enemies. Better safe than sorry, he thought.

At a cue from the altimeter, the thrusters on his *Atlas*'s back switched into high output mode, expending their remaining fuel in a desperate attempt to prevent the 'Mech's legs from shattering on impact.

No matter how many times he went through it, Kanazawa found the impact of a BattleMech landing from a drop as painful as it was exhilarating. The boxy feet of his *Atlas* crashed into the ground at the maximum safe velocity, but he immediately flexed the 'Mech's knees to help absorb the impact. Despite that, a shudder rocked the cockpit that momentarily knocked his main display into static.

Glancing to the right and left, he could see the rest of his lance landing around him, each touching down with professional precision. Without the need for additional commands, his forces began to spread out and search the spaceport.

According to his role in Delta pattern, Kanazawa throttled forward and headed to the northwest. In this case, that led to a gap between two large DropShip hangars. He slowed on approach, the shadows between the buildings making it difficult to see exactly what might be concealed there. He switched to infrared sensors, hoping to penetrate the darkness before moving in for a closer look.

Part of him wished he hadn't seen them coming.

They rose from their underground tunnels on plumes of superheated plasma, one after another, almost touching each other head-to-foot. Boiling up from the ground like a wave of giant cockroaches, they seemed to Kanazawa like alien monsters.

These were no beasts, of course, but men encased in advanced battle armor. Elementals, the Clanners called them. Each armored suit stood three meters tall, with a support-class weapon at the end of one arm and a claw that could tear through 'Mech armor on the other. Rising over the suit's flattened head and V-shaped faceplate was a disposable two-pack missile launcher.

There were at least two dozen of them on the tarmac and firing at him, their small lasers turning the air crimson. They tore at his 'Mech's armor but inflicted no internal damage. At such close range, his long-range missiles were useless, so he raised the arms of his *Atlas* and returned fire with his large lasers.

Training took over, and Kanazawa fired without conscious thought, both lasers hitting their marks and boiling away the armor from the closest two Elementals.

He allowed himself the briefest instant of elation. "That will teach you to tangle with an *Atlas*!" he shouted.

A bit premature, though. He had never faced Elementals in combat before. As the smoke cleared from the attack, he could see the two Elementals standing up, armor melted but repairing itself in a wash of sticky black ooze. As they advanced, all he could do was pull back on the throttle and begin backing up. He thought that the speed of even a slow 'Mech like the *Atlas* should be enough to keep them out of swarming range. Let them get within a hundred meters, and Elementals would jump onto your 'Mech and plant explosive charges between its armor plates.

Looking to finish what he started, Kanazawa triggered his hip-mounted gauss rifle. Recoil shook the cockpit as the 125-kilogram, magnetically accelerated projectile streaked toward its target, the *snap* of the sound barrier breaking the only evidence of its discharge.

This time, the result was much more satisfying. The supersonic sphere slammed into one of the damaged Elementals, shattering armor, bone, and flesh before plowing into the ground, where it gouged a twenty-meter-long trench in the tarmac before coming to a stop. There was nothing left of the Elemental but a memory.

Now that the battle was joined, and his backpedaling was keeping the enemy troopers at arm's length, Kanazawa could spare a few seconds to check on the rest of his command. "*Ichi* Company, report by the numbers!"

The only answer was static.

"Repeat, report by the numbers, *Ichi* Company."

Before he could ponder the implications of the radio silence, his radar scanner beeped for attention. Glancing at the screen and up again at his advancing adversaries, he snapped his head down again in a double take: the entire radar screen was glowing! Not with just a few dozen reports, but what must have been *hundreds*.

Slowing his 'Mech and pivoting at the waist, he saw them through the cockpit windows. As far as the eye could see and from every direction, Elementals painted in mottled Ghost Bear white and blue bounded toward Kanazawa's *Atlas*, none even bothering to fire their weapons. Hundreds, perhaps *thousands* of them.

Alone against them, Kanazawa brought his 'Mech to a stop and raised the machine's arms, beckoning the armored beasts forward. He smiled to himself. This planet, his home, would belong to the Ghost Bears. But this battle would belong to Kanazawa Shiro.

To his surprise, the invitation was not greeted by a hail of gunfire.

The crowd of assembled Elementals parted, as one of them emerged from their ranks to meet the challenge!

The Elemental that came forward wore the standard white/blue camouflage, with the additional adornment of a bear's face painted in scarlet on his helmet. The beastly image snarled and dripped blood from its fangs. Even if the warrior's battle armor had not been uniquely painted, Kanazawa would have recognized him as special by the way he moved. Though encased in a ton of plasteel armor and myomer, he walked with an air of confidence and authority that was also visible through the opaque glass of his visor.

Four more Elementals moved up to flank him, clearly assembling the five-trooper Point that was doctrine among the Clans. Kanazawa expected that they would fight collectively as a unit, for such was the Clan way, but the leader waved them off and hailed on the open channel.

"I am Star Commander Jake Kabrinski of Clan Ghost Bear. I have vanquished Wolves, Hell's Horses, and Blood Spirits and have yet to meet my match. I accept your unspoken challenge."

Now this was bravado befitting the proudest samurai! Perhaps all was not lost, thought Shiro.

"I am *Tai-i* Shiro of the Alshain Avengers," he answered. "I have fought in many battles, but have never faced one such as you. I am honored to challenge you this day upon the soil of my home world."

After a brief pause to acknowledge the transmission, the lone Elemental launched himself directly toward Kanazawa's cockpit on blazing jump jets. It will not be that easy, my Clan friend, thought Shiro.

He shifted the weight of his *Atlas* to the right, tensing the myomer muscles in its left arm and following the ballistic arc of the approaching Elemental with his eyes. At precisely the right moment, he lunged down and to the right, moving the 'Mech's left arm up and forward as he went.

The move caught the Clanner off-guard. In accepting Kanazawa's challenge, this Kabrinski let slip that he had vanquished many Clan foes, but made no mention of Inner Sphere victims. Kanazawa knew that Clan MechWarriors disdained physical combat, so he would not be expecting it. He probably thought the 'Mech would try to shoot him out of the sky.

Unable to change his arc of flight, the Elemental smashed directly into the *Atlas*'s sweeping fist.

The maneuver paid off, but cost Kanazawa dearly. A hundred tons of BattleMech didn't stop on a dime, and the momentum of the flailing attack brought him crashing to the ground. He tried to break the fall with the 'Mech's right arm, but it snapped off at the elbow, unable to support the weight of an entire assault 'Mech.

After what seemed to be an eternity, Kanazawa managed to get the *Atlas* back on its feet with the help of its remaining good arm. Through the ringing in his ears, he could swear the assembled Elementals were cheering his collapse. Quickly scanning the battlefield, he caught no sight of his opponent.

Then, he heard a faint clang from somewhere behind him. Kabrinski must have survived the attack, and had managed to climb onto the back of the *Atlas* while Kanazawa had struggled to get it back on its feet.

He triggered the *Atlas*'s twin rear-mounted pulse lasers, but had no way to tell if they scored a hit. His 'Mech's arms were too clumsy to reach behind and pick the armored warrior off his back, but Kanazawa had an idea. Bracing himself, he stood the *Atlas* straight up, then pushed the sticks forward, causing it to collapse backward. If he was lucky, the Elemental would be crushed beneath one hundred tons of battle machine.

He wasn't lucky.

Kanazawa looked out through the cracked canopy of his cockpit at the sky above, and a shape came into view. Perhaps he had lapsed into unconsciousness and this was a dream, or perhaps he was already dead. Standing on the head of his 'Mech, towering over the cockpit was Jake Kabrinski, or what was left of him. Kanazawa's punch had nearly killed him in one blow: his helmet was gone, and his armor appeared hung about him in tatters.

In those final moments, Shiro Kanazawa studied the bruised and bloodied face of his executioner.

The warrior's eyes were pitch black and set so deeply under his prominent brow that he seemed to be permanently squinting. His head was shaved close, with a single braid of brown hair clinging to his neck, stuck there because it was soaked with sticky blood and a black, tar-like substance.

The Elemental realized that Kanazawa was looking at him, and a horrible grin spread across his Neanderthalic face. In that last moment, when perfect clarity came to the MechWarrior, he saw this Jake Kabrinski for what he really was. *Tai-sa* Shin Yodama-*sama* was right when he first battled Elementals on Turtle Bay so many years ago. They were not human; they were *oni* sent to take their enemies to hell.

None of the Elemental's weapons had survived the impact, but his armor still sported a three-fingered claw on its left arm. He raised it up and prepared to strike, his maniacal grin widening as blood dripped from his mouth to splash on the cockpit window. His tiny eyes burned into his victim's soul as he smashed his claw through the window and beyond. To Kanazawa Shiro, the pain was glorious.

It was, indeed, a good day to die.

2

Sandra Tseng Hospital
Silverdale, Alshain
Ghost Bear Dominion
27 October 3062

Consciousness returned to Jake Kabrinski like dawn rising over a fog-shrouded moor.

He opened his eyes, then instantly regretted it. The harsh hospital lights greeted his gaze with a dazzling array of flashes and sparks. It took a moment for him to realize that he was lying in a hospital bed. He didn't remember being brought here, and he wondered how long he'd been unconscious.

"I see that our patient is alive," he heard someone say. "I suppose I owe you a Timbiqui Dark, Star Captain."

"As I recall, that was the deal, Doctor," a second voice answered.

The words seemed to hover over his bed, mixing with the mental fog in which he floated. The voices were strangely familiar, though not identifiable. He decided to give eye-opening another try.

This time, the light was harsh but bearable. Through the bright haze of his quickly focusing vision, Jake could make out the outlines of two men, one standing on either side of his hospital bed.

"As the subject of this wager, I insist on a cut," Jake said, his voice hoarse and raw. "Or must I issue a challenge for it?"

"I'd say he's more than alive, Doctor," said the one called Star Captain. "I do believe he is awake and back to his old self already." The man spoke loudly and slowly, as if to a foreigner: "Can . . . you . . . hear . . . me . . . ? Do . . . you . . . remember . . . your . . . name . . . ?"

Jake tired of this banter already. He sat bolt upright in the bed and grabbed hold of the man's collar. "My name is Hohiro Kurita," he growled. "Can you tell me the way to Edo?" He pushed his face so close to the man's that their noses were almost touching. Then he realized why the voice was so familiar.

The face greeting Jake's return from the brink of death belonged to Star Captain Carl, one of the most hated and feared instructors from his sibko days. Seeing the old warrior's face—he must have been at least forty by now—brought a flood of memories rushing through the fog in Jake's mind as he sagged back against the pillow.

Carl was an Elemental like Jake, and the streaks of gray in his black hair were an unmistakable reminder of his advancing age. His right eye, clouded with disease, was even lighter than the pale blue of his left eye. Thanks to various scars adorning his tanned, weathered face, Carl looked even meaner than Jake remembered, a feat he would have thought impossible.

What Carl was doing here was anyone's guess, but Jake doubted it was good news. Again, he wondered how long he had been out. He was starting to become aware of the pain in his body, especially the insistent ache in his right leg.

Carl laughed, a harsh, barking sound. "Hohiro Kurita," he boomed. "That's rich. You haven't lost your sense of humor, I see. Even after a week in a coma."

Jake recoiled from the blatant use of contractions. Clearly, his old instructor had spent too much time among Alshain's civilian population. His language had hopelessly deteriorated.

"Be careful, Star Captain," said the other man at Jake's bedside. He peered at Carl over round spectacles. "Your brutish language might push this young warrior back into the land of the dead."

"Point taken, Doctor Svensgaard, but I bring our young hero most urgent news. I will refrain from battering his sensitive ears with further vulgarity."

Svensgaard was blond and tall—by non-Elemental standards—displaying the Nordic features common to many of the native population of the Ghost Bear Dominion. He wore a neatly trimmed, full beard and an antique pair of spectacles to correct his flawed freeborn vision. Jake did not know him, but assumed the doctor's voice was familiar because he might have spoken in Jake's presence while he was unconscious.

"Make it quick, Star Captain," the doctor said. "I have endless tests to run on your 'war hero' before he can be discharged from our care back into your army."

"Not *his* army, Doctor," Jake interjected, "at least not any longer."

Then Jake felt a rush of adrenaline as the unthinkable occurred to him. "What do you want with me, solahma? Have you come to torment me in my convalescence? Am I to join you in some death-seeking squad of old men?"

Carl's laugh was brief and even harsher this time; Jake had cut too close. They both knew that a warrior Carl's age should long ago have been relegated to some cannon-fodder unit.

"Not hardly, Star Commander," Carl said. "I have not yet been tossed into the useless ranks of solahma. Besides, the doctor here tells me you are nearly recovered, though you have been taking your time about it." As if to illustrate the point, Svensgaard absently glanced at his clipboard and nodded.

Jake closed his eyes for a moment, feeling a bit ashamed of his words. "Then to what do I owe the pleasure of your visit?"

"Oh, the pleasure is all mine, Jake. I have kept an eye on your career, you know."

Carl began to pace back and forth at the foot of Jake's

bed. "You have built an impressive codex in the three years since you won your Trial of Position. I particularly liked the slaughter of the Hell's Horses on Bearclaw."

Jake grinned with satisfaction. The aggressive Hell's Horses were long-time rivals of the Ghost Bears. Catching them on Bearclaw last year had been an unexpected feather in Jake's cap. To think he had almost captured a Khan!

"And now that stunt you pulled at the spaceport has caught the attention of Khan Jorgensson. He has recommended you for a promotion."

That was high praise from the Clan's supreme leader. The news stunned Jake, but Carl was not finished.

"As your former instructor, I think your actions in the spaceport battle were reckless, but our Khan seems to think an Elemental who can take on a 'Mech single-handedly has leadership potential. War against the Draconis Combine is a certainty after their honorless assault on our capitol."

The last of Jake's post-coma haze evaporated. His mind began to swirl with images of the impending war against the Combine. Suddenly, he realized why his former trainer had come to visit him.

"A promotion, eh?" Jake said. "And who must I challenge for the rank of Star Captain?"

Carl gave another of his barking laugh, a sound so disagreeable that even Doctor Svensgaard seemed to recoil from the sound. "I think you know the answer to that question already, old friend," Carl said. "Two days from now, you are to challenge me for my rank and the right to command my Supernova Trinary of the 288th Battle Cluster against the Draconis Combine."

Jake felt a jolt of excitement. Carl was too old to lead warriors into combat. The rank of Star Captain and the right to command a front-line unit were more suited to a young warrior with his whole life before him. He had no doubt that he could beat Carl in a Trial of Possession.

Jake grinned with satisfaction, and Carl's face contorted with anger. He leaned in close to Jake and rasped in a spittle-filled whisper, "The powers that be may think otherwise, but I am not solahma yet. Your grandstanding against that pathetic Inner Sphere *Atlas* does not impress me. Three days hence, I will be on my way to the Combine front, and you will be back in this hospital bed—*if* you are lucky."

3

Clan Wolf Headquarters
Tamar
Wolf Occupation Zone
28 October 3062

Stone-faced guards snapped crisp salutes to saKhan Marialle Radick as she strode down the marble-hewn hallway that stretched the entire length of the Clan Wolf's capitol building in the Inner Sphere. Geometric friezes had been chiseled into the walls more than eight hundred years ago, and Marialle could not help but admire them. Her pace did not slow, however, and the rhythmic clack of her gray leather boots echoed on the smooth stone floor.

At the end of the hall were double doors leading to the Clan council chamber, but that was not her destination. She turned the corner and opened the door to the central briefing room.

The room was lit only by the warm glow of a holographic projection of the Inner Sphere some four meters in diameter. It was filled with more than a thousand tiny points of light, each representing an inhabited world. The color of the planet indicated which star empire controlled it; the brightness indicated the estimated strength of the military force stationed there.

Vladimir Ward, Khan of Clan Wolf, stepped out from behind the projection. The crimson glow of the planets held by House Kurita played over his face, accentuating the scar above one eye and exaggerating the deep red "Tamar blush" he had developed from spending so much time on this ozone-depleted world. Some trick of light and shadow transformed his welcoming smile into the grin of a menacing demon.

Marialle blinked at the unexpectedly sinister visage of her oldest friend. "I see you are contemplating the Draconis Combine, Vlad, but they are hardly a threat. Thirteen galaxies of Ghost Bear forces stand between them and us—unless the Bears have decided they want to turn around and go home."

Vlad laughed, a deep, sonorous sound that resonated through the high-ceilinged room. "No, indeed, we have no worries there. It is our *favorite* Clan that I have summoned you here to discuss."

He gestured broadly at the hologram slowly spinning in the air before them. "Take a look at the map, Marialle. What do you see?"

She studied the image for several minutes. "There is an unusual buildup of Combine troops on their rimward borders, including the so-called Lyons Thumb region. That is not news, however. The Combine occupied that formerly Lyran area last month."

Vlad began to walk around the hologram, absent-mindedly rubbing the scar at his temple. "Yes, yes. Go on."

"It looks as though there have been several shifts of Federated Commonwealth troops since my last analysis of their military, but with no discernable pattern. With all the rumblings we hear of a FedCom civil war, perhaps this is a sign that it is about to erupt."

Vlad rounded the map toward Marialle, a smile touching his lips. "That is what I think, too, and I believe that the Combine has relocated troops to be in position to aid Victor Steiner-Davion's cause against his sister, Katherine."

Marialle shrugged. "So the Federated Commonwealth is about to become embroiled in a civil war. What has this to do with the Wolves? We share no border with the Federated Commonwealth, or for that matter, the Draconis Combine."

Vlad's smile changed to a frown as he turned to face the map. "For a moment there, I thought you were on track, Marialle. But you persist in thinking like a warrior first and a Khan second."

Reaching out to touch the point of light representing the Ghost Bear Dominion capital of Alshain with his index finger, Vlad moved his hand in a clockwise motion. The gesture registered in the holotank's motion sensors, zooming on the image until the map showed only the holdings of Clans Wolf, Hell's Horses, and Ghost Bear, and their border with the Draconis Combine. With another hand movement, he brought up a text-display window next to the planet. Data on troop dispositions and recent activity began to stream through it.

"Ten days ago, elements of the Draconis Combine military, supposedly without the approval of DCMS High Command, launched a surprise attack on Alshain. The invaders called themselves the Alshain Avengers, a group of regiments wholly dedicated to reclaiming their lost home or die trying. It was an all-out assault, no quarter asked or given and no *batchall*."

Marialle turned to look at Vlad, her eyes wide. "I had not heard of this. The news must have arrived just today from the Watch?"

"Yes. In fact, it is the reason I called you here. The Avengers jumped insystem with an estimated three combined-arms regiments, veteran troops to the man and possessed of fiery devotion to their cause."

"Was the *Leviathan* operational?" Marialle asked. It was now known that the Ghost Bears had been able to secretly transport their whole population from the Clan homeworlds to the Inner Sphere with the help of two mammoth *Leviathan* WarShips.

Vlad shook his head, looking disappointed. "No, we still do not know what the Bears are up to there. The Avengers were unprepared for the arrival of the *Ursa Major*, however, which is stationed there defending the *Leviathan* shipyard and keeping our Watch agents from getting a decent look at the refit operation. The *Ursa Major* handled the invaders with ease. It joined the battle in orbit and destroyed an entire regiment before the Avenger 'Mechs had even left their DropShips."

"So they landed two regiments of veteran Inner Sphere troops . . ." Marialle began walking her own orbit of the holotank as she worked out the odds in her head. "The Ghost Bears have roughly three clusters on Alshain . . ."

"It was a slaughter," Vlad interrupted. "Khan Jorgensson has his most elite troops guarding his capital world, including an entire cluster of Elementals from Zeta Galaxy. I applaud the Avengers' audacity, but the battle was over before it had begun."

Marialle completed her circuit of the holotank. "The Ghost Bears will never take this lying down. It is a blatant challenge to the security of their Dominion, not to mention a chance for their young warriors to cut their teeth in a real war."

She reached up to touch the map, her finger tracing the length of the blue/red border between the Ghost Bear Dominion and the Draconis Combine. "Soon, this border will be alive with battle as the Bears retaliate against the Combine," she said, "leaving this one virtually undefended." Her finger moved to the blue/brown border with the Wolf Occupation Zone.

She smiled triumphantly. "We shall launch an attack against the Ghost Bear Dominion, seizing many worlds in Trials of Possession before they can shift troops back to deal with us, *quiaff*?"

Vlad shook his head, like a father gently correcting his daughter. It was a look Marialle did not appreciate. She turned away from Vlad to silently regard the holotank once more.

"Neg," he said. "Now you are thinking too much like a Khan and not enough like a warrior. Not only would such a move be entirely too predictable, it would be underhanded, to say the least. We are yet Wolves, are we not? Besides, we could never hold on to what we took from them once the Bears were done with the Combine. Our seven galaxies are already stretched to the limit holding what we have. No, it is too soon. Too soon for *Clan Wolf* to provoke the Bears."

Marialle studied the glowing map again, then reached

out and zoomed the image even further in, to the red-brown worlds of Engadin, Stanzach, and Vorarlberg nestled between the Wolf and Ghost Bear holdings. She turned to Vlad and spoke two words. "Hell's Horses."

Vlad laughed again, but this time the real pleasure in his laughter lightened Marialle's heart. "Yes, the one Clan that hates the Ghost Bears more than we do! *Now* we are making progress.

"It so happens that Malavai Fletcher is en route to the Inner Sphere to review his troops and his holdings and to deliver additional materiel. I will take this opportunity to meet with the Horses' Khan, who so kindly protects the three worlds we ceded to him. It would be only natural to discuss the Ghost Bear situation with him.

"Malavai still bears deep wounds from the flogging he and his Clan took on Niles sixteen years ago at the hands of the Ghost Bears. It should be a simple matter to . . . *encourage* him to launch a series of raids against his most hated enemies while they are occupied in a war with the Combine."

Marialle laughed out loud, too. "And no matter how the raids turn out, the Bears will be weakened. In the end, their ire will be focused on the Horses and not us." She had finally caught on.

Vlad leaned down to flick a switch, shutting off the holotank and bringing up the lights in the room. He turned to Marialle and clapped her on one fur-clad shoulder. "Exactly. And if we are very fortunate, the Bears will be so enraged by the Horses that they will push Fletcher and his *dezgra* Clan out of our Occupation Zone for good."

He turned and began walking toward the door, and Marialle kept up with him. As he pushed open the doors, she suddenly remembered the first part of their conversation. "But what has this to do with the Federated Commonwealth and the civil war?" she asked.

"The Horses raids will draw Bear forces away from the Combine front, prolonging both conflicts. This will keep Combine forces from intervening in Victor's behalf, in turn prolonging the civil war."

They turned the corner and began to traverse the long

hall toward the beaten bronze ornamental doors that led to the sun-baked Tamar day.

Marialle now had the whole picture. "By prodding the Hell's Horses into doing what they want to do anyway, we stand to weaken the entire Inner Sphere."

Vlad paused and turned to her as they reached the huge bronze doors. "And when Ulric's *stravag* truce runs out in 3067, the reborn Clan Wolf will be poised to strike at Terra. We shall trample over the shattered remains of our foes to claim our rightful place as ilClan."

He beamed with confidence as he pushed open the bronze doors to a blast of midday sun. "Come, Malavai Fletcher," he said. "Come quickly to Tamar. We have so much to talk about . . ."

4

Training Facility Beta
Silverdale, Alshain
Ghost Bear Dominion
29 October 3062

Every repetition was pain. Pure, raw pain like a million insects biting at once, driving their mandibles directly into his nerve endings and tearing them apart. It was glorious.

To Jake, the pain was proof that he was alive. And so long as he was alive, he would continue to fight, continue to win.

Despite the pain, or perhaps because of it, he pushed the three hundred-kilogram barbell up and away from his chest, then lowered it until it nearly touched his body. Again and again, the white-hot pain reminding him each time of the injuries he'd suffered at the hands of an Inner Sphere MechWarrior. Each repetition bringing his bruised flesh that much closer to recovery.

"I see you are only up to three hundred kilos," Val said. "I thought you were expected to make a *speedy* recovery?" Val said.

Jake paused his exercises long enough to glance briefly over at her. "*Only* three hundred, Val? I would like to see you do as much ten days after being backhanded by an *Atlas*, Inner Sphere or otherwise."

She sat down on the weight bench next to Jake's and laughed softly. "I suppose you are right, but I would never have gotten myself into that fix in the first place."

Jake pretended to ignore her comment. "Nice to see you too, Val." He continued his next bench press despite his muscles screaming for him to stop.

"We only just finished mopping-up operations yesterday," she said. "Between that and your acute lack of consciousness, this is the first chance I have had to visit you since your . . . duel."

Jake heaved the barbell up onto the brackets above and behind his head, then levered himself into a sitting position facing Val. "What are you saying, Val? You do not consider that it was a duel?"

He took a moment to look at her. An Elemental like himself, she was nearly a head shorter but still more than two meters tall. Her dark-brown hair was woven into a single braid that fell down her back almost to her waist. She tended to fidget absent-mindedly with the braid when the situation was uncomfortable. Sure enough, she was doing it now.

She looked up from her fidgeting and frowned. "There was simply no call for the risk you took, Jake. You are more valuable to your Clan alive than dead, especially when we were fighting to protect Alshain. I know you have only been here a few months, but to many of us this place is home. An attack on Alshain was no time to relive your exploits on Bearclaw."

He fixed her steel-gray eyes with his. "Are you going to turn my victory into an object lesson? Because, if you are, I will have to draw a Circle of Equals right here and teach *you* an object lesson here and now."

Val did not flinch. "Surely you jest, but perhaps a tussle in the gym is what you need to knock some sense into that thick skull of yours."

Jake rolled his eyes to the heavens, and resigned himself to the imminent lecture. They had been together since their sibko days, and she had always taken it upon herself to set him straight.

Val stood up so that she was looking down at him. "What

were you thinking? We fight as a team, Jake. Your point is always there for you—five Elementals fighting as one. Yet you decided all by yourself to disregard both tradition and sanity to show off against that Kurita MechWarrior."

Jake narrowed his eyes and grinned. "Do I detect a note of jealousy? If the whole point had attacked, you would have shared in the kill. As it stands, only my codex was credited with the kill."

That stopped her. Val would never lie. "Aff, Jake. I have to admit that a part of me wanted a share of the glory."

"I knew it!" Jake stood up, triumphant. He crossed the room to grab a towel from a steel rack, and his step showed only the merest hint of a limp. He and Val understood each other so well that sometimes they had no need to speak. Val had always been in Jake's shadow, and sometimes it got to her. Jake wondered for a moment what it must be like to come in second all the time, but quickly banished the thought.

Val tossed her head. "Do not look so proud of yourself, Jake. You do not have me figured out that well. Yes, I am upset that you blocked me from that battle. I am a warrior, *quiaff*? But that is not why I am here."

"Why, then?" he asked.

"Your troops count on you, Jake. That *Atlas* was going to fall one way or the other. There was no need for you to single him out. You worried me, Jake. I was—"

She broke off immediately when a pair of MechWarriors entered the gymnasium. They nodded to the two Elementals and took positions on the weight benches formerly occupied by Jake and Val.

After a few tense moments, Jake cleared his throat and scratched his head, unsure what to say. He didn't know where Val was going with all this, but she obviously did not want to discuss it in front of other warriors.

He gestured toward the nearby punching bag. "If you would be so kind as to hold the bag for me? I might end up fighting Carl hand-to-hand tomorrow, so I had best brush up on my form."

"Sure," she said, and went to stand behind the leather bag hanging from the ceiling. As Jake began hitting the bag with right-handed blows that would crush a man's skull, Val braced against his attacks. "If you win the toss, you will fight the trial augmented, *quiaff*?" she asked between punches.

Jake paused in his assault on the bag, flexing his right arm against a hint of lingering pain. "How so?"

"All your life you have believed that the truest test of a warrior comes when he puts all his skills to the test. Only when wearing his powered battle armor is an Elemental truly using all his skills."

Jake resumed his flurry of blows.

She continued, "Carl always had a preference for un-armed combat. At least, that was what he used to teach the cadets a lesson, *quiaff*?"

"Aff. Carl was a master of all forms, and fast enough to keep up with the younger cadets."

Val smiled. "*Was* a master. The operative term is 'was.' He is well past his prime, which is the reason you got this chance in the first place."

Jake gave the bag a hard and unsuspected right hook, momentarily knocking Val off balance. "You insult me! I got the chance because I earned it."

Val shoved the bag back at Jake, laughing. "Cool down, Jake. Of course your skills are what will prove you worthy of promotion. But if Carl were at the peak of his career, the Khan would never have dishonored him by arranging this trial. I have heard it is one of many being held before we begin our counterassault against the Combine."

Jake stretched, raising both arms over his head until the tips of his fingers brushed the three-meter-high ceiling. Val was right, and he knew she meant no harm. "Yes, I have heard that, too. The decade of peace since the truce has left our Touman clogged with old and complacent officers who have had no war to keep their claws sharpened. The Khan is wise in deciding to inject new blood into the ranks before our campaign begins."

He sat down on one of the benches bolted to the gym wall, pondering the thought. Still sweaty, he mopped his heavy brow with the sleeve of his shirt.

"Here, use this." Val tossed Jake a fresh towel as she walked over. She sat down next to him.

"I wonder if it is wise to change commanders so soon before such a major operation," he said. "The new officers will be unfamiliar with their subordinates, and their subordinates will be unfamiliar with their style of command. It could hurt morale."

Val shook her head. "I trust the Khan. He is wise and far-seeing. Look at how he relocated us to the Inner Sphere, a secret we kept from all the other Clans until the move was complete. Had Khan Jorgennson revealed the plan prematurely, the other Clans would have made a mad rush to seize our holdings, which would have cost us valuable resources and warriors. Now we are firmly established in the Ghost Bear Dominion, and well-prepared to handle our aggressive neighbors."

Jake smiled. One of the reasons he and Val got along so well was that she never failed to fill in the blanks in his thinking. It was only one of many good reasons he planned to keep her in his command staff after he beat Carl tomorrow.

So much had changed for him in the last year, and Jake suspected this was just the beginning. He had no specific criticism of the Ghost Bears' move to the Inner Sphere, and the reality of it was still sinking in for Jake. He trusted their Khan as implicitly as Val did, yet he could not shake the feeling that he was living in an alien place, among a conquered, alien people.

"It is true that the Khan is not one to act rashly," he said. "Perhaps he believes there would be more loss of morale caused by worn-out old warriors leading our forces into battle, *quiaff*?"

Val nodded. "Aff. Besides, he has not changed any commanders of cluster-command or higher rank, so strategic command will not suffer. Yes, I think the benefits outweigh the drawbacks."

"Especially with a warrior like me in charge of a front-line trinary!" Jake said, thumping his chest proudly. That drew dubious glances from the MechWarriors, who were just finishing their sets on the weight benches.

Val slapped Jake's shoulder playfully. "The battle is not won yet, my friend. But you feel you are ready for the trial tomorrow, despite your injuries?"

"Of course." Jake stood up, doing his best to keep the pain from showing on his face. "I am still not back to one hundred percent, but I will not need that much to defeat my *old* teacher."

He crossed the room to the window, which offered a panoramic view of southern Silverdale and the forests beyond. The terrain reminded him of the many places where he had fought since earning warrior status. Every one of those battles had been a victory for him and for his Clan. There was no doubt in his mind that soon he would add another.

He turned to Val, who had joined him. "Wherever we fight, Carl and I, he will learn some new lessons. It is high time the student became the teacher."

5

Encased in more than a ton of steel and myomer, Carl could not feel the cold breeze that whipped past him on its journey from the mountains eastward to the sea. He could just make out the shape of Jake's battle armor on the far side of the ruins. The heads up display in his helmet clearly showed the younger warrior's infrared signature inside his suit, despite the intervening debris.

Any moment, the sun would break over the horizon, signaling the beginning of this Trial of Possession. It would be a fight to remember, Carl thought as he checked his system monitors one last time. In his youth, he had preferred to fight unaugmented. But now, like it or not, he stood a better chance of winning with the armor.

The backpack on his Elemental suit was equipped with the standard short-range missile two-pack, an effective antiarmor weapon with significant range and hitting power. His most potent weapon, it held enough ammunition for two salvoes. The suit's right hand was a modular weapons mount. His carried a support-class laser, accurate enough but not as powerful as the missiles. The suit's left arm ended in a three-fingered steel claw, remotely controlled by Carl's own left hand and strong enough to tear apart Battle-Mech armor like so much rice paper. Slung underneath the claw was a submachine gun. Though too weak to penetrate battle armor, it could prove useful once an opponent's armor was breached.

The first rays of morning light brought little warmth to the combatants arrayed facing off across the burned-out husk of the El Dorado Smelting Plant, just south of Silverdale. The facility had been abandoned after taking grave damage during the Clan invasion. In the decades since, El Dorado had become a favorite spot for Ghost Bear trials of combat because the ruins and the terrain around it—pine woods, foothills, and small, U-shaped lake—offered a variety of tactical options. Add to this the heavy metal content of the surrounding bedrock and countless uncharted basements, and reliable radar detection was a thing of the past.

Carl knew that was why Jake had chosen this spot for their trial. Well, the cub would need all the help he could get if thought he was going to seize Carl's rank and command.

He smiled to himself. *Perhaps it is time to stir the pot.* He keyed the communications circuit, and set the channel to remain open for the duration of the trial. "Soon your trial will begin, young Jake. It is still possible to back out. There would be no loss of honor, in light of your debilitating injuries . . ."

"You must think me a fool," Jake retorted—predictably. "Backing out now might not stain my reputation, but it would save yours. It would also keep you on the front lines, *quiaff*? Well, things will not end that easily for you this day, Star Captain Carl."

"Fair enough, cub. We do it the hard way. I have always said that the most valuable lessons are the ones learned through hardship—"

". . . and the best rewards are earned with pain," Jake said, completing the phrase.

Carl was pleased that the younger warrior remembered his favorite axiom. He glanced up and saw the thinnest edge of sun crack the horizon, turning the cloud-striped sky into a warm orange tapestry of light.

The voice of the trial's Oathmaster crackled through both warriors' comm systems. "Begin."

If Jake knew Carl, the old warrior would immediately press the attack to prove he was still an aggressive and capable fighter. True to form, Carl ignited his jump jets a fraction of a second after the Oathmaster's signal, rising skyward on plumes of superheated plasma.

Too much of the ruined factory lay between Jake and his opponent to see where Carl was headed. Slowly, Jake walked toward the ruined building. *If you are in a hurry, old man, then I will take my time.*

As he reached the shattered factory wall, Jake noticed an unusual signal on his radar display, and spun himself 180 degrees to face the incoming threat. Carl leapt down from the roof directly in front of Jake. Without conscious thought, Jake triggered his own jump jets mere moments before Carl fired his support laser. The quick response put the shot off the mark, but the ruby beam managed to tag Jake's leg, scorching armor and nudging the trajectory of his jump. Rather than arcing gracefully to the roof, he went careening through walls and ceilings like a cannonball, knocking down beams and kicking up a cloud of dust and debris that made it impossible for Carl to immediately give chase.

"Reckless youth!" Carl growled. "Do not dare rob me of my victory by killing yourself through stupidity, Jake."

Cutting off the thrust to his jets, Jake braced for an uncontrolled landing. He smashed through four walls, a ceiling, and a floor, and came crashing down on a pile of empty crates. His suit's breastplate broke his fall somewhat but not without getting severely dented.

Jake looked straight ahead, then glanced down and to the right, where an icon on his HUD detected the position of his pupils and softly glowed in response. Instantly, a schematic of his armor came up, filling the right side of his field of vision with a detailed, color-coded view of his suit's systems. He grunted in satisfaction. It looked like he would need two technicians and the jaws of life to get out of this suit after he won, but at least the armor was still solid.

Dismissing the schematic with a blink of his eyes, Jake quickly took in his surroundings. Carl would not be deterred long by the collapse. Jake would need a moment to counter the ambush, perhaps with one of his own . . .

In the years since he had last seen Jake, Carl had not given much thought to the headstrong boy who had been his charge. It was all coming back now. The cub always seemed to operate on sheer instinct and reflexes, and it looked like he hadn't changed. Well, it would be the death of him now!

Following the trajectory of Jake's armor as best he could, Carl smashed through fallen ceiling beams and stacks of discarded crates with his suit's clawed left arm. Within minutes, he came to a large open area with a telltale hole in the ceiling and a corresponding dent in the floor. It was surrounded by the shattered remains of a stack of wooden crates.

So here is Jake Crater, he thought, but where is our young meteorite off to? Glancing around the area, Carl could detect no clear signs of Jake's exit. There were several open doorways, as well as a large vehicle-access bay whose rolling door had long since been rusted permanently into its retracted position. Beyond the open bay door, Carl could see the lake, where reflections of the morning sun turned its softly rolling surface into a dazzling light show.

Had Jake gone for a swim? A glance to the left of his HUD switched Carl's display to the infrared spectrum. Sure enough, heat traces now made Jake's footprints leading out the bay door immediately visible. Carl followed the prints into the open bay, where he could clearly see the divots of earth dug up by the bifurcated feet of an Elemental suit, leading directly to the lake.

Jake burst through the surface of the water in his battle armor. Twin flashes and puffs of smoke signaled the launch of his SRM two-pack. Carl quickly surmised that the hasty

attack was aimed too high, and dodged it easily by dropping to one knee.

"You really should take aim before you fire, Jake," he
taunted. "I thought you planned on *winning* this trial."

Taking his own advice, Carl raised his right-arm laser as
SRMs corkscrewed over his head.

His targeting cross hairs had just registered a lock when
he heard Jake say, "I was aiming, old man—just not at you."

The shock wave of an explosion over his head threw off
Carl's careful aim, and his laser shot missed Jake entirely.
Carl looked up, but the cowling of his helmet prevented
him from seeing exactly how the missiles had affected the
aging building. Before he could stand and dive forward,
the collapsing structure answered Carl's silent question.
The falling cinder blocks threw him to the ground, and the
rusty mass of the rolled-up steel door smashed into his
back, dislodging his SRM launcher and mangling it beyond repair.

Just before the debris completely buried him, Carl saw
Jake engage his jump jets again, heading toward the pine
forest to the west. "Go ahead and run, *surat!*" he screamed.
"When I get my hands on you, you'll be sorry you ever
stopped running!"

Damn it. Carl told himself that he should have seen this
coming, but he couldn't dwell on that. He had to dig himself out and get back into the fight before the trail got
cold.

The myomer fibers beneath the hard shell of every battle
armor suit acted as synthetic muscles, greatly amplifying
the wearer's strength. If not for the myomers, Elementals
would not be able to move in their suits at all, let alone
jump and fight in them.

Right now, the strength granted by his suit's musculature
was all that stood between Carl and death. Gradually—taking far too many minutes for his liking—Carl pushed and
shoved and dug his way out from under the tons of rubble
dropped on his head by Jake Kabrinski.

Kabrinski—Carl could hardly believe the headstrong
cub had already earned a Bloodname. He was almost
proud, in a perverse way, because he had played a major

role in Jake's training. On the other hand, like all older warriors who had failed to win a Bloodname, he was jealous.

Finally regaining his feet, he took a few steps into the bright morning light, checking his HUD for a status report. His armor schematic showed nearly fifty percent loss, as well as the destruction of his missile pack, while his chronometer confirmed that it had taken more than fifteen minutes to dig out of his tomb. Too long, but Carl figured he could still spot Jake's jump landings on IR.

Sure enough, infrared clearly showed glowing patches of lingering heat, spaced approximately eighty meters apart, which revealed Jake's bounding path directly into the forest. Carl engaged his own jump jets and quickly closed the distance.

Once inside the woods, tracking Jake became far more difficult. There were no signs of jump landings, so Jake must have walked in and covered his path.

"You cannot hide forever, Jake Kabrinski," Carl taunted. "I will find you and destroy you!" When all he heard was silence, it made him even angrier. He charged forward into the woods, scanning right and left for any signs of Jake. He found none, and all he got on his radar screen was static.

"Cease your running, cub!" he called. "Stand and fight like a man."

In his agitated state of mind, and with his radar disabled by the terrain, Carl had no chance of spotting Jake's ambush. As he rushed past Jake's position, Jake slowly raised his right arm to target his support-class machine gun. His HUD registered a clean lock on Carl's dented armor.

Smiling in grim satisfaction, Jake finally answered. "As you wish." Squeezing the trigger, he sent hundreds of fifty-caliber bullets slamming into Carl's back.

The attack shredded chunks of armor from the older warrior's already battered suit, and nearly knocked him off his feet again. Without stopping to assess the damage fully, Jake triggered his jump jets and headed deeper into the woods rather than face the counterattack head-on.

It was a prudent choice. A moment later, he heard a howl of rage over the radio accompanied a blast from Carl's support laser, which destroyed the tree Jake had been using for cover. Sailing over the treetops, Jake allowed himself another smile. Carl's anger would finish the job for him.

He crashed through the leafy canopy and landed on the forest floor. Keeping an unobstructed view of Carl's approach, he raised his machine gun and braced himself to fire. A glance at his HUD released the safety switches on his SRMs. Jake knew he could take a direct hit from Carl, but Carl would not be able to withstand a counterattack. This battle was over.

Carl come crashing through the underbrush into his field of vision, trampling a pair of saplings as he charged forward. Jake held his ground and drew careful aim, bracing for Carl's laser attack. The shot hit him in the chest, melting armor and digging down to the myomer beneath. He could feel the scorching heat, but his suit automatically administered painkillers, which cleared his mind for the counterattack.

Jake triggered all his weapons. The machine gun scored a line of bullet-holes across Carl's left leg and torso, while both SRMs hit him directly in the chest. The twin explosions momentarily hid the scene from view, not that Jake had any doubts about the outcome.

He walked casually toward the fallen Elemental, the spent SRM pack falling from his suit's back automatically to reduce encumbrance, though Jake no longer needed the advantage. As the smoke cleared, he saw without a doubt that Carl was beaten.

Looking up through the cracked and broken visor of his battle armor, Carl saw the approaching form of Jake Kabrinski through the dissipating smoke. Coughing, he struggled to his feet.

"You have come a long way since the sibko," he said.

Jake stopped at arm's length from Carl. "You made me what I am, Star Commander Carl."

Carl winced at the instant reminder of his demotion as

well as the irony of Jake's words. He raised his suit's left-arm claw arm in salute. "You have won this trial, and my respect for your prowess, Jake Kabrinski. Let us hope it is enough to keep you alive on the front lines."

Jake raised his own suit's claw, returning the salute. "More than enough, old man. More than enough."

6

***DropShip* Burning Paw**
Zenith Jump Point, Last Frontier
Ghost Bear Dominion
18 November 3062

Space stretched vast and black before Jake Kabrinski as he gazed out the port of the DropShip *Burning Paw*. For the last hour, the ship had been crossing the deep space separating the starship that had brought him to this system and the WarShip that would be his home during the coming campaign. It was all part of the extensive movement of Bear forces as they massed for retaliation against the Combine. He tried to make out the system's sun, but from this distance the star was just one among billions of others.

Jake sensed the vast emptiness surrounding him, and it stunned him for a moment. He backed away from the window, and sat down heavily in the crash seat of his small, but private, quarters. Though no stranger to travel across the black oceans of space, he had never fully gained what spacers still referred to as "sea legs." He was not as bad as some warriors he had known, but most of those had flushed out of training or been permanently posted to planetside garrisons. He had learned to fight in zero-G, and did not get space-sick very often, but the entire experience still tended to leave him vaguely uncomfortable, and thus irritable.

Not the ideal state of mind for meeting his new commanding officer, he thought. Jake had been reassigned to Rho Galaxy immediately after winning away Carl's rank, and had spent the last few weeks traveling from Alshain to report for duty with the 288th Battle Cluster.

"Attention all decks," said the duty officer over the ship's comm system. "Final docking approach in one minute."

On his way to a new command and a new life, Jake hoped his new commander would be impressed with his bravura performance on Alshain. He pulled the twin seatbelts down and across his chest, securely strapping himself into the crash seat in the unlikely event of a collision during docking. Looking up through the observation window, he now had a spectacular view of the *Nightlord* Class battleship *Ursa Major* as it came into view.

The *Burning Paw* approached toward the WarShip's nose to avoid backwash from the larger vessel's station-keeping drive. At first, the boxy *Nightlord* might have been mistaken for one of the many space stations along the route from the Clan homeworlds to the Inner Sphere. As the DropShip drew closer, angling alongside the WarShip for the correct docking vector, that impression changed completely.

Now he could see the entire length of the vessel, its sheer size was overwhelming. Massing more than a million tons, the *Ursa Major*'s kilometer-long broadsides bristled with dozens of naval-grade autocannon, lasers, and particle weapons, any one of which was fully capable of turning the *Burning Paw* into scrap with a single shot.

Beneath one such cluster of weapons, an enormous cargo bay door, nearly two hundred meters wide and fifty tall, yawned open to the void of space. Within, he glimpsed the hulking shapes of OmniMechs surrounded by tiny, ant-like technicians working as they floated about in null-gravity.

The *Ursa Major*'s jump sail, deployed behind the ship to recharge the vessel's hyperspace drive core, could now be seen in all its glory. Illuminated by the flare of the station-keeping drives, the sail was a vast solar collector only a few millimeters thick. Etched into its surface was a kilometer-tall image of a roaring ghost bear head.

The jump sail retreated from view, along with the rest of the *Ursa Major*, as the *Burning Paw* rotated into its final, nose-first docking position.

"Prepare for docking in ten seconds," the duty officer announced. Within moments, Jake felt more than heard the DropShip's contact with the WarShip's docking collar. The force of the 3,000-ton impact, slow as it was, sent a shudder through the entire ship.

Time for zero-G, he thought glumly as he reached down to release his seat belts. Until now, he'd been under the influence of the *Burning Paw*'s acceleration gravity. Its engines pushed the ship forward with one G of thrust, and the equal and opposite reaction pushed him back into the floor, simulating one G of gravity. Once the DropShip started its docking maneuvers, thrust was no longer expended in one direction or at a steady rate, robbing those on board of the luxury of simulated gravity.

The seat's belts floated up and away from Jake before automatically retracting into the seat back. He pushed off with his hands and floated slowly up toward the ceiling. Another nudge with the toe of his boot sent him flying to the cabin's door. He pressed a button next to the door, which slid open, leaving an oval opening barely large enough for his massive body to pass through. Entering the corridor, he joined the stream of other Elementals heading for the umbilical connecting DropShip to WarShip.

Jake spotted Val in the crowd. "Anxious to get to the grav deck, Val?"

Val laughed cheerfully as she floated toward Jake. "Not as anxious as you, I wager." She had always been more at ease in low gravity.

"I am to report to our new Star Colonel first. His orders were very clear that I present myself to him immediately."

"What do you hear about him?" Val asked. "They say he is a stern taskmaster, but that is true of any Star Colonel, *quiaff*?"

Jake navigated toward a ladder leading to the upper decks, joining a long queue of Elementals. "His name is

Marcus Gilmour. I know he fought in Operation Revival, but that is about the limit of my information. I try to leave the intelligence-gathering to the Watch."

"Seems like a good policy to me," Val said. "Well, whatever he is like, I am sure he is a good commander."

"Why do you say that?"

Val shrugged as best she could while holding the rungs of a ladder. "The Clan way virtually guarantees that no warrior could rise to the rank of star colonel without being worthy."

Jake supposed she was right. The Clan system ensured that only the finest warriors attained positions of command. By the same token, he was confident he would make an excellent star captain. He told himself not to be nervous about meeting his new commander. Gilmour would probably be overjoyed to have a fine young warrior with a shining codex as one of his officers.

As the line began to move again, Jake headed into the umbilical connecting DropShip to WarShip. Val fell back into the crowd behind him, but he heard her parting shot as he continued his climb toward the *Ursa Major* and his new life.

"Look on the bright side, Jake. Nobody could be worse than Carl!"

Jake laughed. Val could always cheer him up. His heart swelled at the thought of the endless opportunities and possibilities that stretched before him. As he reached the War-Ship's corridors and launched himself toward the nearest information panel, he wondered where his unit would be sent first. He hoped it was a nearby planet. All the enforced inactivity of DropShip travel was beginning to get on his nerves. It had been a month since his command performance on Alshain. What he wanted—no, what he *needed*—was a battle.

7

Battleship **Ursa Major**
Zenith Jump Point, Last Frontier
Ghost Bear Dominion
18 November 3062

Jake strode briskly down the hall of the *Ursa Major*'s aft grav deck. Shaped like an enormous donut, the structure was one hundred forty meters in diameter and rotated at a constant speed, its centrifugal force creating the conditions of normal gravity for the people inside. This particular deck contained three exercise rooms, two conference halls, and the commander's office. The spin-gravity holding his feet to the floor put Jake somewhat at ease, but the feeling evaporated as he reached Gilmour's door and knocked once.

"Enter, Star Captain." The deep voice that boomed through the door did little to ease Jake's tense anticipation. The door slid open before him, and he ducked through the narrow opening.

"Star Captain Jake Kabrinski reporting as ordered, sir." Jake stood at rigid attention, his gaze fixed over the head of the man seated behind a desk that was large by shipboard standards.

"Welcome to the 288th Battle Cluster, Star Captain. At ease."

Jake clasped both hands behind his back, moved his legs

slightly apart, and got his first look at his new C.O. Marcus Gilmour was, by Jake's reckoning, a small and old man. Not so old as Carl, to be sure, but with enough gray hair at the temples to mark him as a MechWarrior veteran of more than ten years. He was studying the screen of a small note-puter on his desk, probably reviewing a copy of Jake's codex, the record of all his accomplishments since the sibko.

After several silent minutes, Jake began to suspect that this was some sort of test of patience. Gilmour's face gave no hint of any reaction to what he was reading, so Jake had no clue of what might come next. Eager to make a good impression, he choked back the urge to regale the man with boasts and promises of victory in the battles to come. Instead, he forced himself to remain as impassive as his commander.

When at last Gilmour looked up again, his crystal blue eyes seemed to pin Jake to the wall like a bug on a pin. Jake wanted to look away, but he dared not. He locked eyes with his commander, determined to show no weakness.

Gilmour leaned back in his leather-upholstered chair, still holding Jake's gaze. "I have been reviewing your codex, Star Captain," he said evenly. "I see that you are a rising star, a young warrior who is already making a name for himself. Khan Jorgensson himself has taken note of your exploits."

Jake felt a flash of pride and wondered if he was about to be assigned some special mission.

Gilmour picked up the noteputer and brandished it at Jake with a look of disgust. "Ristar, indeed," he scoffed. "Two kills in your initial Trial of Position started you on the fast track as a point commander. Then two years of sterling service in the Third Bear Regulars, at the end of which you locked horns with Malavai Fletcher himself on Bearclaw. That victory not only got you command of a star, but earned you a slot in the Trial of Bloodright for Xavier Kabrinski's Bloodname."

Jake shifted uncomfortably, wondering where Gilmour was going with this. The man's tone had gone from carefully neutral to openly scornful. Was his commander criticizing him for being victorious in combat, for being aggressive and ambitious? Were these not qualities bred into all good warriors?

"You look confused, Star Captain," Gilmour said. "Well, my point is simple. I do not like *ristars*. I had to read the account of your Trial three times to be sure I was not losing my eyesight. Somehow, a stripling barely out of the sibko bested a field of veterans and walked away with a Bloodname. Then you were given command of a newly formed Zeta Galaxy star, one of the last units to arrive on Alshain from the homeworlds.

"You arrived just in time for your unit to successfully defend Alshain's main spaceport." Gilmour smiled humorlessly. "The high point of which was your single-handed victory over a Combine *Atlas*."

He stood up and walked around his desk. Though he was forced to look up at Jake's commanding height, it did nothing to diminish Gilmour's formidable presence. Jake could almost feel the contempt emanating from him.

"What were you trying to prove with that stunt, Jake? You are in my command now, and the first thing you need to understand is that I do not appreciate my sub-commanders out trying to prove something. I need them following orders, leading their troops, and winning victories. Is that clear?"

"Aye, Star Colonel," Jake said, feeling his face get hot with shame and anger. This was not at all the way he had hoped this interview would go.

Gilmour continued to stare. "Let me tell you the story of another warrior, Star Captain. This warrior scored one kill and tested out of his sibko as a simple MechWarrior. He worked his way up through the ranks, slow and steady, with the patience of the mighty ghost bear. He took risks, but calculated ones, and only when the reward was worth the potential sacrifice. I am that warrior, Jake Kabrinski. Not only did I live to tell the tale, I am still a commander of men. That is because, in all the time, my troops have never failed to achieve their objective. Sooner or later."

Gilmour looked at Jake as though expecting a reply.

"Yes, sir," was the best Jake could do.

Gilmour placed the noteputer back on his desk. "All right, I have had my say, Star Captain. Permission to speak freely."

Jake did not appreciate the insults Gilmour had heaped on him, but he was not a Clan warrior for nothing. He had not come this far just to lose it all without a shot being fired. "Sir, I only do what my Clan has trained me to do, and what I am capable of doing, in the course of fulfilling my orders. I do not flinch from danger, and I do not back down from a fight I can win."

He hesitated, but Gilmour said, "Go on."

"You are not the first to criticize my duel with the *Atlas*, but it was not as foolhardy as it might seem. I knew the 'Mech was damaged and that its pilot was demoralized. I saw a chance for glory and I seized it. Had I failed, the rest of my star would surely have destroyed the 'Mech. There really was no risk to the operation. The victory earned me a place in our invasion of the Combine. I might have died taking that risk, but what Ghost Bear would not have wagered his life for the same prize?"

Jake paused again, waiting until Gilmour nodded permission for him to continue.

"I assure you, Star Colonel, that I am not in the habit of 'grandstanding' when my mission, or the lives of my troops, are on the line. I assure you that you can count on me one hundred percent when I am in command, sir."

"I am glad to hear it, Star Captain," Gilmour said briskly. "I will expect you to deliver on that promise."

He walked back around his desk and sat down again. "I also see from your codex that you have never commanded a combined-arms unit. I will tell you now that I never approved of the formation of Zeta Galaxy. An all-Elemental galaxy—what use is that in *real* combat?"

Jake took a breath. He could not argue with Gilmour the way he might have done with that poor excuse for a warrior named Paul. "I am an Elemental, Star Colonel, born and bred a warrior just as were you. My cadet training required me to qualify in all aspects of combat, including live-fire exercises working hand-in-hand with OmniMechs. I will spend every spare moment between now and our arrival on target to refine my skills. I will also brush up on the finer points of mechanized battle-armor operations if I have to burn the simulators to a crisp. I would welcome any suggestions you can offer, Star Colonel."

Gilmour shook his head. "No need to brown-nose around here, Jake. Just be sure to work closely with your star commanders and *listen* to your MechWarriors. They will save your ass one day."

More likely I will save their asses, Jake retorted silently. Even among the Ghost Bears, where Elementals were revered more than usual, MechWarriors had a tendency to believe themselves higher and mightier than mere infantry.

Gilmour sat back in his chair with his hands palm down on his desk. "Perhaps you are not aware that we cannot claim the honor of being among the first to attack the Combine. That honor went to those units fortunate enough to be stationed directly on the border when this all started: the Fifth Bear Guards, the Tenth Bear Cuirassiers, and the Fifth and Sixth Bear Regulars, among others. So far, their strikes have met with little resistance and exceptional success."

That last sentence caught in Jake's ear, so he risked interrupting. "Little resistance, sir?"

"The planets they attacked were thinly defended—for border worlds, at any rate. We do not know the reason, except that tensions on their other borders may have forces spread thin. Now that our reprisals for Alshain have begun, they will surely move reinforcements into the area as quickly as possible. That is where we come in."

Jake nodded. "We will meet those units head-on?"

"Not quite. The reinforcements are expected to come from the edgeward sector of the Combine. Our unit is being sent to Idlewind, which is in the coreward sector."

"Idlewind is just across the border from our current position. So we will attack soon, *quiaff*?"

"Aff, in six days the *Ursa Major*'s jump drives will be fully charged, and we will jump into Combine space. We will hit hard and fast, so that when reinforcements do arrive, they will have no support on-planet."

Jake was pleased to hear that they would be acting as the vanguard, even though they had missed the initial strike.

Gilmour sat staring at Jake for some moments. "Most of your new command is gathered in meeting hall beta, Star Captain. I suggest you go there straight away and become acquainted. Dismissed."

Jake knew he had his work cut out for him, both as a commander of men and with his own commander. Still, he was satisfied that he had held his own with Marcus Gilmour. He drew himself up even taller, raised his right hand, balled it into a fist, and thumped it against his chest. Gilmour returned the salute.

Jake turned smartly on his heel. Head held high, he walked toward the door. He was a ristar and proud of it, as any Clan warrior would be. He would find a way to win the approval of Marcus Gilmour if it was the last thing he did.

The star colonel sat thinking about the interview with Jake Kabrinski that had just concluded. After a moment, he picked up his noteputer and tapped a notation into Kabrinski's file.

"He wants the glory, but can he handle command?" Gilmour wrote. "Will need strong MechWarrior support."

The press of a button brought up a roster of the Mech-Warriors of the 288th. He scrolled down through the names and selected one, bringing up the file on Star Commander Lita. He nodded to himself as he put the noteputer back on his desk.

Yes, Lita would do nicely. He just hoped she would not be wasted trying to save a lost cause.

8

Battleship *Ursa Major*
Zenith Jump Point, Last Frontier
Ghost Bear Dominion
18 November 3062

Twenty-nine expectant pairs of eyes greeted Jake as he entered the grav deck's largest meeting hall. His command waited silently as their new star captain reached the front of the crowded space to address them for the first time. As Jake looked around at the faces, he felt a little nervous that all but two were unfamiliar. He smoothed the front of his gray uniform jacket and took a deep breath. His voice carried easily through the small space as he began to speak.

"At ease, warriors. This hall is not large enough to hold all fifty of the Elementals serving in this command, but I thought spin gravity would be more hospitable than floating around in a fighter bay while we got acquainted. I trust that the point commanders present will accurately relay my words and sentiments to their point members."

Jake was rewarded with a smattering of laughter over the pitfalls of zero-G. He was sure that many of them shared his preference for solid ground over floating in space.

"In six days the *Ursa Major* will finish recharging her drives. At that time, we will jump into Combine space as part of the Ghost Bear counterattack being launched all along their border. We will be the first Ghost Bears to set foot on the planet Idlewind, and I know we will be the first to win our battle."

Jake was glad to see heads nodding here and there. They were looking forward to the chance for combat as much as he was.

"Our Clan has awarded me the honor of leading this Trinary into battle against an opponent we have not faced in organized combat for a decade. I won this command because of what I have already accomplished, but it will be my deeds yet undone, and yours, that will carry us through the battles ahead. Our war against the Draconis Combine will demand more from me, and more from all of you, than we have ever been asked to give. They fight with different weapons and different tactics, and we must never underestimate them. As Clan warriors, we claim strengths our enemy can never hope to equal, but we will learn their shortcomings and add them to our arsenal of advantages."

Jake paused to look around again. He knew that the words he spoke now would set the tone of his command from this day forward.

"During the long space journey from Alshain to this system, I had plenty of time to review all of your codexes. They are impressive, and I will be proud to fight alongside you in the coming months. I earned this command in a Trial of Possession with your previous star captain. He was a strong warrior and a worthy opponent. I do not consider myself Carl's replacement, however, nor should you. Let this be a new day for our Clan and a new beginning for all of us."

Jake felt good standing there before his new Trinary, and he was gratified by the ripple of approval that ran through the room. He took a few steps toward a nearby chair, which he dragged over to where he had been standing. He turned the chair around, and sat down, straddling the chair-back.

He smiled. "I am glad the formalities are over with. Before we adjourn to duty stations, are there any questions? Comments?"

One young warrior stood up right away. He was tall for a

MechWarrior, and his curly black hair was shorn close. Jake recognized him at once, and gestured for him to speak.

The young warrior stepped forward slightly and cleared his throat. "MechWarrior Ben, Battle Nova, Point Two. A comment, sir."

Jake nodded, leaning forward with his arms resting on top of the chair-back.

"It was my privilege to fight alongside you and your Elementals against the Hell's Horses on Bearclaw last year," Ben said. "I was there at North Gryphon Falls and on Talon Ridge, although I did not have the pleasure of witnessing your victory over Khan Fletcher. It will be an honor to serve under your command."

Jake smiled. "Of course I remember you from Bearclaw, Ben. I look forward to having you in my nova. Anyone else?"

This time a female MechWarrior spoke up. "Star Commander Alexa, Striker Nova," she said. "I wish to ask you a question—if I may speak freely." She had the size and stature typical of her genotype, with short blond hair and cool gray eyes.

This warrior Jake did not recognize, but something in her tone hinted at trouble. He braced for the inevitable counterpoint to Ben's enthusiasm. "Speak freely now, Star Commander, or we may all regret it later."

Alexa folded her arms defiantly. "I have served with this Trinary, in this Cluster, for three years. Two years ago, I earned my star commander's bars. My codex speaks for itself. I am not ashamed to admit that I was surprised when you were given the right to challenge Carl over me."

Jake felt himself tense up, but he let her finish.

"My question is this," Alexa said, "why should I follow a warrior into battle who has no experience leading Battle-Mech forces, let alone leading a combined-arms trinary?"

Slowly, Jake stood up. At his full height of 210 centimeters, the top of his head nearly touched the ceiling. He decided that the only way to deal with the situation was to fight fire with fire.

"You need only one reason, Star Commander Alexa. I earned my rank and this command through fair Trial. My codex *also* speaks for itself. I have earned this command through my deeds. That is the way of the Clans."

Jake pushed the chair out of the way. "If any of you believe that I am unfit for command, it is your right to challenge me for it, just as I challenged Carl."

He looked back at Alexa. "I have no desire to fight you or anyone else in wasteful Trials on the eve of war. But let me be very clear. If any of you challenge me, I *will* defeat you, just as I defeated Star *Commander* Carl. I suggest that you carefully consider the consequences to our Trinary and our Clan if warriors are lost to such a challenge."

Alexa looked around the room, seeming to weigh her next words. "I agree that it would be wasteful to expend machines and warriors on frivolous Trials mere days before we attack the Combine. See to it that our trust in you is not misplaced, Star Captain Jake, and no such Trials will be necessary."

Jake nodded slowly. "Let me worry about that, Star Commander. All you have to worry about is doing your own duty to the Clan, *quiaff*?"

Her eyes flashed angrily, but Alexa nodded and said no more.

Satisfied that he had asserted his authority without too heavy a hand, Jake looked around again. "If there are no more questions, I am sure we all have duties to attend to. Dismissed!"

With that, the assembled warriors began to break up and file out through the exits. Jake noted that Star Commander Alexa was one of the first, as though she could hardly bear one more minute in the same room. MechWarrior Ben, however, was coming toward Jake.

As he made a formal salute, another warrior also advanced upstream through the crowd. She came up alongside Ben, just as he began to speak. "I just want to say once again, sir, that I am proud to be assigned to your nova. We have been training constantly since Bearclaw, and we are all anxious to strike back at the Combine. With you leading us, I am sure there is no enemy we cannot defeat."

The new arrival nudged Ben playfully with her elbow. The two were obviously comrades. "I think that is enough praise-heaping for one day, Ben," she said. "Give the man a rest."

Jake read her rank off her insignia. "Star Commander, I do not believe we have met . . ."

She stiffened and saluted, her voice dropping an octave as she feigned formality. "Lita, Battle Nova Commander, reporting for duty, sir."

Jake extended his hand and smiled broadly. "So, you are to be my second-in-command. Your codex is quite impressive. It is a pleasure to meet you in person."

Lita accepted his handshake, which gave Jake a moment to size her up. For a MechWarrior, she had a firm grasp, although he guessed that she had probably overcompensated because he was an Elemental. Lita was also quite tall for a MechWarrior, nearly as tall as some Elementals but much thinner. She would never fit in a 'Mech cockpit otherwise. She had lively green eyes that gave her a youthful air, despite the advanced age signaled by her gray-streaked auburn hair and sun-weathered skin. He knew her age, of course. At thirty-two years, she was old for a Clan warrior. Yet, her demeanor and expression seemed closer to that of the decade-younger Ben, but tempered with experience.

"I have served under Lita ever since being relocated to the Inner Sphere," Ben said. "She and I have been members of this Trinary for nearly a year. You are in good hands with her, Jake. She is the best *Mad Dog* pilot I have ever seen."

Jake smiled at their banter. "You should be proud, Lita. Coming from Ben that is high praise indeed, considering he is a *Mad Dog* pilot himself."

Lita slapped Ben on the back and laughed, a soft, musical sound that belied her obvious warrior nature. "Not such high praise, ever since he switched to a *Nova*, but appreciated none the less."

Jake was already beginning to like this Lita, yet her informal manner was cause for concern. And it was not just Lita. He had observed the same lax standards among other warriors who had spent more time in the Inner Sphere. Discipline was everything in a warrior, and Jake could not help but wonder about the wisdom of the Ghost Bear relocation.

He decided he would speak to her about it later, before it became a problem.

"Speaking of my *Mad Dog*," Lita said, "I had best go attend to it before my tech puts its arms on backwards. But you and I need to know each other better, Jake Kabrinski. I do not want to wait until we are on the field dodging Kurita missiles to get acquainted."

Jake laughed. "Indeed. Since our esteemed star colonel has insisted that I log extra time in combined-arms simulations, I think that would be an excellent way to begin our partnership."

Lita winked. "I look forward to it, Star Captain. I will make sure you get a good workout."

Jake looked from Lita to Ben. Although he had only just arrived, this was already feeling like home.

"Come, warriors," he said, starting toward the door. "I have had enough of sitting at a desk poring over codex files. Let us have Battle Nova report for simulations at 0800 tomorrow. And make sure Star Colonel Marcus is invited to observe. I definitely do not want *him* to miss our first day."

9

"**E**nemy drop zone at two kilometers and closing. Battle Nova, prepare for Elemental deployment on my mark."

Lita's voice crackled over Jake's commline, the static a result of radioactive impurities. Radiation was not a problem for him while encased in his battle armor, but the doses in this planet's atmosphere could kill an average-size human in a matter of minutes.

Of course, that would not happen because this was a simulation. Yet still the signals and images registering in Jake's HUD were the same as if he were actually riding the hull of Lita's *Mad Dog* as it raced across the countryside at eighty-five kilometers per hour. In reality, the two warriors were on entirely different decks of the *Ursa Major*, separated by more than a hundred meters, but connected to the same computer-controlled simulation.

No matter how many times he ran these simulators—twice or three times daily since joining the 288th—the virtual reality they created remained almost entirely convincing, thanks to advanced Clan holography and biofeedback. Jake could hear the wind howling outside his helmet, and the *Mad Dog*'s every footfall sent tremors through his armor. The 'Mech's pace was slowing to a walk now in preparation for his point's dismount.

Lita signaled again. "Mark."

Although Jake was in overall command of Gamma Trinary, Lita was the unit's senior MechWarrior. She performed as the unit's commander while his Elementals were mounted, a common arrangement in nova stars led by Elementals. For one thing, a BattleMech's sensors were more advanced than an Elemental's, and an Elemental was not much more than cargo while clinging to the sides of an OmniMech.

"Star One, dismount!" Jake called, his words setting the twenty-five battle-armored Elementals of Gamma Trinary's Battle Nova into motion. Jump jets flaring, the warriors leapt clear of their mounts in practiced unison, landing to the rear and sides of the still-moving Omnis so as not to be trampled underfoot.

"Delta and Epsilon points, flank left to the hills and await my command," Jake said quickly. "Alpha, Beta, and Gamma Points with me. Star Two, flank right." They had dismounted in a gorge running through some rolling hills.

"Aye, Star Captain," Lita confirmed. "My 'Mechs will draw them out."

The objective was an Inner Sphere company of twelve BattleMechs that had made a low-altitude drop into the hills directly north of Jake's position. His plan was simple: divide and conquer. Orbital surveillance indicated that the enemy's three lances had scattered somewhat on landing, so the plan was to engage each lance individually rather than face the entire company at once.

The nova's five OmniMechs presented the most tempting and visible target to the Spheroids, so they were acting as decoys. Meanwhile, the main body of Elementals would move straight up the middle, directly toward the enemy drop zone. Depending on the enemy's reaction to the flanking 'Mechs, the Elementals stood a good chance of hitting them in the rear. Two stars of Elementals would also take the left flank, acting as a mobile reserve and blocking the avenue of retreat in case the enemy force tried to withdraw.

Jake switched to the private frequency he shared with Val, who headed up Beta Point. "Everything is going according to plan so far," he said.

Interference over the channel added a high-pitched squeal to her reply. "Aye, but do not forget that Star Colonel Marcus is running the show today."

"I have not forgotten. In fact, I am counting on his determination to prove me unfit for command."

"Why is he still on your case, Jake?" Lita asked.

Jake had no answer, though he had pondered the same question more times than he could count. "He and Alexa seem to have some kind of grudge against Elementals."

Val spoke through another wave of static. "From the way Alexa snapped at you in yesterday's exercise, I think she is jealous of your rank. But the star colonel?"

"It does not matter why he has it in for me. I intend to use it to beat him today."

"How?" Val asked, though her signal became weaker and the squeal became stronger as she ranged away from Jake's position. Her point was scouting the hills to the east of the main body.

"They say Marcus is a fine tactical commander, but his dislike of me could blind his judgment and give us the advantage we need to defeat a numerically superior force."

Val's signal was getting weaker. "I suppose . . . your Point, Jake. Hold on . . . signal at . . . confirm?"

"Val, I am losing you. Repeat all after 'hold on.'" Jake tried to boost his radio's signal power, guessing that Val was having the same trouble receiving him.

The only reply was static.

Lita and her command were eager for battle, even a simulated one. Now that her Star had delivered its Elementals, she ordered them back up to full speed. Easily outpacing the Elementals, they would circle around the hills to the east.

"Do you think Jake's plan will really work?" Ben said over Star Two's frequency. "Why not hold our ground in a more defensive stance rather than risk being flanked in the open field?"

"Jake thinks Gilmour wants to make us look bad, so we have to prove something today. He is not going to sit on his haunches among the hills simply waiting for us to attack, but Marcus can be unpredictable. We must stay alert."

This seemed to set off a chorus among her Star.

"We are always alert, *quiaff*?" said Petra, the *Stormcrow* pilot.

"Aff," said MechWarrior Reese in his gruff voice, "but in this situation we are at a disadvantage. Not only are we facing the Star Colonel, we do not know the composition of his force. He could have anything from old Succession War 'Mechs up through the latest models to walk off the assembly line. My *Hellbringer* is more than a match for any vintage 'Mech, but I do not know about the others. Have you seen the readout on the *Templar*?"

"I have," said Umbriel this time, "and it is a fearsome design indeed. One thing we know is that Gilmour has configured his force to approximate a Kurita company, to better prepare us for the battles to come. They would be unlikely to have access to one of the Federated Commonwealth's newest OmniMechs." Umbriel was the star's resident expert on BattleMech specifications, not surprising since she had been born into the technician caste and had actually fought her way up to a front-line warrior assignment.

"Enough talk for now," Lita cut in. "Let us concentrate on the scanners. Umbriel, scout ahead but stay in visual contact."

Umbriel's forty-ton *Viper*, the lightest and fastest 'Mech in the star, made an excellent heavy scout. "Aye, Star Commander. The radiation interference might cut me off from the rest of you if I range out too far."

"I confirm your situation, Star Captain," said Point Commander John. "We have no sign of Beta Point, either. It must be the radiation." John's Gamma Point had stayed closer than Beta.

Jake considered their options: search for Val or stick to the plan? It was possible that Beta had been ambushed, in which case they would probably need help. On the other hand, if they were merely out of radio range, they would be sticking to the plan, too, and might be heading back to rendezvous with the rest of the force even now. Furthermore, the delay caused by a search could jeopardize the Elementals' coordination with Star Two.

John radioed Jake again. "What should we do, Star Captain? My point could split off and check the hills to the east—"

"Neg, we will stick to the plan, John. Keep your point close to mine and continue to advance to the north." Jake didn't like the idea of potentially abandoning Val, but he liked deviating from the plan even less. Besides, Val could handle herself if her point got into trouble.

"We are in trouble, people. Spread out and keep firing!"

Val squeezed off a laser shot before engaging her jump jets again, narrowly avoiding a flight of long-range missiles. Her mind raced over the few available options. Her point had ranged out on the right flank, according to their standard deployment pattern, but had lost radio contact with the rest of the nova. Before she could reestablish contact, a lance of enemy 'Mechs converged on their position. Although a point of five Elementals could usually defeat a single 'Mech, an entire lance of four was more than a match, forcing her point into a fighting retreat toward Jake's last known position.

By ordering her point to spread out, Val hoped the enemy 'Mechs would split up to give chase, preventing them from concentrating their firepower. She was fortunate that her tactic worked, but unfortunate that the heaviest 'Mech in the opposing lance, a forty-five-ton *Wolf Trap*, had chosen her as its target. With a running speed three times that of her battle suit's jumping speed, it was only a matter of seconds before it closed for the kill.

Glancing at the rear-view portion of her HUD, she could see the humanoid *Wolf Trap* thundering toward her, raising its right-arm autocannon in preparation for flattening her with a hail of bullets the size of her leg.

"Alpha Point, this is Beta Point. We are engaged with an

enemy lance. Over." Val tried the radio again, but had little hope it would save her point from her current predicament.

Suddenly, she smiled as she remembered her technical briefing on the *Wolf Trap*. "Jake, can you hear me? We are outmatched here and in need of reinforcements. Over."

Nothing.

Well, there was more than one way to skin a surat. The *Wolf Trap* thought she was running. Let him continue to think that.

She crested a hill, then dropped prone, and rolled to a stop, lying face-up just beyond the hilltop. She could feel the thrumming footfalls of the *Wolf Trap*, approaching at a full run into point-blank range. As long as it did not step on her, this should work.

Looking up, Val saw the bottom of a huge, oval-shaped foot pass overhead, easily large enough to squash her like a bug. She held her breath as the foot came crashing down, but it landed just shy of her.

She slowly let her breath out and raised her right arm, taking aim on the 'Mech's right-rear torso plating as it ran past her position. The *Wolf Trap* got its considerable speed from the huge, extra-light engine that filled the 'Mech's entire torso. The armor on the 'Mech's back was thin enough to be breached with just two shots from Val's support laser, unless the 'Mech turned around fast enough to stop her from getting the second shot.

Here goes nothing, she thought. Val fired her first shot, a ruby lance of energy that streamed toward the back of the *Wolf Trap* at the speed of light. She saw that she was right on target. Yes!

It would take a few seconds for the laser crystals in her weapon to cool off before she could fire again. In the meantime, she could see the *Wolf Trap* slowing down to begin its about-face. Fortunately, forty-five tons of metal and myomer could not stop on a dime. Dirt and rocks were kicked up as the *Wolf Trap* decelerated and began turning to the right.

Val could see her target point disappearing, and glanced at her HUD. The support laser's indicator was still red.

"Damn it, cool down!" she said, as if that could speed up the weapon's recycle rate.

She looked forward again, just in time to see the *Wolf Trap*'s autocannon arm swivel around to face her. Her laser indicator turned green.

"Eat this, freebirth scum!" she shouted, triggering her laser.

The shot landed squarely at the spot she had scorched with her previous attack, lasing a hole through the exterior armor and stabbing into the complicated machinery within. Her years of training were well spent. If she was lucky, the shot would superheat one of the ammo bins residing in the 'Mech's torso, causing a massive explosion.

She was not lucky.

Undaunted, the *Wolf Trap* continued on, finishing its circle and unleashing a stream of projectiles from its autocannon arm and beams of crimson from its twin, torso-mounted medium lasers. As the weapons found their mark on Val's battle armor, her HUD display filled with static, then went black.

She could hear the voice of Marcus Gilmour clearly over her radio now that the simulated static was gone.

"Bang," he said. "You are dead. Congratulations, Point Commander Valerie. You are the first casualty in today's exercise. Report for debriefing once you have recovered from your untimely death."

"Star Commander, I have a radar contact." It was Umbriel's voice over the static-ridden radio waves.

Lita responded quickly. "I copy, Point Kappa."

"I see a group of 'Mechs ahead. By my estimation, they are very close to the drop point. It is a group of six to nine machines."

"I would say two lances, eight 'Mechs," Val said, "most likely the main body of their company. I wager their scout lance is out in the hills. Are they moving?"

"Neg. They appear to be motionless. Possibly arrayed in a defensive circle. It is hard to be sure. The radioactivity is playing havoc with my radar."

"Then, they either have not seen us, or do not care. They will care soon enough. Point Eta?"

"Here, Star Commander," Ben said.

"Ben, go on ahead and rendezvous with Umbriel. You two can use your jump jets to cross the hills wide to the right. We will probably lose radio contact, so do not wait for a signal from me to attack. Rather, strike their flank in exactly two minutes."

"Excellent plan!" Ben said, excitement in his voice. "You will draw them out, and we will hit them where it hurts."

Lita revved her *Mad Dog* up to a full sprint. "Aye. And if Jake is on schedule, he will be coming in on their other flank right along with you."

Jake glanced at the chronometer in his HUD, then looked toward the hills in front of him. There was still no sign of Val's point, but he forced that out of his thoughts. The rest of his force was on-target and on time.

"Point Alpha, Point Gamma, halt." At Jake's command, the nine other Elementals stopped their bounding leaps across the hills. They formed up into a rough line fifty meters long.

"The enemy drop zone should be directly over the hills to the north. The radiation has rendered radio contact with our OmniMechs impossible, and our own radar is virtually useless for the same reason."

John interrupted with a question. "My estimate on the enemy position agrees with yours, Star Captain, but how will we coordinate our attack if we cannot contact Star Two?"

Jake smiled. John was an excellent warrior and an able point commander, but not very imaginative in his approach to challenges.

"Listen," Jake said.

The ten Elementals stood motionless and silent. As if on cue came the faint sounds of BattleMech footfalls and distant weapons fire. "There they are, and right on time," Jake said. "All Elementals, advance!"

With that, he engaged his jump jets and leapt onto the

crest of the hill. Looking out across the valley, he could see that his estimate of "right on time" was perhaps a bit premature. Lita's OmniMechs had already engaged the enemy, and they were outnumbered nearly three-to-one.

"Have they lost two 'Mechs already?" It was John again.

"Let us hope not. But if they have, then we must not delay. Follow me in, low and quiet."

Rather than use his jump jets, Jake ran toward the target zone. He and the others would be well concealed by the gently rolling terrain, and the radiation interference would render them nearly invisible to radar.

When he was almost in attack range of the nearest Combine 'Mech, a fifty-ton *Blackjack*, Jake heard a faint crackle on the nova's open channel. A glance at the radio icon of his HUD engaged the automatic tuner, which began to wrestle with the faint signal. Before he could get the results, his force was in range.

"All Elementals, fire on the *Blackjack* on my mark," he ordered.

Ten Elementals slowed and stopped, concealed behind a low rise some two hundred meters behind the medium 'Mech.

"Mark," Jake said. Twenty short-range missiles burst free of their launchers and raced toward the back of the *Blackjack*. Eighteen found their mark, exploding all over the 'Mech's ten-meter-tall body, nearly half of them slamming into the right-rear torso. Jake could see the telltale "aftershocks" rattling the *Blackjack* as its autocannon ammunition stores began to explode in sequence. The MechWarrior ejected from the cockpit mere seconds before the entire machine was engulfed in a brilliant orange fireball.

A cheer went up from his Elementals, but Jake was still watching the smoke drifting where the *Blackjack* had been. As if reading his thoughts, a flight of missiles burst from the cloud and smashed into the ridge his troops were using for cover, knocking most of them off their feet.

"Well, that got their attention!" It was Lita, barely audible but still in the game.

Jake smiled to hear her voice. His concerns about whether she was too lax about discipline had proved unfounded. Over the past few days, he had learned that on the battlefield she was all business. "So much for the element of surprise. My troops will continue to draw their attention."

"Much obliged, Star Captain. And yours is not the only surprise in store for the Spheroids."

As a pair of spider-like Combine *Bishamon*s came bursting through the smoke toward Jake's position, a blinding fusillade of green pulse-laser blasts came at them from the north. One of the 'Mechs, hammered by more than a dozen hits, ceased its advance and turned north to face Ben's *Nova* and Umbriel's *Viper*. The other *Bishamon* continued toward the Elementals, launching a swarm of medium-range missiles from the oval canister on its back.

Some of the Elementals ducked behind the ridge, where they were safe from the MRM attack. Jake and four other Elementals lit off their jump jets, flying up and away from the approaching attack. This turned out to be the wrong move. The *Bishamon*'s aim was high, catching the jumping Elementals at the apex of their flight. Five missiles rammed into Jake, knocking him out of the air.

For a moment, Jake could neither move nor breathe. Electrodes, drugs, and countless other devices implanted in his "trainer suit" simulated endless battlefield conditions, including having the wind knocked out of you by twenty kilograms of missiles. It was a painful, but accurate, representation of the punishment Jake would have received on the real battlefield had he made the same mistake.

Lifting himself into a sitting position, he glanced at his HUD. Radar showed that the Ghost Bear and Inner Sphere forces were now well and truly engaged. With the interference, it was hard to tell which side was winning, let alone who was where. Jake decided that, since none of the enemy was likely to leave the area, he should call in his reinforcements.

Then he realized they would not be able to hear his signal or respond.

Pulling himself to his feet, he steeled himself for more combat. This battle was not over yet . . .

*   *   *

"The battle was over before it began."

Star Colonel Marcus Gilmour paced pack and forth across the front of the room, where the sweaty smell of Battle Nova's thirty soldiers still lingered in the air. The general debriefing was over, but Jake had remained behind.

"I disagree, sir," he said, straightening up in his chair. "My plan was sound, and it nearly worked."

Gilmour stopped and turned toward Jake. "Wrong. You knew about the radiation interference and the problems it might pose for communications, but you failed to plan for that contingency.

"And besides, 'it almost worked' is what I should be hearing from some used-up solahma—or the dead. Not from one of my front-line star captains."

That hurt, but Jake had to agree. His plan had a flaw, and he had failed to realize it until it was too late.

"You are right, Star Colonel. I do not dispute my error in judgment. What I am disputing is your assessment of the result. At worst, the battle was a draw, and some might even call it a marginal Clan victory."

Marcus Gilmour turned away from Jake to face the white-board at the front of the meeting room. Its surface was covered with hand-sketched diagrams of the simulated battle they had just run. "I knew you were going to be trouble the moment I saw you. A typical, big-headed *ristar*. I think they must have invented the term for you."

That got Jake's blood pumping, launching him to his feet. "No, sir, not a typical *ristar* at all. A typical *warrior.*"

Gilmour spun to face Jake. "You contradict me, soldier?"

"You have been waiting for me to fail ever since I first set foot on the *Ursa Major*. You thought I would not be able to command a combined-arms unit and that I might take unnecessary risks because I am an ambitious young warrior."

Gilmour nodded. "Exactly."

"Today's simulation was my first defeat since joining this unit—and only a marginal defeat at that. I might remind you that I survived to the end of the simulation. It was you who called an end to it, Star Colonel, declaring it a 'tactical defeat' for my side before I had a chance to fell the one remaining enemy 'Mech."

Gilmour crossed his arms over his chest. "Yes, yes. We all know your penchant for head-to-head duels with Battle-Mechs. But what is your point?"

"My point is simply that I failed to take the environment enough into account when I made my battle plan. Today's 'tactical defeat' came from the radiation present on that simulated world and your own counter-strategy. It had nothing to do with my lack of combined-arms experience or my *ristar* ambition.

"My plan was flawed," Jake continued, "and I accept responsibility for my nova's performance in today's simulation. All I ask is that you do not take this single event as proof that your theories about me are correct."

Gilmour did not speak right away, but his expression was unreadable. Then he began, uttering each word as though it had been carefully selected. "I think you have made your point abundantly clear, Star Captain. Now let me make my point abundantly clear: If I have seen nothing this day that confirms my 'theories' about you, I have also seen nothing that disproves them. Until that occurs, I will continue to watch you very closely, Jake Kabrinski."

Jake sighed inwardly, but was careful not to let his exasperation show. He could see that he would need more than a few simulator victories to convince Gilmour that he was worthy of his command position.

He snapped a sharp salute. "It will be my pleasure to prove you wrong, sir."

The barest hint of a smile crossed Marcus Gilmour's lips as he returned the salute and told Jake he was dismissed.

"We shall see about that," he said in a voice just loud enough for Jake to hear as he left.

Khan Malavai Fletcher was deep in a review of the state of his touman when he was interrupted by a communication from the main deck. He tapped a button that connected the commline in his private quarters with his officers.

"My Khan, there is an incoming holographic message for you," the communications officer said.

"Put it through," Fletcher snapped.

He spun his chair around to face the corner of the room where the holoimage would appear. Within moments, he was looking at a full-length projection of Wolf Khan Vladimir Ward.

"Greetings, Malavai Fletcher. The Wolves welcome you to the Inner Sphere," Vlad said, smiling in that arrogant way of his. "I understand you have only just arrived from the homeworlds. Once you have completed the review of your troops, I invite you to visit me on Tamar.

"I have some information you may find useful, but its sensitive nature requires that I only communicate it to you in person. I can guarantee it will be worth the trip. Until we meet . . ."

The image dissolved into empty space once more.

Fletcher leaned back in his chair, still staring at the place where Vlad's image had been. He rubbed his jaw in thought. What possible "information" could the Khan of the Wolves have that would interest the Khan of the Hell's Horses?

What were those cursed Wolves up to now?

"Whatever it is," Malavai Fletcher growled to himself, "we will be ready."

10

Approach Vector, Idlewind
Pesht Military District
Draconis Combine
25 November 3062

With the *Ursa Major* on its approach vector for Idlewind, Marcus Gilmour had called his commanders together for a staff meeting. The meeting would be held on the *Ursa*'s bridge, which Jake had not yet found time to visit. As the double doors slid open before him, he marveled at the sight. He had never seen a spacecraft as large or advanced as this cutting-edge *Nightlord* Class vessel.

The bridge was shaped like a trapezoid—about one hundred meters long and seventy-five meters wide at its widest point aft, where Jake had entered. The ceilings were high enough to allow BattleMechs to walk through without stooping over. To his right and left were pressure doors also large enough to allow them access from the main cargo bays if need be.

He had entered on the bridge's upper level, where the ship's captain and her immediate subordinates had their stations. A pair of staircases led down some five meters to the lower level, whose walls were lined with dozens of secondary duty stations. Huge plasteel windows ran above them along the fore, starboard, and port walls, each pane ten meters tall and twenty-five wide. The panoramic view they offered of the space surrounding the *Ursa Major* was truly breathtaking, and Jake stopped in his tracks to take it in.

"I do not remember the techs installing a wall here," someone said from behind him, but when Jake turned around, all he saw were the bridge doors sliding shut.

It took a moment for him to get the joke. Squeezed between him and the door was a type of Clan warrior bred exactly opposite of an Elemental. At a meter shorter than Jake, he was invisible until Jake dropped his gaze. The man had the enlarged cranium and eyes that were an offshoot of the genetic engineering to increase an aerospace pilot's perceptive ability and reaction times. He was barely 165 centimeters tall, however, and as thin as a rail to better squeeze into the cramped confines of a fighter cockpit. His skin was pale, and his black hair was a mere fringe around his face.

Jake knew immediately the identity of the warrior. He wore the insignia of a star captain, and only one trinary commander in the whole cluster was a fighter pilot.

Jake stepped back to give the smaller warrior some space, and extended his hand. "You must be Star Captain Rai," he said.

The diminutive warrior accepted Jake's handshake enthusiastically. "Indeed I am. And you must be Star Captain Jake Kabrinski. I have heard much about your exploits, and I must say I am impressed. You seem to be quite capable for a ground-pounder."

Jake smiled and looked sideways at the pilot, assuming the slight was merely good-natured ribbing. Pilot-bred warriors were a rare sight among the ranks of the Ghost Bears because the Clan judged that the negative aspects of the breed outweighed the positive. The Bears had never adopted the fighter pilot phenotype into their breeding program, as had the other Clans. Rai must surely have been taken as a bondsman and then later accepted into the Ghost Bear warrior caste.

He was about to ask, but the doors opened behind him again. This time Star Colonel Gilmour stepped onto the bridge. He was accompanied by his aide, Star Commander Willem, a bald Elemental even larger than Jake.

"Well, I see you two arrived early," Gilmour said. "Admiring the view, Rai?"

"As always, sir," Rai said as he and Jake saluted.

Gilmour gestured toward the center of the bridge. "Come, join me at the holotank while we wait for the others."

He led the way to a circular platform about five meters in diameter, which stood just behind the captain's station. Star Commodore Angelina Devon turned in her chair and stood up as the group approached. Gilmour offered her a quick salute. Although the two officers held equivalent rank, this was *her* ship.

"Request permission to engage holotank," Gilmour said with stiff formality. Jake wondered if that was due to the usual rivalry between spacers and ground-pounders, or something more.

She returned the salute. "Of course, Star Colonel. But see to it that your staff meeting does not disturb my bridge crew. We *are* in hostile territory, after all."

"You will hardly know we are here, Star Commodore," Gilmour said, but he looked visibly irritated.

The bridge doors opened again, admitting Star Captain Zira Bekker, commander of Beta Trinary, the last remaining officer of Gilmour's command staff. She had a mane of shoulder-length, platinum blonde hair and a seemingly permanent scowl on her face. Jake had passed her in the corridors a few times, but he and she had never exchanged words.

"Right on time, Zira. Now we can begin." Gilmour reached out with the toe of his boot to tap the activation stud at the base of the holotank.

Immediately, the area above the platform was filled with light, then quickly dimmed and coalesced into a star map of the Inner Sphere. Gilmour stepped onto the platform and touched a red point of light representing a Draconis Combine world. He turned his hand clockwise, and the image zoomed in on the border between the Combine and the Ghost Bear Dominion.

He looked down from the holotank platform, surrounded by a halo of stars. "As you all know, the Ghost Bears were only too happy to accept the challenge after the unprovoked and unannounced attack on our capital world of Alshain some five weeks ago. This act clearly demonstrated that the unspoken truce between the Dominion and the Combine was null and void. For ten years, we have been waiting and preparing for just this moment."

Jake looked around at his fellow officers. They were nodding in agreement. Everyone was glad that the time for war had finally come.

"As you know, we launched counterattacks almost immediately. Those units already stationed along the border were among the first to move into Combine territory. Staging from their garrison posts, they attacked the targets closest to them."

As he spoke, Gilmour reached out and touched three Combine worlds spaced evenly along the border. Their color shifted from red to pale blue, representing Ghost Bear control. "Already the planets Richmond, Schuyler, and Kanowit are firmly under our control. Battles from this first wave continue on no fewer than ten Combine border worlds. Other units are being deployed as quickly as possible from their Dominion postings to Combine targets.

Intelligence indicates that many of the Combine's best units were stationed along the Federated Commonwealth border when our first wave began. We can expect stiffer resistance as the enemy also rotates more troops to the Dominion border. This is where we come in. Willem?"

Gilmour stepped down and gestured to his aide, who came forward and took his commander's place on the holotank platform. The hulking Elemental's voice was as forbidding as his presence. "Our cluster is part of a second wave of attacks striking at worlds not touched by the first wave. We will attack planets along the entire length of the border, which will prevent the enemy from being able to concentrate their forces on a few specific targets. In this way, their superior numbers will be negated, and they should prove no match for our superior skills and equipment."

Willem reached into the holographic field and touched a red world as he closed his hand into a fist. The point of light rapidly expanded until the stellar map was replaced by the three-dimensional image of a slowly spinning planet.

"Our part of the plan is the planet Idlewind. We arrived at the system's nadir jump point twenty hours ago. Since then, we have encountered no resistance and received no transmissions from the planet. Our transit from jump point to planet will take seven more days, but I expect no aerospace resistance until we reach orbit."

"I doubt we will be attacked in orbit either," Rai said.

"What makes you so sure?" Zira asked, her tone scornful. "Perhaps you are anxious to lead your trinary from the safety of this bridge?"

Rai frowned, but otherwise ignored the insult. "From what we know of Kurita warriors, they favor a combat style not unlike our own. They value honor, albeit a different flavor of it, and also have been known to duel."

"I had heard that they ceased their dueling practices some years ago, *quiaff*?" Jake interjected.

"Aff, but so did we, if you recall," Rai said. "My point is simply that they, like us, would rather fight on the ground than in space. If they had wanted to destroy us inbound, they would have attacked us at the jump point while we were recovering from the jump."

"Perhaps they sent their space forces to the zenith jump point," said Star Commander Devon from her captain's chair, without turning around.

"I doubt they would commit all their forces at one jump point or the other," Gilmour said quickly, probably to regain control of the briefing. "It is far more likely that they will engage us when we reach orbit, or as Rai suggests, they will not meet us in space at all. Assuming for the moment that such is the case, we have our choice of landing zones."

He reached out and touched the image of Idlewind, and three pulsing points of light appeared on its surface. "Alpha, Beta, and Gamma Supernovas will land at three separate drop points, as shown here. These three targets represent the planet's main production and defense sites. It is expected that the DCMS will array the bulk of their forces to defend those sites, which will allow us to fulfill our primary goal of neutralizing the planet's defenders.

"Alpha will disembark from the *Arctic Cave* via low-altitude drop here, and secure what appears to be the planet's primary munitions manufacturing and storage facility. Beta will execute a drop some two hundred kilometers to the north, attacking Idlewind's only military-grade spaceport and holding it for our later use if need be. The *Cave* will continue north with Gamma, then land among the concealment of Fakir's Canyon. Our analysis suggests that the caves there are the likely location of an underground command center. Gamma will seek out that command center and destroy it. If that proves unnecessary, they will act as a mobile reserve for Alpha and Beta, as they will be stationed with the *Arctic Cave*."

Jake bristled at the idea that he might not get a chance to strike back at the Combine after waiting so long. He consoled himself with the thought that the most scrupulous analysis would have identified the caves as a target, and that there would indeed be something to fight in those canyons.

"What units defend the planet?" Jake asked when Gilmour paused for questions.

The star colonel glanced over at his aide, who looked down at his handheld noteputer as he spoke. "Our latest information places the Ninth Pesht Regulars on Idlewind. An unexceptional regiment, but their commander is said to be ruthless."

Zira Bekker grinned and raised one clenched fist. "Ruthless like their *dezgra* attack on Alshain, *quiaff*? They will find that we are even more ruthless when provoked."

Gilmour raised an eyebrow. "Indeed, Star Captain."

He switched the holotank off and stepped down from the platform. With a glance back toward Angelina Devon, he spoke in a low voice. "I fear we are wearing out our welcome here on the bridge."

His offhand comment drew a chuckle from the officers, but Jake guessed that the uncharacteristically conspiratorial comment was the colonel's calculated attempt to create sympathy among his officers.

"Well, that is the gist of it," Gilmour said, his voice normal again. "The briefings on your individual targets have been downloaded into your noteputers. Study them well. In a week, the long wait since Tukayyid will finally be over. Soon, the Ghost Bear flag will fly over Idlewind."

11

Tomita carefully slid the *shoji* panel shut behind him and stepped into the small garden. For a moment, its simple beauty replaced the sense of dread that had accompanied him from the Newbury HPG station to this little country house. A wall three meters tall enclosed the garden, but it was concealed by the leafy boughs and blossoms of trees growing all along it. A flower garden had been placed at each corner of the garden, each one surrounded by a ring of carefully placed stones.

At the center of the garden, a fifth ring had been crafted into the tiled walkway. Sitting inside the circle was a lone figure, dressed in a simple white *gi* and with his legs folded under him. His shoulder-length white hair and neatly trimmed white beard suggested that he had lived many seasons, but he gave off an aura of inner strength that belied his ancient appearance.

Tomita approached the man slowly, stopping just outside the circle. He waited to speak until formally recognized. Although he had carried messages to and from this man many times, this time was different. He knew it was not customary to kill the messenger, but in this case, he feared bringing bad news.

After a pause long enough to give gravity to the interruption without wasting either man's time, the white-haired man slowly opened his eyes and looked up at Tomita. "You bring news of the Ghost Bear war."

Tomita bowed deeply at the waist, and held the bow for several beats before straightening again. "*Hai,* the fighting proceeds as expected. Combine troops have fallen to the Clan at nearly every turn."

The old man watched Tomita intently but did not speak.

"The DCMS is pulling veteran and elite regiments from the Federated Commonwealth front, but those troops will not arrive quickly enough to offer immediate reinforcement. It is predicted that at least a dozen worlds will fall to the Ghost Bears before the year is out."

Tomita paused, and the old man simply waited. He knew that Tomita was not getting to the point. Tomita took a deep breath and forged ahead, determined to get this over with.

"There has been a . . . complication on Schuyler. On that world, Aletha Kabrinski, the Ghost Bear saKhan, led her troops personally into battle. *Tai-shu* Teyasu Ashora happened to be onplanet at the time, and he apparently believed honor demanded that he personally meet such a worthy opponent in combat."

The old man finally spoke, stroking his thin beard with one hand as he did. "So, the warlord of the Pesht Military District is dead. For once, things move our way without the need for us to pull any strings. After the setback we suffered on Alshain, this is indeed fortunate. From the look of you, I thought you were bringing *bad* news."

Tomita opened his mouth to speak, but no words came. The old man narrowed his eyes ever so slightly, just enough to raise Tomita's blood pressure. "His replacement as warlord?" he asked.

"Of course, these appointments normally take weeks or months, but in time of war—"

"Out with it, Tomita, lest this meeting take weeks or months."

The even tone of the old man's voice was far more chilling than if he had shouted in anger. Tomita swallowed, then spoke two seemingly simple words. "Tomoe Sakade."

A long silence passed between the two men, but only Tomita showed any outward signs of emotion. He did his best to hide it, but he was nervous about the old man's reaction—whatever it might be.

The white-haired man closed his eyes, returning to his silent meditation. Without permission to leave, and not daring to speak out of turn, Tomita had little choice but to remain at rigid attention. He dared not glance at his chronometer, but he estimated that a good twenty minutes passed before the old man finally spoke.

He did not open his eyes or in any way alter his serene pose. "So, Theodore has installed his own low-born *wife* as warlord of the most important military district in the Combine. Once again, he shows us that he failed to inherit his father's strength of character. Once again, he reminds us that only the Black Dragons can restore the strength and glory of the Draconis Combine, no matter the cost."

A few moments passed before he spoke again. "This time our esteemed Coordinator has gone *too* far."

Tomita bowed, holding it longer and deeper than before. "Understood."

Another few minutes of silence passed. "Has the replacement for her prefecture command been named?" the old man asked.

"Not yet, but several candidates are known to be under consideration. The Coordinator is expected to make the appointment next week."

The old man nodded slightly, a slight smile crossing his thin lips. "The Seventh Sword of Light is fully rebuilt. It is high time that Kiyomori Minamoto stepped forward to accept the promotion Theodore has so repeatedly offered him. How could such a loyal son of the Combine refuse this honor in the Dragon's time of need?"

Tomita bowed again, knowing the meeting was finally over. Taking a few steps backward before turning to leave the garden, his head swam with the implications of this day's events. He had believed himself the bearer of bad tidings. Instead, he seemed to be the herald of a change that would bring the Combine to its most crucial turning point since the Kentares Massacre.

Tomita's heart swelled with pride. Soon, so very soon, the Black Dragons would return the Draconis Combine to the old ways and to its rightful position of dominance in the Inner Sphere.

12

Fakir's Canyon was something of a misnomer. It was not simply a single gorge cut into the earth by an ancient river but a vast network of canyon systems at the intersection of three of Idlewind's tectonic plates. Some of the canyons had been cut by rivers, others by earthquakes and continental shifts, and still others were dug centuries ago by Star League-era mining operations.

The net result was a series of twisting trenches, which provided an ideal setting for cat-and-mouse games like the one a Combine *Hunchback* had been playing with Lita for the better part of an hour. She would come out from behind a corner, let off a hasty shot with her Tomodzuru autocannon, then duck back into cover. Lita's *Mad Dog* was just fast enough that the *Hunchback* could not get away, but it always seemed to be one step ahead of her, as if the Mech-Warrior was enjoying the game.

She did not share his pleasure.

"Battle Nova, what is your status?" came Jake's voice over the radio.

"I am about to teach an old samurai a new trick," she

said. "I trust your Elementals are keeping the local infantry entertained?"

"Aff, that we are. Just give me the short-form report, Lita."

Checking her radar screen, which was static-ridden because of the high metal content of the surrounding walls, Lita could see the *Hunchback* moving around to hit her right flank. Pivoting her 'Mech ninety degrees to the right, she lined up her HUD's targeting cross hairs with a narrow crease in the canyon wall.

"Just wide enough for a *Hunchback*."

"What was that?"

Lita smiled, "Just thinking out loud, sir. I am occupied with a *Hunchback* at the moment—a stalemate that will soon be resolved. The rest of my star is divided into two teams. Points Beta and Epsilon are using their jump jets to scout the upper parts of the canyon for snipers, while Gamma and Delta are just north of my position. On last report they were crushing a Kurita heavy lance."

She could hear machine gun fire behind Jake's reply. "See if you can rendezvous with my Elementals in Sector D after you are finished there," he said. "The *Ursa Major* just sent some new orbital images that require immediate attention."

"Acknowledged, Star Commander." As Lita watched, the shadow of a 'Mech fell across the opening in the canyon wall. "I will be but a moment."

She pressed the throttle all the way forward, first walking, then running toward the emerging *Hunchback*. It took a few steps back, raising its stubby arms defensively.

The *Hunchback* pilot had obviously not expected her to close. Armed with a huge autocannon that was most effective at short range, it was a 'Mech that other 'Mechs ran away from, not toward. Especially when the other 'Mech was armed with long-range missiles.

Fortunately for Lita, she was not armed with long-range missiles. She twitched the control stick, jinking her *Mad Dog* to the left just enough to avoid the *Hunchback*'s hasty shot. Dozens of massive slugs buried themselves in the canyon wall behind her, sending a shower of rocks raining down from above, a few clanking noisily off of her 'Mech's armor.

As she neared point-blank range, Lita throttled down and flicked the ammunition selection switch on the heel of her control stick. The HUD registered the selection of "HE Ammo" as the cross hairs pulsed gold over the *Hunchback*'s chest, indicating a positive Artemis IV lock-on.

Say hello to my advanced tactical missile system, House Kurita, she thought, then pulled the trigger. Twelve missiles shot from each shoulder-mounted launcher, corkscrewing toward her opponent.

The ATM was a recent development of Clan Coyote. The weapon had two options. It could be loaded with extended-range missiles that would have a range far superior to LRMs. Lita had chosen the other option, high-explosive missiles that exchanged fuel for larger warheads, giving them limited range but destructive power rivaling short-range systems.

Nearly all of the twenty-four missiles launched from her *Mad Dog* found their target. Explosions blossomed all over the hapless *Hunchback* as it staggered back against the canyon wall. Throwing her 'Mech into reverse, Lita continued firing with her arm-mounted lasers as she backed up.

The explosions continued, most likely from a missile or laser touching off the *Hunchback*'s autocannon ammunition. Something rose up through the billowing smoke pouring from the Kurita 'Mech, and Lita could just make out the shape of an ejection seat rocketing the MechWarrior to safety.

Lita hailed Jake's frequency as she turned her *Mad Dog* around and headed north. "Star Captain Kabrinski, I am on my way to Sector D."

"You spoke truly, Star Commander. That did not take long."

Lita laughed. "Now that warrior knows which of us was the cat and which the mouse."

Pressing down firmly on both foot pedals, Ben engaged his *Nova*'s jump jets. The exhaust port mounted center and rear on the 'Mech's torso sent a rumble through the cockpit as fifty tons of OmniMech were launched in a ballistic trajectory that would—if all went well—result in his landing on the far side of a chasm one hundred-fifty meters wide.

In mid-jump, Ben received a radio message from his Umbriel. "Any sign of snipers, Beta?"

"Neg, Epsilon. Nothing on your side of the canyon either, then?"

"It is odd, considering Inner Sphere doctrine, that we have found nothing up here. It is almost as if they *want* to fight us toe-to-toe in the canyon."

"Could be," Ben said. "But we have not searched the entire area yet. Who knows what tricks they might have up their sleeve."

The message light flashed again on his console as he feathered the foot pedals to bring the *Nova* into a landing that sent shock waves through the cockpit.

"Point Beta, do you read me?" demanded Lita.

"Loud and clear, Star Commander. We must be right on top of you."

Ben could hear laughter in Lita's voice. "Good. Follow me north to Sector D. Jake says the eye in the sky has spotted something interesting."

"Roger that. You take the low road, and we will take the high road."

Lita sang her response. "And I'll get to Scotland before ye."

Ben adjusted his neurohelmet, thinking his connection was faulty. "Excuse me?"

Lita laughed again. "Sorry about the vulgar contraction. It is an old song."

"I am not familiar with it. Learned during your Inner Sphere captivity, I presume."

"Add it to the list, Ben. Hold on. I think I see the rest of our star up ahead. Keep sharp up there."

Ben checked his radar screen, realizing he had been briefly lost in the conversation.

"Sharp as a tack, Star Commander," he said.

Petra focused on her opponent and thumbed the trigger. Monstrous shells the size of trash cans poured from her

Stormcrow's left-arm autocannon into a Combine *Centurion*, battering its armor mercilessly and sending the machine staggering backward as its pilot struggled to keep it upright.

It was a wasted effort.

As she continued her barrage, smoke billowed from the other 'Mech. Its heat sinks were rupturing, their chemical contents reacting violently with the air and the fires starting in the 'Mech's body. Within seconds, the smoke was so thick that she could no longer see the *Centurion*.

Reese's voice came grumbling over the comm. "Save your ammo, Petra. He is dead."

Lifting her thumb off the trigger, she radioed back. "How can you tell?"

Reese laughed, an unusual, guttural sound that was mercifully rare. "See for yourself."

One foot of the *Centurion* appeared through the smoke, as if the 'Mech were staggering forward. When the other foot came forward, Petra understood. The 'Mech had been literally cut in half. There was nothing at all above the waist as the machine's legs stumbled forward a few more steps before collapsing to the ground.

Petra grinned with satisfaction. "So much for that lance. It is good to finally be in battle."

"A sentiment with which we all agree." Reese brought his *Hellbringer* alongside her *Stormcrow*. "I would normally say two against four was a fair match, but this was almost too easy."

"The briefing did mention that some of the Pesht Regulars might be green troops, only recently transferred from the sibko—I mean, the academy."

"That would account for the poor showing they have made so far today. What is your status, Petra?"

She checked the profile in the lower-right corner of her HUD. "So far so good. I lost some armor and one of my medium lasers, but nothing critical. You?"

"Armor is thin on the left side, and my anti-missile system is empty, but other than that—wait a second . . ."

Petra reflexively glanced at her radar screen, but saw

nothing. Her *Stormcrow* did not have an active probe. "What do you see, Reese?"

"A weak signal, to the north. It is difficult to make out, but—"

Suddenly, dozens of missiles came streaming through the smoke, most of them falling short of Petra and Reese's 'Mechs, but forcing them back a few steps in reaction as the explosions shook the canyon.

"Weak signal, indeed!" Before waiting for a positive visual contact, Petra pulled the finger trigger on her control stick, sending five ruby beams from her 'Mech's right arm into the rapidly thinning smoke left by the *Centurion*.

Through sheer luck, one of the beams hit a *Sunder* as it emerged through the smoke, but its pilot seemed not to mind the damage to its massive leg. The blocky, ninety-ton OmniMech of Kurita design strode confidently forward. The pilot returned fire, unleashing blue-white beams of energy from the twin, long-barreled particle projection cannon on its right arm.

Petra slammed the control stick to the right and braced for impact. By sidestepping, she had narrowly evaded one of the two PPC beams. The other slammed into her 'Mech's already weakened right arm, destroying what remained of its armor and ruining another medium laser.

Petra keyed the commline. "Well, Reese, it seems that at last we have a real opponent to face on this rock."

As if in response, a transmission came in over the open channel. "I am *Tai-sa* Mark Graham, commander of the Ninth Pesht. You shall not pass."

"And it gets even better, Petra. He is not alone," Reese said over the star's channel.

As Petra continued circling to the right, Reese began moving his *Hellbringer* to the left. The last of the smoke cleared to reveal the *Sunder*, flanked by a pair of *Mad Dog*-like *Avatar* OmniMechs, each one mounting large missile launchers in both shoulders.

"I was wondering where those missiles came from," Petra commented dryly.

The five 'Mechs held a stand-off position for a moment, as if each side was waiting for the other to make the next move. The three Kurita 'Mechs effectively blocked off the canyon, preventing any further progress to the north.

"There must be something very important to the north that they send the regimental commander himself to guard it," Reese said.

Jake Kabrinski's voice broke in over the Battle Nova channel. "You are correct, Point Delta. Orbital surveillance confirms that the planetary command center is buried in the canyon just beyond their position, as we suspected."

Petra grinned. "No wonder the C.O. has come out to play. This is his last stand." On her radar screen she saw the signals of Jake and more than a dozen Elementals approaching from the south.

"Let us make it a good last stand, then," Reese said, firing a blinding beam of energy toward the nearest *Avatar*.

The next instant Petra saw scores of missiles beginning to rain down from the canyon ridge above, exploding all around Reese. He backed up the *Hellbringer* as fast as he could, trying to get out of the way.

"They must have spotters on the ridge, calling in indirect fire," she said. Then she saw Jake running toward her, reaching the feet of her *Stormcrow* as the last of the missiles came down.

"This last stand just got more interesting," Reese said.

Petra sighed. "Indeed, but whose last stand is it?"

=== 13 ===

Fakir's Canyon, Idlewind
Pesht Military District
Draconis Combine
2 December 3062

"**R**eese, break left. Petra, break right," said Jake.

"Right on it, sir," Petra said. "By pressing up to the canyon walls, we minimize our exposure from above."

"Precisely. Now move it!" As missiles rained down from above, Jake's mind raced to come up with a plan of attack. To the east and west were sheer cliffs concealing unknown attackers. To the north were three of what must be the best MechWarriors of the Ninth Pesht Regulars. No enemy units were to the south, but withdrawing was precisely what the enemy wanted him to do.

And there was no way Jake was going to play into their hands a second time in one day. He would not give them the satisfaction. Or Star Colonel Gilmour, for that matter. Gilmour had let it be known in a multitude of subtle ways that his opinion of Jake had not improved a single notch. On top of that, Alexa seemed intent on undermining Jake's authority, not letting up since the day they had first met. Jake knew he had to press into the canyon and locate the suspected Combine base—both for the good of the Clan and for his own honor. As missiles continued to fall

all around him, the beginnings of a plan formed in his mind.

"OmniMechs, keep the pressure on the enemy 'Mechs. Cover my Elementals while we close to that outcropping of rocks just south of their position. Point Zeta, are you close yet? Over."

After a brief pause, Lita's voice came through. "Moving as fast as I can. I am close. I can hear the fighting from where I am. I should be coming up from the south in one minute."

As Jake charged toward the cover of some massive boulders strewn over the canyon floor, machine gun and laser fire exploded around him, striking several of his Elementals as they ran alongside him. "Make it thirty seconds, Lita. We are a little outnumbered here."

Reese took his *Hellbringer* to the left, but the *Sunder* and one of the *Avatar*s started closing the distance with him, probably seeing his heavier 'Mech as the real threat. Before reaching cover behind some fallen rocks along the cliff face, Reese let loose a salvo of SRMs, medium lasers, and one of his PPCs at the *Avatar* he had already damaged, scoring hits with all but the PPC. He didn't wait around to see what kind of damage his attack inflicted, most likely hoping the pause behind cover would give his 'Mech enough time to cool down.

As he ran, Jake saw Petra bring her *Stormcrow* forward and to the right, closing in on the second *Avatar* to bring her autocannon into play. Her opponent took a few steps back and launched a double-salvo of LRMs from its shoulders, following it up with a shotgun-like blast from its right-arm autocannon. Her speed made her a difficult enough target that the cannon shot went wide, but her *Stormcrow* weathered a spread of twenty long-range missiles before she raised her 'Mech's left arm and let rip with the autocannon.

Massive shells burst forth from her weapon, each shot making an unmistakable choking sound as it began its supersonic journey to the target. Even on the move, her aim was true if a bit low. The weapon stitched a staggered line of bullet holes big enough for a man to crawl into all the way up the *Avatar*'s leg, across the right side of its torso, and over its shoulder. It was a testament to the Combine pilot's skills that he managed to keep his 'Mech upright under such a barrage.

"Star Captain," Petra said. "I am about to lose my lasers."

Jake heard warning tones in the background of Petra's transmission. Glancing over toward her 'Mech, he could see that one of the *Avatar*'s missiles had dug its way into her machine's right arm before exploding, nearly blowing the limb off and ruining the myomer controls from the elbow down.

Jake's Elementals had just reached the boulders. From his position, he could see the *Sunder* advancing toward Reese's *Hellbringer* to the west. All was not lost if they played their cards right. "Conserve your autocannon ammo then, Gamma. We need to hold on until Lita arrives," he said.

"Roger that, sir. I will hold this flank."

Ben raced his *Nova* along the top of the ridge, his 'Mech's oversized feet kicking up clouds of dust as he sprinted along.

Glancing out his cockpit window to the west, he could see Umbriel's *Viper* racing along the opposite side of the canyon. "My scanners show enemy units up ahead, in the canyon and up here as well. Can you confirm, Umbriel—I mean, Epsilon?"

Ben could hear laughter behind her response. "Confirmed, Beta. There seem to be at least two targets up ahead. I am slowing to cruising speed."

Umbriel always seemed to get a good chuckle at Ben's expense, even at the tensest moments. Ben did not take it personally, though. He respected the fact that she had worked her way up from the tech caste. And she had bailed him out on more than one occasion.

He brought his attention back to the battle. "Focus, Ben, focus," he muttered to himself. It seemed like nothing was up ahead, but Ben's radar showed definite enemy contact. Suddenly, a massive salvo of missiles launched vertically from behind a cluster of rocks, arcing up and to the west, and then went sailing down into the canyon. Zooming in on his HUD display, Ben scanned the terrain where the missiles came from. He made out the shapes of two boxy tanks parked behind some jagged rocks and covered in tan camouflage netting.

"There they are," Umbriel said. "A pair of LRM carriers just out of range of the canyon."

"I have two on my side, too. I think the weather is about to clear up for them down in the canyon."

Umbriel laughed again. "Aye, Ben. Less rain, I think."

Ben engaged his 'Mech's jump jets. As he approached, the carriers began to roll backward, trying in vain to keep range between themselves and his approaching OmniMech. Both let loose missile salvoes just before he landed, but their long-range guidance could not deal with such a close target. Only a few missiles glanced off his *Nova*'s armor as the 'Mech's feet came down in front of the nearest carrier. Ben opened fire with six pulse lasers and four machine guns.

LRM carriers were designed to hide and fire, as they had been doing quite effectively just moments ago. Lightly armored and slow-moving, the vehicle had no chance against the full firepower of a Clan *Nova*. The carrier was literally torn to shreds, its crew scrambling to leap out of the vehicle's hatches before its ammunition exploded.

Which it did, in spectacular fashion.

The crew of the second carrier had already abandoned their vehicle by now, dropping their weapons and running for cover. Ben could see two or three squads of infantry approaching from the direction of the canyon, ineffectually firing their rifles at his 'Mech as they ran.

"Two down, but the spotters are putting up a good fight. How are things on your side, Epsilon?" Ben glanced out the cockpit window again. He could see the smoking wreck of one LRM carrier and Umbriel's *Viper* chasing the second off to the west.

As her 'Mech dropped out of sight, Umbriel said, "You will forgive my tardiness. My *Viper* is not as heavily armed as your *Nova*. The second carrier will be dealt with in a moment. You can join the rest of them down on the canyon floor now, *quiaff*?"

Ben's cockpit shook with the violent impact of multiple laser hits before he could utter a word. Cursing himself for becoming distracted, he saw his new opponent on this side of the canyon. Striding toward him was a virtual doppelganger of his own *Nova*, but bulkier and sporting a white and gray Pesht Regulars paint scheme with jade-green accents.

Ben steeled himself for the fight. He keyed the open channel. "So this is the Draconis Combine's . . . *Black Hawk*, is it?" he said. "Let us see how the imitation compares to the real thing, *quiaff*?"

Surprisingly, the enemy pilot answered him in a deep male voice with none of the expected Japanese accent. "Aff. I think you will find me a more fitting opponent than those LRM carriers, Clansman."

Ben was surprised by the respect shown in the use of Clan language. "I am MechWarrior Ben of Clan Ghost Bear. Who do I have the honor of fighting this day?"

"I am *Chu-sa* Minoru Tetsuchiba, executive officer of the Ninth Pesht, and the honor is all mine."

As Lita's *Mad Dog* rounded the corner, it was obvious that she had arrived in the proverbial nick of time.

Jake's Elementals were swarming around a damaged *Avatar*, which swatted at them with its boxy arms like a human beset by bees. Reese's *Hellbringer* was backing up toward Lita's position, smoke rising from multiple armor breaches as he fired at the *Sunder* and the *Avatar* pursuing him. Petra's *Stormcrow* sniped at them with laser fire from behind a pile of boulders. She must be out of autocannon ammunition as well as severely damaged.

Switching her selector to long-range munitions, Lita signaled her arrival with a twin salvo aimed at the *Avatar* not currently covered with Elementals. Her missiles arced up and over Reese's backpedaling 'Mech, then slammed down into the already-damaged *Avatar* to devastating effect.

Missiles erupted into balls of flame all over the Omni-Mech's body, but none so damaging as the rounds that found their way into the left torso and the ammunition bin therein. Multiple follow-up explosions rocked the seventy-ton machine, the force of them causing the *Avatar* to stagger and fall to its knees.

"That ought to get their attention!" Lita broadcast confidently.

Indeed it had. The *Sunder* lurching toward them past the smoking wreck of its lancemate let loose with both PPCs and the massive autocannon that comprised its left arm. It was not shooting at the *Hellbringer*, but at Lita's newly arrived *Mad Dog*.

Fortunately, the autocannon was barely within its operational range, and narrowly missed. The PPC shots struck her 'Mech's torso, melting off most of the armor but leaving the advanced missile launchers undamaged.

Lita switched the ammo selector to standard, then signaled Reese. "I do not want to be around when he lands a shot with that autocannon, Delta."

Reese sounded tired but determined. "Aye. Let us finish this quickly."

Taking cover behind a nearby pile of debris, Reese fired all his weapons at the advancing *Sunder*. At the same time, Lita and the *Sunder* exchanged fire again. The Combine warrior landed a solid autocannon hit on the *Mad Dog*'s right leg, knocking Lita to the ground.

The combined noise of weapons fire between the three BattleMechs was deafening, and the smoke from missile launchers and battlefield fire made it difficult for Lita to tell what exactly had happened to the *Sunder* amid all that shooting. All she could see was that the 'Mech had stopped firing.

As the smoke cleared, the *Sunder* stood completely still, damaged but apparently intact.

Lita was first to break the brief silence as she worked the *Mad Dog*'s controls to get it back on its feet. "What is he doing?" she called to Reese.

Then, slowly at first, the humanoid machine began to fall backward. As it bent at the knees, the slow fall accelerated, and all ninety tons of OmniMech came crashing down.

Reese brought his *Hellbringer* out from behind the rocks

and walked it over to the *Sunder*, which he prodded with his 'Mech's foot. "If I had to guess, our friend took one too many SRMs to the cockpit, and was either knocked out or killed."

Lita laughed out loud. "Or perhaps he just wanted to take a nap? What do you say we go see how our star captain is doing up north?"

There was one thing Jake liked about the Inner Sphere's recent deployment of OmniMechs. Because Omnis were designed to carry battle-armored troops on their hulls, they were that much easier for armored infantry to hang on to when attacking at point-blank range.

Jake was clinging to the *Avatar* just above its twin medium lasers and just below the cockpit. He gripped a hand-hold with his suit's left-arm claw as the Combine MechWarrior shook his 'Mech violently in an attempt to knock the Elementals off.

From her position clinging to the same 'Mech's left leg, Val radioed Jake. "You have to hand it to this guy. Even without jump jets, he puts up one hell of a fight."

Jake grimaced. "Aye. He knows that if he stops for even a moment, I will have all the opportunity I need."

The words were barely out when the *Avatar* stopped moving.

"What is he doing?" Val asked, but Jake was already in action. With the briefest burst of his jump jets, he leapt up to the *Avatar*'s cockpit, kicking at its sloped surface with both feet.

BattleMech cockpit windows, subjected to heavy weapons fire on a daily basis, were constructed of sturdy polymer compounds that could withstand incredible punishment. The micro-fractures Jake's kick made in the canopy would serve two purposes.

First, the MechWarrior inside would be startled by the sudden, unexpected noise and the interference on his HUD. Second, it would weaken the window material enough to be breached by a well-placed laser shot.

Kneeling down on the canopy, Jake placed the muzzle of his support laser a fraction of a centimeter above the spider web of cracks from his kick, pulled the trigger, and held it down. The canopy heated up, glowing first red and then white-hot. Warning lights flashed on his HUD as his laser also heated up, but the sustained shot was what was needed to soften up the polymer for the coup de grace.

Releasing the trigger, Jake drew his left arm back, curling his armored claw into a crude fist. "Too late," he said as the *Avatar* started to move again.

He smashed his fist into the still-hot canopy window, punching through to the interior of the cockpit. Opening the claw to full extension, Jake braced with his right arm and pulled with every drop of the suit's myomer-enhanced strength, tearing the center of the window free and tossing it to the ground some ten meters below.

As he looked down into the cockpit, now open to the midday sun, he realized that the 'Mech had again ceased moving. The MechWarrior inside was slumped over the console, either unconscious or dead.

Val climbed up the immobile 'Mech next to Jake and also peered into the cockpit. "What happened to him?"

Jake reached into the cockpit and pulled the warrior's head back. "There is your answer."

Protruding from the warrior's belly was the ornately crafted handle of a bladed weapon. The dead man was still clutching it with both hands, while viscous blood and coolant from his cooling vest mingled and dripped down to the cockpit floor.

Jake let go, and the warrior slumped back over the controls. "The ritual of bondsref. He would rather die than become a bondsman to us."

Val engaged her jump jets and leapt toward the ground as Lita's and Reese's 'Mechs walked over and joined them.

Lita's voice was uncharacteristically somber over the commline. "They call it seppuku. For many of them, it is the only honorable way out if they cannot prevail."

Jake shook his head in disbelief. It was just another amazing instance of how different the people of the Inner Sphere were from the way of the Clans. The warriors of the Draconis Combine were said to be most like Clansmen in their conception of honorable combat, and yet they were nothing like the Ghost Bears in this barbaric custom of sep-puku. Jake wondered if he would ever feel at home in the Inner Sphere.

Petra's *Stormcrow* staggered out from behind her pile of boulders, her 'Mech clearly the worse for wear. "That looks like the end of the command lance, then, *quiaff*?"

"Neg," Jake said. "Inner Sphere lances normally consist of four 'Mechs, Petra." He thought her offhand comment was callous, then he realized that Petra could not see what he was seeing. Shrugging off his disgust at the enemy com-mander's action, he jumped off the *Avatar* to where Val was standing on the ground. He could see Umbriel's *Viper* leap-ing down from the western wall of the canyon, slamming into the ground on twin spires of fire to join the rest of the nova.

Looking around, Jake realized that one of them was missing.

"Where is Ben?" he asked over the nova's channel.

Ben was beginning to worry. His radio and half his jump jets had been destroyed by the *Black Hawk*'s second attack, and now the 'Mech was successfully barring him from en-tering the canyon. Every time Ben made a move to the west, the enemy pilot would use his greater speed to inter-cept and attack.

Changing his tack, Ben began to run the *Nova* to the east, away from the canyon's edge. The *Black Hawk* immedi-ately gave chase, then suddenly stopped.

Ben circled his 'Mech around in time to see the Combine 'Mech turn and begin to run directly north. He turned in the direction of the canyon just as Umbriel's *Viper* rose up over the edge and landed at his side.

"You finally got that second carrier!" he said jubilantly, momentarily forgetting that his radio was out.

He popped his canopy open as the *Viper* approached, waving to Umbriel to do the same. She pulled up in front of him and opened her canopy, then crawled out and jumped onto Ben's 'Mech. "What were you messing around with up here?"

Ben laughed. "Only the second-in-command. I thought

he was going to finish me off, but then he just stopped and ran off to the north."

Umbriel pulled a tool from her belt and leaned into Ben's cockpit. Demonstrating that she had lost none of her tech skills since becoming a warrior, she opened a panel, twisted two wires together, and closed the panel with the turn of two screws. She patted it with her palm and smiled proudly. "That should do the trick until you get back to base and a proper tech has a look at it."

Ben grinned sheepishly. "Thanks, Epsilon."

Tucking the screwdriver back into her belt, Umbriel brushed her sun-bleached hair away from her face and stood up. "Ben, look," she said, pointing to a lone Elemental hopping up from inside the canyon. The jury-rigged radio crackled to life.

"What is the situation up here?" The voice was Jake's.

"The regiment's XO was up here in a *Black Hawk*," Ben said. "He headed north just before Umbriel got here to lend a hand."

Jake bounded toward Ben's 'Mech on his suit's jump jets. "Well, his commander—along with the rest of his lance—just went down," he said. "Our surveillance suggests that their command center is to the north."

Lita's voice came through faintly, the additional distance taxing the makeshift repairs to Ben's radio. "Perhaps he is withdrawing there to coordinate the rest of his regiment's strategy."

Then came Val's distant voice. "Or, if they have a hyper-pulse generator there, maybe he plans to call for off-world reinforcements."

Jake grunted, which Ben took to be agreement. "One way or the other, we have to stop him," Jake said. "Battle Nova, move out!"

=== 14 ===

DCMS Command Center
Fakir's Canyon, Idlewind
Pesht Military District
Draconis Combine
2 December 3062

Jake rounded another corner in the twisting canyon, then raised his hand to signal the rest of his point to stop. "Another dead end. Lita, any readings yet?"

"It should be here somewhere," she said from some fifty meters behind him. The 'Mechs of Jake's command were using their scanners to try to detect the entrance to the Combine base while the Elementals searched on foot. "Orbital surveillance picked up heavy concentrations of metal, as well as unidentified radio transmissions coming from this part of the canyon."

"Aff, but where?"

Jake looked around the canyon, using his HUD's infrared sensors to penetrate the fading afternoon light. The east and west walls of the canyon were split as though two giant hands had torn them asunder. Jake guessed that this end of the canyon must have been cut by an earthquake. At the northernmost end, the canyon came to a narrow point draped in shadows. The opening was far too small for a BattleMech to enter.

"Reese's active probe has not turned up anything," Lita said. "You ground-pounders will just have to find it on foot."

Val came up beside Jake. "My point takes the left side again?"

"Neg. I think I see something. Follow me." Jake trotted toward the deep shadows at the far end of the canyon, switching on the external spotlights mounted on either side his backpack's SRM tubes.

The brilliant light revealed a narrow opening in the rock face, and the glint of reflections from within suggested a man-made tunnel.

Val gave a long and very audible sigh. "There is no way we are fitting inside that tunnel."

"I beg to differ, Point Commander." Jake glanced at the red diamond in the lower right corner of his HUD and spoke the command word "egress."

With a loud hiss of depressurization, the helmet and faceplate of Jake's battle armor hinged up and away from his face as the chest plate hinged down, exposing his head and torso to the warm Idlewind air. He carefully pulled one arm and then the other out of the suit, reached up to grab the top of the backpack, lifted his legs out, and sprang to the ground dressed only in a lightweight sensor mesh.

"Alpha, Beta, and Gamma Points, egress." All around him, the Elementals of Battle Nova began exiting their armor, while the MechWarriors dug jumpsuits out of storage compartments in their OmniMechs and tossed them down to the Elementals.

After getting into a gray camouflage jumpsuit, Jake went over to his battle suit. Slung beneath its left-arm claw was an antipersonnel submachine gun. He took the barrel with one hand and pressed a release switch at the base of the ammo feed with his other. With a flick of his wrist, he turned the barrel ninety degrees clockwise and pulled it free of the suit's arm.

Then he reached into a belt pouch on his armor and pulled out a small headset radio, an extending stock for the SMG, and two additional clips of ammunition. After slapping the stock into place on the weapon, he brought his radio to his ear and called to Lita. "We do not know how far or deep these tunnels run, so I can offer no estimated return time."

"I understand. Do you want my 'Mechs to stay here in case anyone slips past you?"

"Post two 'Mechs here, but take the rest and see if you can find any other entrance points. I will take three points of Elementals in with me. Epsilon Point remains here at the entrance and Delta Point goes with you in case you find another way in."

There was a hint of concern in Lita's voice. "You think you can handle whatever is in there with fifteen troopers?"

It was a fair question coming from a MechWarrior, but Jake knew better. Looking up at Lita's cockpit towering above him, he gave a short, humorless laugh. "In those narrow tunnels, they will only be able to fight us one on one. There is no doubt in my mind that any one of my Elementals is a match for any one of their soldiers."

"I suppose you are right. The Spheroids always underestimate our Elementals when they are not wearing their metal and myomer."

"I will call for reinforcements if things get out of hand. Do not worry about me challenging an *Atlas* one-on-one in there."

"See that you do not. We are just getting used to having you around, Jake."

Her comment hit home with Jake. He was also growing accustomed to his new unit, and it crossed his mind that he would miss his new comrades if reassigned.

Mentally brushing aside the sentimentality, he wrapped the strap of the communicator firmly around his head. Then he walked to the tunnel entrance and peered into the darkness.

"All right, Elementals," he said, waving for his troops to follow. "Let us pry these cubs from their den."

The entrance to the tunnel network was clearly not designed with Elementals in mind. The narrow crevasse was barely wide enough for their huge bodies to squeeze through.

After ten minutes of this, Val was ready to give up. "Is there no end to these rat tunnels?"

Jake glanced over his shoulder at where she was trying to squeeze her muscular body around a stalagmite that reached from floor to ceiling, cutting the already narrow tunnel in half. "No stomach for closed-in spaces, Val? Have no fear. I think I smell fresh air up ahead."

Jake could see brighter light from around the next corner, and sure enough, the tunnel widened at that point into a room hewn from the stone. At the far end was a metal wall that mated perfectly with the surrounding stone. In its center was a closed steel door with no window. Alongside it was a small rectangular box with a glass face.

Val stepped forward and breathed a sigh of relief. "A palm-lock door? Very advanced for the Inner Sphere."

They called John forward to have a look. "Not as rare as they used to be, Val," he said. "The Spheroids are always working to advance their technology. Look at how much they learned from ours."

Jake nodded. "It also reinforces the theory that this is their planetary command center."

Val stepped up to the door, raising the muzzle of her pulse-laser pistol and leveling it at the place where the door met the wall. "It is certainly hidden well enough."

Jake took hold of the door handle as Val turned a knob on the side of her weapon, then pulled the trigger. Instead of the usual stream of laser pulses, the pistol emitted a steady, low-frequency beam. Squinting with concentration, Val used the laser as a cutting torch, slowly running the beam all around the edge of the door.

With the last of its hinges cut, the door began to fall into the hallway beyond. Jake grunted as he held the heavy door by its handle to keep it from clattering loudly to the ground. Still holding the door, he stepped back, and Val and her point rushed through the doorway, weapons at the ready.

Jake leaned the door against the rock wall, then went to stand in the open doorway. Iron beams supported the rock tunnel that stretched into the darkness, lit periodically by a simple light bulb dangling from a wire.

Val came over. "No guards here. They knew we were pursuing, *quiaff*?"

Jake nodded and went forward to take the lead. "Perhaps there is another strongpoint further along," he said.

"No time to lose, then."

Nodding, Jake waved his troops forward. If all went well, he would soon have his chance to prove Marcus Gilmour wrong once and for all. The prospect buoyed his spirit as he began to jog forward into the darkness.

"Zeta Point, this is Delta Point. I think we have found another entrance to the tunnels."

Lita sighed and leaned heavily on her control panel. "Roger that, Kris. Continue your search pattern."

"That makes three entrances in addition to the one Jake used," Ben said over the radio.

"That we have found so far. Who knows how many ways in and out of those warrens there are?"

Ben laughed in a vain attempt to cheer Lita up. "Well, I suppose the enemy commanders know."

Lita allowed herself a smile, but only a small one. "Aye, but we do not have one handy to ask, and I am running out of guards to post at these entrances."

"Then we will have to hope Jake gets to the command center before they all start running."

"Hope will not be enough," Lita said. She keyed the radio channel to her and Jake's private frequency. "Alpha Point, come in. This is Zeta, over."

Interference broke up the signal; Jake was deep in the tunnels by now. His voice sounded faint and distant. "What have you got, Lita? Let me guess: *another* tunnel entrance."

"Aff, and there could easily be more. I am continuing my search pattern, but I cannot guarantee that we will be able to cover all of their exit points."

There was a pause, followed by the stutter of SMG fire. Jake's voice carried the stress of combat. "Enemy contact, Zeta. We will march double-time and hope the Idlewind brass have not found an unknown exit."

Lita did not like the sense of helplessness she felt. It was all up to Jake's Elementals now. "Roger that, Alpha, and good luck. Zeta out."

Jake's heart pounded with a fresh rush of adrenaline as he ducked back around the corner. Thumbing the release catch on his SMG, he ejected the empty clip, which clattered to the ground. "I count seven of them."

Kneeling below Jake, Val poked her head around the corner, snapped a few bursts of emerald laser fire down the corridor, and then snatched her head back. "Make that six."

The Kurita infantrymen's assault rifles continued to lay a suppressing fire down the corridor, preventing the Elementals from rounding the corner and advancing any deeper into the complex. Ricochets drew sparks from the metal paneling lining the walls, making talk difficult and forcing Jake to keep his head down.

Reaching into a leg pocket, he pulled out a clip and slapped it into his SMG. He cocked the slide back and waited for a pause in the enemy fire. The stutter of weapons fire gradually slowed and stopped. As one, Val and Jake dove around the corner and opened fire—on no one.

The room previously filled with Combine infantry some fifty meters down the corridor was now vacant.

Jake charged back down the hall and waved for the rest of the Elementals to follow. "They are pulling back," he called out. "Ghost Bears, press the attack!"

When he reached the guard room, Jake quickly took stock of the situation. It was another small, square room, furnished with only a table and two folding chairs. The table, up-ended for cover during the firefight, was riddled with bullet holes and laser burns. Shell casings littered the ground around it. The other three walls of the room each possessed a closed wooden door.

"Three exits. Which way did they go?" Val walked to the center door and tested the latch. She looked over her shoulder at Jake. "It is not locked."

John shouldered his way through the Elementals lining the hall and stepped into the room. "Even if we knew which way they went," he said, "that way might not lead to the command center."

Jake thought John had a point. The Combine soldiers might be deliberately trying to lead them away from the heart of the complex. "We cannot chance missing the command center, so we will split up. My point will take the right-hand exit. Beta point, take the left. Gamma, take the center. Check in every five minutes."

Val and John each gestured for their points to follow, then led them through the left and center doors, respectively.

Opening the third door quickly with a jerk of his left hand, Jake pointed the muzzle of his SMG down the hall. It stretched at least sixty meters into the rocks, again lit by only a few bare bulbs.

"Keep sharp, Alpha," he said, then began loping down the hall, followed by the four other members of his point. He began to wonder if this complex was a decoy for the real command center or had merely been evacuated before they got here. Right now, all he could do was hope that neither possibility was true.

"There must be a private escape tunnel for every soldier in the Ninth!" Ben said in exasperation as he radioed the discovery of yet another tunnel opening.

Lita looked out her canopy at the slowly setting sun. "I would not be surprised if many of these tunnels extend only a few meters into the rocks."

"Decoys? Very devious, but I suppose you could be right. We cannot fully investigate all of them."

The incoming transmission light flashed for Lita's attention. "Battle Nova, what is your status? Over." It was Star Colonel Gilmour checking in from his drop zone at the munitions plant on Idlewind.

"Star Captain Kabrinski is still inside with three points, sir. The rest of us have located no fewer than thirty possible entrances into the tunnel complex, but I am stretched too thin to effectively guard them all even with Assault and Striker Novas pulled back in."

"So some of the command staff may have escaped?" Gilmour sounded concerned.

Lita frowned and leaned forward, closer to the cockpit

microphone. "Aye, Star Colonel. That is, if this complex is indeed the planetary command center. We still have no direct evidence of that, sir."

"No, we have not, but the DCMS went to a great deal of effort to construct those tunnels, *quiaff*?"

"Aff, Star Colonel. We will proceed under the assumption that this is the command center. If I may ask, sir, how fares the rest of the campaign?"

There was a pause before he responded. "The fighting is going as expected. Beta Trinary met with no worthy resistance and took only minimal losses while destroying the heavy battalion defending the spaceport. My Alpha Trinary is engaged now with mixed forces to your east, but the enemy fights without spirit. It is only a matter of time before they surrender or are destroyed."

Lita thought about how poor was the quality of most of the troops they had encountered. "The loss of their commander seems to have had a negative effect on them."

"We have a few bondsmen already, and their reports indicate that the tai-sa was—how did they put it—a 'slave driver.' Without him cracking the whip, the rank and file cannot stand."

Lita thought that sounded typical of what she knew of the DCMS. "Theirs is such a top-heavy command structure. The Clans might have the same problem if each warrior was so dependent on his superior officer."

Gilmour laughed sharply. "Well, see that you do not get too independent of my command, Star Commander. Inform me the moment there is a change in your status, *quiaff*?"

"Aff, Star Colonel. Over and out."

After what seemed like hours of jogging through tunnels more twisted than the canyons above, Jake thought he heard something as he paused to catch his breath.

A gruff whisper came from one of his point-mates. "What is it, sir?"

Jake gestured for silence. He touched his ear, then pointed toward the next corner in the tunnel. The other four warriors acknowledged the signal with a nod, then Jake began to advance slowly down the tunnel, his point right behind him. He stopped just before reaching the corner.

Listening carefully, he could just barely make out words being spoken in a strange tongue. The sounds were distant enough that he could not have deciphered them even if he had understood the language.

Jake nodded his head sideways toward the corner, and readied his SMG. He was down to his last clip, and it was at least half-empty. He peered around the corner, and the sight that greeted him was both fully anticipated and totally unexpected.

Before him opened a vast natural cave easily large enough to house assault-class 'Mechs. Steel walkways were riveted to the walls of the cave at irregular intervals, linked to one another by tubular ladders and short staircases, creating multiple uneven levels within the space. On the ground floor and some of the walkways were numerous computer work stations and radio receivers. The facility could easily accommodate fifty-odd staff, but it now stood virtually abandoned. Two men in drab jumpsuits—technicians certainly—hurriedly worked on adjacent ground-level computers.

The room's only other occupant was a single figure covered head to toe in black clothing. By the body proportions, Jake judged the figure to be female. Bits of enameled black armor were visible through the cloth, and the cowl over her head framed an expressionless, reflective faceplate. She stood facing Jake directly, as if she knew he was coming. Her SMG remained slung, her katana sheathed. She stood, arms folded, as if awaiting a command—or a challenge.

It hit Jake suddenly what he had been looking for all this time they were searching the twisting tunnels. No, farther back than that. Ever since taking over his new command, he had been waiting for *something* to happen. Now, encountering this enemy commando deep beneath the surface of an alien world, he understood what he had been waiting for: a truly worthy opponent. It was his only chance to prove himself to his new command and his new commander in one fell swoop. This was his moment.

Handing off his SMG, Jake calmly stepped out into the

open and walked toward the figure. The four Elementals of his point followed at a cautious distance.

As he approached, the woman in black dropped her arms to her sides, but otherwise remained motionless. The techs behind her, on the other hand, gradually noticed Jake's entry into the room. Hastily, almost convulsively, grabbing at piles of papers, they rushed for one of the countless exits and disappeared.

Jake's team moved to follow, but when the figure in black took a step forward, Jake waved them off. Nothing those techs were carrying could be as important as what he was about to do. He stopped just beyond arm's reach of her. Up close, he could see how tiny she was.

Straightening to his full height, he thumped his fist to chest in salute. "I am Star Captain Jake Kabrinski of Clan Ghost Bear. I hereby invoke the ritual of *zellbrigen* and challenge you to a duel of warriors."

The figure in black remained silent as the echoes of Jake's challenge reverberated through the cavern. When the sound of his voice finally faded away, she made a deep bow, folding her small body a full ninety degrees at the waist. She held the bow for only the barest of moments, then smoothly drew herself to attention.

Her obvious grace—not to mention her bravado—impressed Jake. Without a word, she moved into a ready stance, shifting her left leg back and bending slightly at the knees and elbows. She made no move for either of her visible weapons.

Jake nodded. This was getting better by the moment. "Then we shall fight unarmed," he said proudly. "In this solemn matter, let no one interfere." The four Elementals standing anxiously at the cave's opening lowered their weapons.

Without apparent effort, the black-clad figure sprang into action, leaping directly toward Jake and snapping her left foot around for a hard kick to the head.

Jake guessed that she thought him slow merely because he was large. Shifting his weight to the left, he raised his right arm to deflect the kick, his hand open to grab her pant cuff if the opportunity presented itself.

It did not.

Jake realized too late that she was not actually launching a kick. Her left foot landed solidly on his massive forearm, and with surprising momentum, the rest of her body followed. Her right foot rebounded against Jake's chest, too quick for him to catch, and she literally leapt off of him, over him, and behind him.

Jake whirled around, swinging his fist. She was already darting around him, crouching below his powerful left hook and sweeping out her right leg to catch him off-balance. He wasn't off-balance enough to be felled by the attack, but he did stumble forward.

By the blood of Kerensky, she was fast!

Following the momentum of her leg sweep, she tucked herself into a roll, then sprang up into a crouch immediately to Jake's right. With power and precision, she jabbed her right elbow into the back of his right knee, the force of the blow lancing through Jake's whole body and buckling his leg under him.

The shock and pain of the attack forced a bestial howl from his lungs as he tumbled to the ground. Battling the pain and rolling with it as best he could, he quickly returned to a crouching position facing the warrior in black. "You are fast, but speed alone will not win this duel!" he said, not caring whether she understood his words.

He knew she could use her speed to wear him down; he had seen the tactic many times. And almost as many times, he had won the day by ending the duel on his terms, not his opponent's. With a fierce battle cry, Jake lunged at her, arms wide to grab hold of her and apply the advantage of his strength. His eyes widened in surprise as she remained in place, accepting his charge.

Raising his yell to a fever pitch, Jake hammer-punched down with both his enormous fists, and came within centimeters of landing two bone-crushing blows against his tiny opponent.

At the last possible moment, she fell backward and dropped to the ground, her right leg levering straight up into Jake's sternum. Without stopping her motion, she continued to roll backward as Jake fell forward onto her extended legs. Then she sent him sailing over her prone form. He flew through the air on the momentum of his charge, and crashed into the bank of computer terminals recently abandoned by the two hasty techs. Bits of shattered equipment flew in every direction as Jake came to rest on a heap of mangled computers and the remains of a cheap aluminum desk.

The incessant ringing in his ears, coupled with the flashes of light in his field of vision, prevented him from seeing what was coming. In a single, fluid motion, continuing the roll that had sent him flying, she leapt to her feet. Whirling around to face him, she drew her katana from its sheath on her back.

Jake's heart nearly stopped as the sword sliced toward his exposed neck. He willed his arms to lift and block the attack, but they would not respond. The edge of the blade stopped just as it touched his skin, drawing the faintest of nicks.

As consciousness faded, Jake gazed into the featureless faceplate of his opponent. All he could see there, reflected in its polished surface, was the face of a defeated man.

15

Outbound Vector, Idlewind
Pesht Military District
Draconis Combine
14 December 3062

The vast emptiness of space stretched into infinity through the port window, a sight that usually filled Jake with awe and anticipation of the next world, the next battle. Today, as the *Arctic Cave* burned away from Idlewind, the planet shrinking into the distance, it only made him feel small and insignificant.

Gradually, the sounds of the mess hall behind him began to intrude on the cold silence in which he had wrapped himself ever since the battle in the tunnels of Fakir's Canyon. The clatter of plates and flatware, the clanking of metal cups, seemed almost as faraway as the planet. The sound of voices raised in celebration, the exact words muffled by the din of dozens of warriors basking in the afterglow of victory, seemed just as foreign. Jake wondered if he was the only Ghost Bear on the ship who was not rejoicing.

Lita's voice finally broke through his deep funk, though at first he did not even hear her. "Star Captain Kabrinski, are you going to eat or stare out the window all day?"

Then he heard Ben's amiable laugh. "This slop is not getting any warmer sitting here, either."

With a start, Jake realized he had been ignoring the rumblings of his belly in favor of the endless ruminations about what had happened back in the caves of Fakir's Canyon. He decided that his hunger was the easier of the two problems to resolve at the moment, and he turned away from the window.

He walked over to where Lita and Ben were sitting. He winked at Ben. "Will it really make a difference in the flavor?" he joked.

"Jake is right," Lita said cheerfully. "Slop is slop, be it piping hot, room temperature, or frozen on a stick."

Ben laughed again, and Jake felt his own mood begin to lighten.

"Frozen on a stick, that is how we left them on Idlewind, *quiaff*?" Ben quipped. He meant well, of course, but the young warrior's words plunged Jake right back into his glum mood.

He grunted, looking down at his plate of food as though it had personally insulted him. "Aye, the Ghost Bears taught the Combine a thing or two," he said tonelessly.

"Once the command center fell, their whole defense fractured," Ben went on, too full of his own exuberance to notice the hollowness of Jake's voice. "They thought they could take us one on one as true warriors. Even in honorable combat, they were no match for us."

Jake picked at his food, unable to shake the gloom of the past two weeks that had all begun when the mysterious, black-clad woman defeated him, then spared his life. More than a week in the sick bay had given him plenty of time to replay the event over and over in his head as the battle for Idlewind—and the subsequent Ghost Bear victory—raged on without him.

Sitting across the room was Star Commander Alexa. When Jake happened to look up, she intentionally caught his gaze. A slight smile of satisfaction played over her lips as she gave him a cool and barely perceptible nod. Jake went back to his food without acknowledging her.

Lita noticed the brief exchange of glances and turned to Ben. "Indeed, the victory on Idlewind was a worthy one, but we cannot rest on a single conquest. We must put that battle behind us and prepare for the next."

Ben nodded slowly. "Now we are on the way to Garstedt."

"Aye," Jake muttered, pushing away his plate of congealing food.

"They say the Combine has finally rotated some front-line troops to face us," Lita said through a mouthful of reconstituted vegetable matter. "I hear that we will fight a Sword of Light regiment on Garstedt."

Jake almost smiled. "It would be an honor to combat such skillful and renowned warriors . . ."

Ben was excited. "Let the rumors be true!" he cried, slamming his fist down onto the table for emphasis. "What an opportunity!"

"Calm down there, cub," said Zira Bekker walking over to them, her tone venomous. "No need to lose your lunch over a pile of baseless hearsay."

"To what do we owe the pleasure of your company, Star Captain?" Jake asked.

Zira smiled thinly. "Pleasure, indeed. Star Colonel Gilmour has summoned the senior officers to a staff meeting. Big news, or so I hear."

Lita cracked a smile. "More baseless hearsay, Zira?"

Bekker, senior to Lita, glanced over at her but did not respond, while Ben looked grateful for Lita's defense.

Jake pushed his unfinished lunch away for good and stood up. He doubted that fate could harm him more than it had already.

"To the star colonel's office, then," he said.

As Jake and Zira walked off, Lita pulled Jake's plate over to her side of the table and continued where he had left off. Ben watched as she eagerly dug in. "How do you pack in so much food?" he asked. "If I ate that much, I would explode!"

Lita shrugged. "High metabolism, I suppose."

A worried look crossed Ben's usually cheerful face. "I do not understand what is bothering Jake. Is he still stewing over what happened down in the tunnels?"

"I think so," Lita said between bites, "but I have no idea why. Every warrior meets defeat at one time or another. I have known my share, but none that hit me as hard as Jake is taking this one."

Ben nodded. "I lost count of how many times the instructors beat me in sibko training."

"That is different, Ben. In training, it is easier to view defeat as a lesson. It is not so easy in real combat."

Ever the optimist, Ben grinned. "He will get over it once he is back in battle again."

Lita paused in her voracious eating and looked toward the door. "I hope you are right, Ben. For all our sakes."

Jake and Zira passed wordlessly along the grav deck's narrow hallway. When they reached the door to Marcus Gilmour's office, it slid open with a barely audible hiss.

Gilmour was standing behind his desk, and Star Captain Rai and Star Commander Willem were sitting in chairs facing him. Jake and Zira took two empty seats.

Gilmour acknowledged them with a nod as he walked around to the front of his desk. "I want you all to know that the war goes well," he began. "Besides our victory on Idlewind, I have received reports confirming inroads on a half-dozen other worlds. However, other reports confirm that Combine reinforcements will reach worlds in our assault sector by the time we arrive on Garstedt."

Jake shifted in his chair. Anticipation and trepidation mixed inside him to create an unfamiliar brew. Fortunately, he still had the presence of mind to focus on what his commander was saying rather than what he was feeling about it.

"I think we can all agree that this is welcome news," Gilmour was saying. "I, for one, was not impressed with the troops on Idlewind, and I look forward to crossing swords with the best of the DCMS. But that is not why I summoned you all here."

He lowered his voice, despite the fact that no one could possibly overhear his words. "Thanks to the delays inherent in interstellar intelligence-gathering, we have only now received news of a significant event that occurred nine days past."

Jake looked around, but the others looked as blank as he did.

"On December fifth," Gilmour said, his voice as solemn as if he were announcing the naming of a new Khan, "Arthur Steiner-Davion was killed in an explosion while addressing a large gathering on Robinson."

Rai raised his hand, and Gilmour nodded for him to speak. "Pardon my ignorance, Star Colonel. We are all familiar with Victor, but who is this *Arthur* Steiner-Davion?"

"It is obvious from their matching surnames that they are born of the same sibko, Rai," Zira Bekker asserted.

Gilmour frowned at her interruption. "Arthur is Victor's sibling, yes. What is interesting about this news is that the explosion was apparently no accident."

Jake wrestled with the implications of such an event. To carry out murder like a thief in the night was alien to the way of the Clans. Alien to the way of a true warrior, which was to be direct and forthright and settle matters in honorable combat.

"Assassination? But why?" he asked. "If someone sought to weaken the Federated Commonwealth in such a cowardly fashion, why not eliminate Victor himself?"

Gilmour shrugged. "I do not know, Star Captain. Such deceitful, dishonorable behavior is beyond my understanding, too. I am told the young man was speaking out against the alliance between the Draconis Combine and his own realm."

"Perhaps the Kuritas wanted to silence him," Zira offered. "They could never resume their ancient war with the FedCom while they are fighting a war with us!"

Jake looked at her. She was probably right. "I think it will be a long time before I understand the ways of the Inner Sphere," he said.

For once, Gilmour looked like he agreed. "I am told that Khan Jorgensson believes that this act will be the spark that finally ignites a civil war between the two halves of the Federated Commonwealth."

Jake and the others exchanged silent glances again, totally baffled at what any of this had to do with the Ghost Bears.

Gilmour walked around to stand behind his desk. He planted both hands on its smooth steel surface. "The implications are far-reaching and impossible to predict. But the fact is that we had better get used to the way things work here, and quickly. For better or worse, the Inner Sphere is our home now. That does not mean we must descend to their level, but we must learn to understand how they think. They are deceptive and tricky, so we must be prepared to anticipate what they will do. This has never been the way of the Clans, but we are in the Inner Sphere now. We must adapt to survive. We shall call on all the strength and courage of the mighty ghost bear. In all our history, the Bear has never forsaken us."

Gilmour looked at each of his officers, letting his words sink in. Jake thought he sensed something different in the look his star colonel gave him, but he was too full of inner turmoil to be sure.

"We have much to prepare before the next battle," Gilmour said. "Go now, and bring this news to the attention of your commands. Dismissed."

16

At that moment, Jake's entire universe consisted of the rhythmic thud of massive feet pounding against the ground. As he clung to the exterior of Lita's OmniMech running across the Northern Plains of Garstedt by night, there was nothing to see, and no other sound. Yet.

The darkness of the battlefield concealed the hundreds of combatants gradually maneuvering into position. Jake thought of it as a gigantic game of chess played between opposing commanders. In this game, the pieces were multi-ton war machines, and the first shot fired could spell the difference between victory and defeat. The prize for the winner was nothing less than control of the planet. Ghost Bear intelligence suggested that the entire defending regiment was arrayed against them on the plains this night, but that was impossible to confirm visually.

In this game, the first move came from a humble source: a lance of Pike support tanks positioned on the crest of one of the few hills on these plains. They let loose with a fusillade from their combined total of twelve long-range autocannon, the high-pitched wail of their high-velocity shells announcing to all that the battle was joined.

Lita did not wait for a signal from Jake. "We have enemy contact, bearing one-one-oh. Gamma Trinary, break and engage. Fire at will!"

She throttled her *Mad Dog* into a run while Jake and the rest of his point hung tightly to their handholds on the hull of the sixty-ton Omni.

He glanced at the corner of his HUD, bringing up a tactical map of the area supplied by the *Mad Dog*'s computer and sensors. Red icons on the map flagged the enemy 'Mechs Lita had spotted: a lance of unidentified heavies at the edge of long-range. Icons representing his Battle Nova showed their own positions to the right and left flanks of the *Mad Dog*, forming an inverse V formation sweeping in on the left flank. The other two stars of Gamma Trinary were barely visible to the south, toward the center of the enemy formation.

His helmet microphone automatically picked up his voice as transmitted to Lita. "Do not rush to close range just yet, Lita. Let us press the range advantage of our weapons while we can."

"Aye," she said, firing twenty-four missiles from her shoulder-mounted launchers, the glow from their propellant piercing the night sky as they followed a gentle, arcing path toward the lead enemy 'Mech more than eight hundred meters away. Even at that distance, the blossoming explosions on the target *Dragon* were clearly visible to Jake.

"I would not dream of holding your Elementals back one moment longer than is necessary, Star Captain," she added, with just a trace of sarcasm.

"Of course, you would never intentionally delay my entry into battle, Star Commander. But closing with the enemy eventually would be appreciated."

Lita let loose another salvo of extended-range missiles. "This is a crowded battlefield. I am sure you will get your chance for glory this night."

After the twisting corridors of Fakir's Canyon, Jake welcomed the wide-open plains of Garstedt. And the battle plan was equally straightforward: meet the enemy head-on and overwhelm them with superior skill and firepower. Although the two sides had not engaged in a formal challenge, the direct combat was due largely to the Combine's massed deployment here on the plains surrounding the planet's only major industrial center.

That the Ghost Bears held the advantage in firepower was not in question. Unlike other battles in this war, the question of skill was not so easily answered. Arrayed against the Ursine Inferno was the Second Sword of Light, one of House Kurita's most elite and loyal regiments. Jake had read the briefings. On paper, the battle was an even match. But every commander knew that, in practice, something could always go wrong.

Explosions rocked the *Mad Dog*, nearly knocking him loose from his perch.

"What the hell was that?" radioed Ben.

"Surely not ranged weapons fire," Umbriel said. "Maybe a minefield?"

As the *Mad Dog* slowed to a stop, Jake looked down from his position on its chest, and immediately saw the answer. The explosions and strange tremors had been caused by charges blasting the metal covers off carefully prepared pits. Emerging from them were dozens of Combine battle-armored infantry, the carapaces of their Raiden suits painted dull tan and emblazoned with the rearing Kurita dragon.

Enemy battle armor! Great Kerensky, this was exactly what Jake had been hoping for. "Elementals, detach on my mark," he called. "Lita, after detachment, advance on those Combine 'Mechs. We will handle this."

"Roger that, Star Captain. Enjoy yourself."

Jake ignored that as he deactivated the magnetic clamps holding his suit securely to the OmniMech. "All Elementals, detach!"

He extended his legs and briefly engaged his armor's jump jets, which sent him back and away from the *Mad Dog*. Just before hitting the ground, he gave his jump jets the slightest touch to ease the landing of more than a ton of metal and man combined. The impact still forced him down on one knee, a rather ungainly position for a battle-armored trooper.

Once Jake and his point were dismounted, Lita immediately throttled up again. The Elementals did not move until she had cleared the area.

Jake glanced to his right and left, checking that the star's other twenty troopers had recovered from their landing maneuvers. "Star One, engage enemy battle armor at will. Let us show them how an Elemental truly fights!"

He got to his feet, but not before a lone figure emerged from the drifting smoke left by the explosions. The warrior was clad in Raiden armor like the others, but was clearly not one of them. His armor was painted dull black from head to toe, its only insignia a bright red Kurita dragon in the center of the breastplate. The suit's visor was crafted to give the appearance of a pair of glowing red eyes that peered menacingly from under the edge of its helmet.

The warrior began to walk casually toward Jake as if merely out for a stroll. The battle raging around Jake faded into smoke and obscurity as his mind raced back to the caves of Idlewind and the mysterious commando in black. Time seemed to stand still.

He saw again the tiny, black-clad figure bowing politely before raining a flurry of kicks and punches on his unsuspecting body. The worst humiliation of all was her holding a blade to his throat in a gesture that said, "I could kill you, but I will not."

Like an echo, the Raiden bowed easily at the waist, as if the armor was specially engineered to allow the maneuver at the obvious expense of mid-torso protection.

"I accept your challenge!" he transmitted over the open frequency. He raised his right arm as if to salute and fired the support laser mounted there.

The Raiden warrior did not rise from his bow as Jake had anticipated, but continued to stoop over and then tuck himself into a roll. Though the ungainly maneuver should have been impossible in battle armor, this trooper pulled it off with apparent ease.

Jake was stunned. His laser blast sailed over the rolling body of his enemy, who gave Jake a stiff-arm punch as he leapt to his feet. The punch carried the momentum of the roll, landing on the muzzle of Jake's support laser with a resounding "clang" that vibrated through his entire suit.

The hit snapped Jake into action, and he swung his left-arm claw around for a blow to the Raiden's head. Again, the Combine warrior seemed to be a step ahead. He used his right-arm weapon to block the blow while simultaneously opening fire with the submachine gun slung under his other arm.

Such a light weapon was not usually much use against battle armor. But at point-blank range, and aimed precisely at the joint between armor plates as this one was, any weapon could chip away at the nearly impenetrable hide of an Elemental.

The shots sent lances of pain through Jake as the Raiden raked his body with bullets. At the same time he forced Jake's claw away with his support weapon and brought up his knee to smash Jake squarely in the groin. Jake's armor helped ease the pain of that blow, but it was still powerful enough to send him crashing to the ground.

Move and counter-move. Jake was sure now who he was fighting. Her moves were unmistakable and her skill without flaw. Although he could scarcely believe it, this had to be the same warrior who had bested him in the caves three weeks ago.

He scrambled to his feet and let loose a pair of SRMs. In his haste, the shot went wide, entirely missing the Raiden and sailing off into the night on corkscrews of smoke and fire.

The Raiden ignited her jump jets, rising into the sky and passing directly over Jake to land behind him. Jake spun, firing his support laser. The weapon let out an unusual hum as it fired, and it seemed to be hotter than it should. Jake wondered if her punch had damaged the laser emitter.

This time, his attack was well-timed and scored a hit, but damage to the laser had reduced its power. The attack barely scorched the Raiden's armor as she came crashing down some fifty meters in front of him.

Jake triggered his second SRM salvo as his mind raced. She had beat him last time, but now they were in battle armor, in *his* realm. He needed to press that advantage and regain the upper hand.

One of his SRMs scored a hit, exploding against the Raiden's leg as she jumped again. Jake switched his HUD to infrared mode as she sailed into a drifting cloud of smoke. The smoke was still warm, making it difficult to track her.

A signal flashed on his HUD. "Jake, are you there?" Lita called over the command channel. She sounded anxious.

He continued to scan the smoke for signs of the Raiden, silently cursing the interruption. "Aye, Star Commander," he said. "What is your status?"

Relief flooded Lita's voice. "I am glad you are all right, sir. We have them on the run."

"That is good to hear," Jake said, wondering why she sounded so worried. "Once we are finished here, I will round up the Elementals and rejoin you for the final push."

"No need, sir. The rest of Gamma's Elementals have already advanced to regroup with us. I thought you must have fallen in battle."

Jake was stunned. How could that be? It was not possible that so much time had passed.

Remembering his black-clad nemesis, he resumed scanning the smoke. A strong gust of wind swept across the battlefield, clearing the remaining smoke.

There was nothing there.

No battle raging around him, none of his fellow Elementals fighting, and no elusive black Raiden. Lita was right. The fight had moved on without him. Glancing at his chronometer, he was shocked to see that the duel had lasted nearly thirty minutes, not the brief, tension-filled seconds it had felt like.

"Do you want me to send Umbriel to pick you up, Jake?" Lita asked.

"Neg," he said, barely getting the word out as he began to trudge toward the front lines. He could not believe that he had been bested and abandoned again, left alive to ponder another humiliating defeat.

═══ 17 ═══

Glenwood, Garstedt
Pesht Military District
Draconis Combine
27 December 3062

Lita emerged from the repair tent and breathed deeply the sweet night air. Up here at the Ghost Bear camp high on Skyview Plateau, she had a spectacular view of the city of Glenwood stretched out below. The city lights sparkled in the darkness, mirroring the countless stars overhead.

She walked over to Jake, who also seemed to be admiring the view. "The Second Sword of Light seems ready to admit defeat," he said, without turning his head. "Another few days and Garstedt will be firmly in our control."

Lita was surprised by the dull tone of his voice. Things were going well, yet he seemed detached, as though not part of this battle at all.

"The view is most impressive, *quiaff?*" he said, his voice just as dead and indifferent.

Lita took another deep breath to clear the residue of coolant and grease from her lungs. "Aye, Jake. That it is. We must try to enjoy the moments of peace and beauty between the moments of war and bloodshed. There is more to being a warrior than making war, you know."

Jake looked down at her and raised an eyebrow. "Perish the thought."

She laughed and gestured grandly at the city below. "Truly, if we cannot pause to enjoy our success, what is the point?"

Jake looked down at the city, then up at the sky, and shrugged. "I do not know or care. Such reflections are best left to oathmasters. I am a warrior. I live to fight, and fight to live. Such is the way of the Clans."

The tone of empty resignation in his voice disturbed Lita deeply. She looked up at Jake with concern. "I have heard—and spoken—those words many times. But if I may speak frankly, it sounds like you scarcely mean what you say this night."

Jake turned back to her, and his deep-set black eyes looked almost menacing. "You presume too much, Star Commander. *Never* allow yourself to doubt my convictions or my dedication to the teachings of Kerensky again."

Lita backed off. "Understood. I did not mean to insult your honor or integrity, Jake. I am sorry."

She was not about to be put off so easily, however. "I only say such things because I am genuinely concerned for you, Jake. Has the star colonel been on your case again? Or maybe Alexa?"

Jake shook his head slowly. "No, it is not that . . ."

Lita took a deep breath, mustering her courage. "You have not been the same since Idlewind, Jake."

She saw him flinch ever so slightly. The whole unit knew the story by now. Maybe that was why it was eating away at him.

"I have heard what happened in the tunnels, Jake, but there is more, *quiaff*?"

He turned to her, despair in his eyes. "Aff. During the battle on the Northern Plains, a warrior appeared among the Combine battle troops and challenged me. Her armor was painted black, and she countered every move I made as though she knew what I would do before I did it."

Lita could hardly believe what she was hearing. "You think it was the same warrior, the one from Idlewind?"

"I *know* it was. Without a doubt."

Lita smiled, and Jake's eyes flashed angrily. "Did I say something funny?" he demanded.

"No, Jake, I was just thinking you have nothing to be ashamed of. If the same Combine warrior fought you—and defeated you—both in and out of battle armor, I can think of only one possibility. She has to be DEST."

"What kind of name is that?" Jake asked. "Is it Japanese?"

"Not a name, an acronym: Draconis Elite Strike Teams. From what I know of the Combine's military, they are the only ones cross-trained so extensively. She is almost certainly a MechWarrior, and possibly a fighter pilot too."

"Seems like a waste of effort, heaping so much training on a single warrior," Jake said. "How can she possibly be expert in so many disparate methods of combat?"

Lita shrugged. "I do not know, but she did manage to beat you—"

Jake looked down at the ground, his whole body sagging.

"And you are one of our best," she added quickly.

He shook his head morosely and did not look up.

"If it is any consolation, House Kurita fields very few DEST troopers," she said. "They are 'the best of the best.' But so are you. Given the right circumstances, I am sure you could defeat her in combat another time."

"What evidence is there of that?" Jake mumbled, still staring at the ground.

Lita touched his arm and made him look at her. "As a Clan warrior, you have certain expectations. Expectations about the kind of enemies you will face and the forms they will take. This commando took you by surprise, her actions counter to everything you have been taught and everything you have seen on the battlefield till now. It is no surprise that you were not at the top of your form against her. You are a very accomplished Elemental, Jake Kabrinski, but you are also a very specific kind of warrior. She, on the other hand, fits no profile you have ever seen. In war, knowledge is often power. In both your encounters with her, she held all the cards."

Jake shook his head again. "Then how can you say I shall defeat her next time?"

"Because you hold some of those cards now, Jake," she said, turning to head back to the repair tent. "Play them right, and your next duel will be her last."

18

The earth shook as the six mammoth engines of the egg-shaped *Overlord-C* DropShip slowed its descent to the tarmac. Dressed in his full dress uniform of gray leathers and fur, Vlad Ward stood at a safe distance. He was flanked by dozens of similarly dressed warriors, as well as an honor guard of ten battle-armored Elementals. Behind them stood his domed headquarters building, its entrance flanked by two flagpoles, one bearing the Clan Wolf banner and the other bare. The building's marble columns and ornate carvings conjured images of ancient times and fallen empires.

None so powerful as the Clans, mused Vlad as he watched the DropShip gradually touch down. Once it was securely on the ground, a ramp telescoped down from one of the vessel's lower bay doors. A lone figure appeared at the top of the ramp, then began to descend, his form strangely back-lit by the bay's work lights.

The man looked small compared to the huge DropShip as he strode down the ramp, but Vlad knew that was an illusion. This was Khan Malavai Fletcher, a gigantic Elemen-

tal if ever there was one, and decked out in the Hell's
Horses striking black and red dress uniform.

As Fletcher's feet touched the tarmac, warriors standing
at the second flagpole quickly hoisted the banner of Clan
Hell's Horses, careful to halt its ascent a few centimeters
below the Wolf banner.

Fletcher approached and snapped a smart salute. Vlad returned the salute. "Welcome to Tamar, Malavai Fletcher,
Khan of the Hell's Horses," he said, with great formality.
"The facilities of Clan Wolf are at your disposal for the duration of your stay."

"You may dispense with the pleasantries, Vlad Ward.
Your hospitality is most appreciated, but I will not be stay-
ing long." Fletcher's voice rumbled like an approaching
freight train, with a disconcerting metallic tone from the
countless replacement parts that formed most of his skull
and neck.

Vlad smiled slightly. "Brief and to the point as always,
my friend," he said. Fletcher's guard had also debarked by
now. All Elementals, the dozen men and women formed up
behind their Khan.

Fletcher grunted acknowledgment, but his expression
showed the mental gears turning within his massive head at
Vlad's claim of friendship.

"Come," Vlad said, turning toward the domed headquarters. As the two began to walk toward the Wolf capitol, the
honor guards of both Khans fell into formation behind
them.

"I have heard some interesting news since arriving in the
Inner Sphere," Fletcher said. "Details were scarce, so I am
hoping you can fill me in."

"At your disposal, Malavai," Vlad said, smiling up at the
giant beside him.

"I understand that the Ghost Bears went to war with the
Draconis Combine some months ago. Perhaps you would
bring me up to date on the war's progress."

Vlad hid his pleasure at the question. Fletcher had just
made his job easier. It was no secret that Malavai Fletcher
hated the Ghost Bears.

"There is no love lost between the Wolves and the Bears,

but I have to hand it to them," Vlad said. "The first wave of their assault was a stunning success."

Fletcher's eyes narrowed under his protruding brow. "But their second wave . . ."

Vlad gave a short laugh. "What second wave? It is as if Khan Jorgensson had no long-term plan when he started this thing, and now the whole offensive has bogged down into a series of drawn-out shooting matches on a dozen worlds."

Fletcher nodded in grim satisfaction. "Yet the fighting goes on."

"—and on, and on. There is no sign of either side stopping any time soon. In fact, this may be what both of them want."

"How so?" Fletcher asked, and Vlad could have sworn his red bionic eye glowed even brighter just then.

They had by now reached the double doors of the capitol building. Vlad waved away the guard and personally held the door open for Fletcher. "It goes without saying that all Clansmen, even the accursed Ghost Bears, are natural warriors," he said. "Our preferred state is war. The same holds true, more or less, for the samurai culture of the Combine."

Their respective entourages took up guard positions outside the building as the massive doors swung shut behind the two Khans. Vlad led the way down the long main hall.

"I am puzzled," Fletcher said. "If the Combine is so anxious to fight, why have they made peace with their ancient enemies in the Federated Commonwealth? They did not need to wait for the arrival of the Clans to make war."

"This is your first visit to the Inner Sphere, *quiaff?*" Vlad said, and Fletcher nodded. "Ironically, it was the arrival of our own Clans that forged the alliance between the Combine and the FedCom. They united to fight a common enemy. That was fine while it lasted, but the *bushi* of House Kurita have been eager for war ever since the Truce of Tukayyid."

Fletcher grinned, a toothy, metallic grimace that Vlad was not sure indicated pain or pleasure. "So they suffer in peacetime much as we do. Hmm . . . I wonder if I might come to like these Kuritas."

Vlad returned the smile. "Perhaps. You know the old saying. The enemy of my enemy . . ."

". . . is my friend," Fletcher said. "So, I suppose we are friends after all, you and I."

Vlad and Fletcher turned the corner at the end of the hall and came to the central briefing room. "Which brings us here, *my friend*," Vlad said, pushing open the doors to let his guest enter first.

Following him in, Vlad tapped a button on the wall, and the holotank in the center of the room came to life. Glowing points of light representing the worlds of the Ghost Bear Dominion and their neighbors on both sides spun slowly in three dimensions, offering a complete view of the current state of the war.

Fletcher circled the holotank, studying it with his mismatched eyes. Vlad stood back, knowing he must let the Horses Khan speak first.

Fletcher reached up to the holomap, running his finger along the dimly lit worlds on the Wolf/Bear border. "The Bears seem to have abandoned all caution. They have nearly stripped their border with you, presumably to fight their war with the Combine."

Fletcher's back was turned, so he did not see Vlad's smile of satisfaction. Vlad doubted he would have been clever enough to catch on even if he had.

"You catch on quickly, my friend," he said. "I wanted to bring this to your attention as soon as possible. I understand your fleet carries fresh troops and materiel?"

Fletcher glanced toward Vlad, who offered him a bland, unreadable expression. "Aye, troops and other necessities to reinforce my holdings in the Inner Sphere."

Vlad walked over to the holomap and ran his finger over the trio of red-brown worlds belonging to the Hell's Horses. They were nestled snugly between the Wolf zone and the Ghost Bear Dominion. "Yes, your Inner Sphere holdings. Only three worlds . . ."

Fletcher began to pace, obviously agitated. Vlad assumed that the big man's ire was directed at the Bears and not at him for trying to subtly manipulate the conversation.

"Only three worlds," Fletcher growled, ". . . when the Ghost Bears have so many . . ."

". . . and they defend them so lightly . . ." Vlad said, keeping his voice completely even.

Fletcher stopped his pacing, and stood silently for a moment, probably considering his options. "The high and mighty Ghost Bears cannot be allowed to drop their guard so easily without paying for it."

"No, indeed," Vlad said, spreading his arms in an expansive gesture that seemed to take in the whole glimmering holomap.

Malavai Fletcher glanced over at Vlad, a look of fierce determination on his brutally knit-together face. "And who better to exact the fee than the Clan that has suffered countless indignities at their hands?"

Vlad knew he need say no more. Fletcher was on autopilot now. Nothing could staunch his rage once it began to build.

Fletcher nodded in satisfaction. "Thank you, Vlad Ward, for bringing this to my attention. I will not forget what you have done for my Clan."

He turned toward the door, and Vlad followed him out into the hall. He stood watching as the Elemental strode powerfully down the long hallway back toward his waiting DropShip.

Vlad indulged in another smile of satisfaction. *You have no idea how right you are, my dear Malavai. When this war is done—if you survive it—I have no doubt that you will never forget what I have done for your Clan.*

19

Clan Ghost Bear Field Headquarters
Drake Woods, Luzerne
Pesht Military District, Draconis Combine
3 August 3063

It had become a familiar scene to Jake over the last three months: the weekly meeting of the cluster's entire command staff, from Star Colonel Marcus Gilmour all the way down to the individual star commanders. In total, seventeen officers gathered in a tent normally used as a mess hall to get the latest news from the front and to discuss strategy.

At least that was the theory.

Standing before the assembled warriors, Gilmour cleared his throat and the various conversations in the tent finally died down. "When we arrived on Luzerne in May, our analysis predicted a swift victory like those that came before. Reinforcements from deeper within the Combine, as well as unexpected resistance from local civilians, blunted our initial assault."

Lita leaned over to Jake and whispered, "So we get the history lesson again today, *quiaff*?"

Jake nodded slightly. "Aff. Maybe this time there will be a point."

Although it was unlikely Gilmour had heard Jake's actual words, he shot him a cold stare for talking out of turn.

"That was three months ago, and not much has changed. Worse, we have spent the last five weeks in this cursed forest fighting a—what do they call it?—yes, a 'guerrilla war' against an unknown number of enemy 'Mechs and infantry."

And as far as Jake was concerned, the whole mess was Gilmour's fault. After serving under the aging star colonel all these months, it was obvious the man was overly methodical and cautious. Those qualities might have served him well in other campaigns, but here on Luzerne, they were a liability. Jake briefly considered interrupting to demand swift action. Perhaps guerilla tactics called for something similar in response. He opened his mouth to speak, then shut it again. Anything he said would be useless, considering his commander's dim opinion of him.

Jake told himself that the only way he would ever get through to Marcus Gilmour was on the battlefield, not the briefing room. It shocked him that he would even conceive of such dishonorable tactics. Being in the Inner Sphere was affecting his thinking in ways he did not like. On the plus side, at least the DEST woman was off tormenting someone else . . .

Gilmour turned to the back wall of the tent and pulled down a retracted map that showed the local area in some detail. He pointed to the center of the map. "This is our problem—the forest itself. It seems that we will never finish with the enemy forces in here, if only because we cannot even determine how many of them there are."

"Now we are finally getting somewhere," Lita whispered.

Jake was glad to know he wasn't the only one growing impatient with the star colonel's super-caution.

Gilmour pointed to a large, hilly area north and west of the forest. "Based on our limited orbital reconnaissance, as well as analysis of the enemy's attack patterns over the past weeks, I have concluded that they must have some kind of staging base in these hills for keeping their forces supplied and repaired. We must find this base and destroy it, all while maintaining the illusion that we are simply continuing these forest fights so as to catch them unawares."

Jake could hardly believe what he was hearing. For the past few weeks, he and some of the other warriors had discussed the possibility of a base, but he had hesitated to bring it up with Gilmour. His loss of confidence was developing into a disturbing pattern.

An indignant Zira Bekker shot to her feet. Gilmour sighed, waving his hand in permission to speak.

"Sir, I must protest!" she fairly shouted. "Deceiving the opponent in such a manner is inappropriate and honorless, is it not?"

Gilmour crossed his arms over his chest. "Star Captain, your protest is duly noted, but I must disagree. The enemy has prosecuted a continuous campaign of sneak attacks and hit-and-run strikes. We have tried to maintain our standards of honor, but all we have to show for it is this stand-off. If we now have a chance to break this stalemate, it is time to dispense with formalities and get on with the business of victory!"

A murmur of approval swept through the room as Zira sat down heavily, unhappy but resigned.

Gilmour walked forward a few steps to stand directly in front of her. "If it makes you feel better, Zira, your Beta Trinary will stand alongside my Alpha, continuing the same fight of the last five weeks. Jake Kabrinski . . ."

Jake sat bolt upright. "Sir?"

"Your Gamma Trinary will sweep out to the northwest while the rest of us 'fight the good fight.' "

The words drew a smattering of laughter from the officers, especially Lita.

"You will take your Elementals out under cover of darkness to locate the staging base," Marcus continued. "When you have located it, the rest of us will join you and bring this campaign to its long-overdue end."

Immediately, unexpectedly, Jake's heart sank. His trinary would be used as mere scouts for the rest of the cluster! He barely heard Marcus's closing words.

"As per standard procedure," Gilmour was saying, "Delta will act as a mobile reserve, which you may call on as needed. That is all."

As everyone began to stand up and leave, Lita elbowed

Jake in the ribs. "Cheer up, Jake! You drew the best assignment this rock has to offer. At least we get out of this forest for a few hours."

The jab seemed to wake Jake from the doubts that plagued him. Lita was right, although perhaps not in the way she intended.

He cracked a smile. "Aye, Lita. We must make the best of this opportunity. Get your MechWarriors ready for departure. We have less than eight hours to find the base."

And, he told himself, to destroy it before the others arrived.

Jake and his point were making another sweep through the western sector, investigating some unusual magnetic-scan readings. Like so many scouting missions, the search was interminable. It was the reason scouting was detested by true warriors. He told himself that this one would be different—assuming he ever found the enemy, that is.

It occurred to him that his own cluster's troubles on Luzerne mirrored the entire war. Gilmour had stopped giving out regular updates on the war's progress on other worlds, which Jake had assumed was because the unit needed to focus on their own situation. Thinking about it now, he wondered if the whole damn war had bogged down for some reason. Gilmour had been eager enough to announce morale-building reports of Ghost Bear successes in the early stages of the war.

He was still wondering about all this when he got the news he was waiting for. Gamma had located the Kurita base! It took less than ten minutes to rendezvous with the rest of his Elementals at Gamma's position, and what he saw when he got there was breathtaking.

A massive cave had been carved into the rock face of what must have originally been a quarry or strip mine. The entire base, consisting of three large 'Mech bays and at least a dozen lesser buildings, was concealed within the cave walls. A canopy of stone rose more than thirty meters above the cave floor, covering the whole base. This ingenious arrangement made the base visible only when viewed from the west—and only from ground level.

Val came up alongside Jake. She let out a low whistle that was heard only over their private channel. "No wonder we did not find this place before."

"Aye," Jake said. "Imagine the work that must have gone into it. Impressive."

"Quite. I wonder how many other armies have been fooled by it?"

"I wish those Elementals would hurry up and find that base," Ben said to Umbriel, who was sitting on the shoulder of his *Nova* doing some repairs.

Umbriel shook her head at his impatience. "All in good time, Ben. I am sure Jake and his troops will find it soon."

Ben leaned back in his cockpit seat and gazed at the stars through the 'Mech's open canopy. He gave a long-suffering sigh. "If we were back with the other trinaries, we would be in combat right now."

With one more turn of the wrench, Umbriel finished tightening the connector between the actuators in the *Nova*'s shoulder. She leaned over to look down at Ben from her perch. "Perhaps, but we are not there, so it is irrelevant. At any rate, your 'Mech's arm should rotate more smoothly now."

"Thank you, Umbriel. With the rush to get out here tonight, my tech had no time to look at it."

Umbriel looked up and joined Ben in his stargazing. "Look at the bright side," she said. "We may not be in combat, but at least it is not raining on us!"

Ben smiled. "Yes, I suppose it could be worse, if that is what you mean."

A few minutes of silence passed between the two. Ben thought he could make out the sound of distant fighting to the south, and sighed again.

"The sky here is beautiful, *quiaff*?" Umbriel said softly.

Her comment elicited a chuckle from Ben. "Nice try at changing the subject, Umbriel. It is beautiful, yes, but I cannot stop thinking about how different these stars are from the skies over Bearclaw."

She looked over at him. "That was where your sibko was stationed, *quiaff*?"

"Aff. You know, I think it is the stars more than anything that remind me of home. Even more than the differences in language and customs, the stars in the sky are a constant reminder of how far we are have traveled. I wonder if we will ever see those stars again." Ben sighed again.

"But we are only a few jumps away from the Dominion, Ben."

"You know what I mean, Umbriel. I am talking about the Kerensky Cluster, our true home."

Umbriel shook her head. "No longer. The Ghost Bears are here to stay. Besides, was it not the great Kerensky's aim that the Clans return to the Inner Sphere to save it from itself? All humanity calls this their true home, *quiaff*? Why not us?"

Ben leaned back and folded his arms behind his head, still looking up at the stars. "I cannot answer for the entire Clan, but I just do not feel . . . comfortable here. You will at least admit that the people have not exactly greeted us with open arms."

Umbriel leaned over so she could see Ben. "Oh, I do not know. On the streets of Alshain, the populace seemed to react positively to my uniform, and they certainly appreciated our defense against the Combine invasion. I am sure they prefer us to the Kuritas."

"Maybe you are right as far as Alshain goes. But the outlying planets are never going to be a Ghost Bear fan club."

This time, Umbriel sighed heavily. "Perhaps, but now I think you are making excuses for your own uneasiness."

Before Ben could protest, the incoming-transmission light began to flash its angry red on Ben's instrument panel.

"Eta Point, this is Zeta," said Lita, her tone urgent. "Do you copy?"

Ben sat bolt upright at hearing his commander's voice. "Aye, on station and ready, Star Commander."

"Good, because nap-time is over. Star Captain Kabrinski has found the Kurita base."

Umbriel began laughing so hard she nearly fell off the *Nova*'s shoulder. "Nap-time! I love it!"

Ben frowned at her levity, valiantly maintaining his composure. "Copy that, Zeta. I will proceed immediately to the rendezvous point. Umbriel, do you not have a 'Mech waiting for you?"

Wiping a tear from the corner of her eye, Umbriel flashed Ben a mock salute. "Aff, Point Commander. On my way!"

Umbriel expertly maneuvered the Elemental hand-holds on the *Nova*'s hull to climb down to the ground, then ran for her *Viper* standing ten meters away.

Ben pulled his cockpit canopy down around him, turning the locking clamps to seal the cockpit. He had not even begun throwing the switches to fire up the 'Mech's reactor from standby to full power when another message flashed. It was Lita again.

"Point Eta, come in!" She sounded agitated.

"I am on my way, Zeta."

"Ben, Jake's Elementals are under attack and outnumbered! The Combine forces protecting the base must have spotted them. Forget the rendezvous and double-time it directly to these coordinates."

As numbers transmitted from Lita's computer flashed across his secondary monitor, Ben's mind raced. Judging from the coordinates, it would take Gamma's OmniMechs nearly an hour to reach Jake's position. He did not dare speak aloud the words that Lita must surely be thinking, too.

Would they make it in time?

20

Drake Woods, Luzerne
Pesht Military District
Draconis Combine
3 August 3063

Explosions lit up the night from all directions, their force creating shockwaves that knocked dozens of Elementals off their feet. A few tried to avoid that fate by igniting their jump jets, but their hasty action turned out to be worse. Those unfortunates went careening into overhanging trees obscured by the darkness.

Amid this chaos, Jake Kabrinski tried valiantly to hold his troops together. "Point Delta, status report! Striker Nova, hold your position! Point Beta?"

"Here, Jake," Val said a moment later. "A little busy, though. I have a lance of enemy 'Mechs here on the left flank."

Jake cursed under his breath. "Delay them, Val. I am still gathering data on the enemy force. Point Delta, are you there?"

Static made it difficult to make out the reply. "This . . . Delta. Sorry . . . delay, Star Captain."

"Spare me the formalities. What is happening on the right flank?"

". . . least two . . . 'Mechs and infantry here . . . send support, over?"

Jake took a deep breath to control his temper, then turned quickly and fired his support laser at the enemy foot soldier who had managed to sneak around behind him. The weapon, designed for use against armor, left nothing but a pair of high-gloss combat boots trailing wisps of smoke where the DCMS soldier had been. In Jake's agitated state, the disturbing image almost made him laugh out loud.

He took another deep breath, then remembered Delta. "Delta, your transmission is breaking up. Are you requesting support on your flank? Over."

More explosions ripped through the woods, nearly throwing Jake to the ground. Instead of Delta, it was Val who answered, her signal also breaking up. "Jake . . . cannot hold this . . . very long. What . . . your order? Over."

Bullets from infantry rifles bounced off Jake's armored carapace, the noise of their ricochets lost to the dull buzz in his mind. Out the corner of his visor, Jake glimpsed a slight, black-clad figure approaching through the woods.

In an instant, his fog cleared. He spun quickly to face *her,* raising his support laser and firing again and again and again. He had let loose a pair of SRMs and forty rounds from his left-arm SMG before it dawned on him.

There was nothing there. A moment of panic welled up. Was he losing his mind?

Val's insistent voice dragged Jake back to reality. ". . . Jake, dammit! What . . . want us to do? Are . . . there?"

Turning back in the direction of the Kurita base, Jake could see the shadowy images of four assault-class Battle-Mechs approaching through the forest. In the lead, a massive *Akuma* knocked trees aside as it went, its demonic, red-lacquered face grinning as if mocking Jake's indecision and confusion.

Engaging his jump jets, he leapt up and back, away from the advancing 'Mechs. His mind was suddenly, perfectly clear.

"Star One, this is Alpha Point," he called. "All Elementals, pull back to rendezvous with the advancing Omni-Mechs. I repeat, all Elementals pull back!"

* * *

To say that Lita was frustrated would have been an understatement. She was pushing her *Mad Dog* as fast as it could go, but the need to constantly dodge around trees kept her speed down to half what her 'Mech could do out in the open. Glancing out her cockpit screen to the right, she saw Umbriel's *Viper* come up alongside her. The *Viper* was the star's fastest 'Mech, so Lita was not surprised that Umbriel had caught up so quickly from behind.

"I can forge on ahead using my jump jets, Star Commander," Umbriel said.

Lita did not think it a good idea for her Star to get too spread out, but Jake's last transmission made it clear that the situation was dire. "Go on, Umbriel. Get to them as fast as you can, but do not fully engage until the rest of us arrive. I do not want you to be overwhelmed before we get there. Understood?"

Umbriel did not hide her excitement. "Aff. I will not waste an instant!" She blasted her *Viper* into the air on pillars of flame shooting from its three-toed feet. In moments, it rose above the forest canopy and out of sight.

Lita heard the 'Mech come crashing down some two hundred meters ahead of her position, then heard it jet into the air again.

She was sure Umbriel would get there in time, but would a lone *Viper* be enough to make a difference?

"The trees are slowing their pursuit, Jake, but it is only a matter of time before they catch up to us!"

The desperation in Val's voice was uncharacteristic, but not surprising in their current predicament. Jake did not know how to reassure her as a commander should. Perhaps Gilmour was right in thinking that he had risen to command too soon.

No! This was supposed to be a redeeming victory, not another humiliating defeat. The battle was not lost yet. Jake steeled himself and transmitted back to Val. "By the time they catch up, we will have reached our OmniMechs. Then we can turn and fight together."

"Copy that, Alpha." Val sounded unconvinced.

Another tremor hit, knocking Jake to the ground. This time it was not from an explosion. Looking up, he saw the unmistakable shape of a *Viper* OmniMech, tilted down as if looking at a bug. In this case, the bug happened to be him.

Umbriel's cheerful voice came over the trinary's channel loud and clear. "I heard a rumor you could use some 'Mech support, Star Captain."

Relief rushed through Jake's body like a fast-acting drug. "You are a welcome sight, Umbriel. We have enemy 'Mechs on our tail. See what you can do to harass them, but—"

"—do not engage. Yes, I got that speech from Lita already. Over and out."

Jake watched as the forty-ton 'Mech again bounded off on jump-jet flames, then he sent out a call to his Elementals. "Star One, listen up. The first of our 'Mechs has arrived, and the others cannot be far behind. Halt your withdrawal and prepare to about-face and meet the enemy."

His point commanders had just begun transmitting confirmation of the orders when Ben's *Nova* came crashing down next to Jake on its jump jets.

"The cavalry has arrived, Star Captain," Ben said. "Time for a little payba—"

Deafening noise obliterated the rest of Ben's transmission. A massive explosion erupted less than fifty meters away, tearing up trees by their roots and sending them flying in all directions. One hit Ben's *Nova* square in the shoulder, and the 'Mech staggered back a few steps.

"Stravag!" he cursed. "Umbriel just fixed that arm. What the hell was that?"

Jake could hear the sounds of other, similar explosions landing all around him. "Could be artillery, or—"

Then the sonic boom hit, the unmistakable sound of aerospace fighters tearing through the sky faster than sound could follow.

An air strike! Jake berated himself for not seeing it coming. "Delta Trinary, do you read? Are you there, Rai?"

"Ready to fly at a moment's notice, Star Captain. What can I do for you?"

"Here is your moment's notice, Rai. Get those OmniFighters in the sky right now. We are getting bombed back to the Age of War here!" Jake did not mean to sound harsh, but things were quickly going from bad to worse.

"On my way. Your airborne hostiles will have too much to worry about to bomb you in—three minutes. Maybe less. Over and out."

As Rai signed off, Lita's *Mad Dog* appeared in the clearing. It trotted up alongside Ben's *Nova*. Jake's ears were still ringing as she spoke.

"Glad I did not miss the fireworks, Jake. Star Captain Rai is on his way to deal with the air support, *quiaff*?"

Jake sighed. "Aff, but it will take him at least three minutes."

"We had better dig in then," she said.

"What about those 'Mechs approaching, sir?" came Ben's voice. "We cannot just sit here, *quiaff*?"

To make things worse, another incoming message was flashing for Jake's attention, and he realized it had been doing so for some time. It was Star Commander Maxwell of the Assault Nova.

"Star Captain, do you read?" Maxwell shouted. "We are being hammered by enemy artillery. Please advise."

Before Jake could reply, another set of explosions shook the ground. Lights flashed before his eyes, and this time he could not tell whether they were on his HUD or in his head. After a few seconds, he realized he was lying on his back.

More explosions followed, then the rhythmic beat of BattleMech footfalls and the chatter of machine-gun fire. Voices dueled for attention on all channels of his communicator, but they blurred together in an incoherent mush. Jake tried to get up, but he was losing consciousness faster than he could move. Oblivion had already begun to draw him down into its dark arms. Thanks to the painkillers automatically administered by his battle armor, Jake had no idea how bad he was hurt.

21

Ghost Bear Field Headquarters
Drake Woods, Luzerne
Pesht Military District
Draconis Combine
5 August 3063

"**D**o you have any idea what you were doing out there? Do you have *any idea* what kind of damage you caused this Cluster? *Do you . . .*"

Star Colonel Marcus Gilmour's voice trailed off, as if he were searching for words in some other language. He stood up and began pacing behind his desk again. Jake was not surprised that his commander had run out of things to say. The tongue-lashing had already been going on for twenty minutes.

Gilmour sighed heavily and ceased his pacing. He cast a sideways glance at Jake, then immediately looked away as if he could not bear the sight of the warrior standing before him at rigid attention. He planted his fists on his hips and looked up, as if the heavens themselves would open to help him.

"What happened to you on Idlewind, Jake?"

Jake would have responded, but his commander's rant was not over. Gilmour turned around, and for the first time since the dressing-down began, he looked directly into

Jake's eyes. "I had my doubts about you from the start. I told you as much the first time you walked in here. But this . . ."

Shaking his head in disgust, Gilmour pulled up his chair and sat down. Resting his elbows on the desk, he steepled his fingers in thought. Several long minutes passed.

"You tell me, Jake," he said finally. "What should I do with you?"

It was a good question. Jake knew that begging for another chance to prove himself would be too desperate a move. Besides, it might play right into the star colonel's hands. It shocked him to realize that even he was beginning to wonder if he deserved a second chance.

"Never mind, Star Captain," Gilmour said impatiently. "I know the proper Clan answer to my question. Quite frankly, I do not think you deserve a Trial of anything right now."

His eyes narrowed, and the thin, predatory grin that formed on his lips gave Jake a chill. "No, you will not fight any Trials, at least not at my request. I have just the assignment for you . . ."

Leaning forward, Gilmour tapped a few keys on his computer terminal. The glow of the screen reflected in his strangely glittering eyes. "Your Trinary suffered heavy losses out there, Star Captain. Twenty percent personnel and nearly fifty percent materiel, from the latest reports. Is that correct?"

"Yes, sir," Jake managed to croak out.

Gilmour nodded as he tapped a few more keys. "Your unit is overdue for rest and refit, then. Once this business on Luzerne is finally straightened out, you and your Trinary will hitch a ride with the merchant transport *November Wind*. It will take you back to the Dominion—to Predlitz."

The words hit Jake like a sucker-punch to the gut, even though it felt like someone else was standing there in his place and he was watching the events from afar.

A few more key taps, and Gilmour turned back to Jake, folding his hands on the desktop like the most well-behaved cadet in class. "On Predlitz, you will work with the local garrison commander—" he paused and smiled, as if he had said something funny—"to get your Trinary back to full combat strength. The planet's usual garrison, the 140th Striker Cluster, is here at the front. So, until your unit is up to strength, your combat assignment will be to supplement the planetary defense. I do not want to hear from you until your *entire* unit is fit for duty. Do I make myself clear?"

As Marcus Gilmour began to stand, the scraping of his chair gave Jake such a start that he blurted out, "Crystal clear, sir."

"Very well, then. I suggest you brief your subordinates on their new assignment immediately. I am sure they will have plenty of—questions for you. Dismissed."

A voice inside Jake's mind screamed for him to say something—anything—to change the outcome of this meeting. Yet, all he could think about was the phantom image of the DEST woman stalking him through the forest shadows. It had been two days and it still haunted him. Relentless. Unforgiving. Unstoppable.

Jake extended his fist in a perfunctory salute, then turned to leave. All he wanted was to get out of here as fast as his boots could carry him.

A half-dozen conversations thrummed through the Gamma Trinary MechWarrior barracks, all of them mirroring to some extent Ben and Lita's current dispute.

"If we could only get rid of their *stravag* artillery, then we would have them for sure!" Ben was saying.

Lita did not know whether to be refreshed or frustrated by Ben's naivete. "There is more to the Kurita defense than artillery, Ben. Without effective infantry and armor support, artillery alone is not an effective defensive weapon."

"Or an offensive weapon, for that matter," Ben retorted. "That is why the Clans dispensed with it centuries ago."

"Not *all* the Clans," Umbriel said sarcastically, pulling up a chair next to Ben. "Let us not forget Clan Wolf's *Naga* OmniMech . . ."

Lita nodded. "Armed exclusively with Arrow IV missile artillery and deployed on the front lines."

Ben rolled his eyes. "You know what I mean. The use of artillery as a warrior's weapon was long ago discontinued"—he turned to Umbriel and added—"among *most* Clans."

"The *Naga* notwithstanding," Umbriel said, "the Clans do use artillery under certain circumstances. As a front-line warrior, you simply do not see it."

"Artillery has no place in the ritual dueling of *zellbrigen*," Lita said, "so most trainers—and commanders—do not speak much about it. But it is deployed with garrison troops to round out their combined-arms forces. Which brings me to my original point, Ben."

He looked genuinely interested. "Which was what?"

"I agree that the Kurita artillery is key to their defense," Lita said, "but only because it is effectively combined with infantry, tank, and BattleMech forces."

Umbriel rejoined the fray. "The last five weeks may have been annoying as hell, but we will walk away from this having learned a thing or two about combined-arms tactics."

A new voice joined the discussion. "A good thing, too, for that is a lesson we have sorely needed since Jake Kabrinski took command." Alexa swaggered over from a gathering of her own unit.

Ben glared at her, but Lita spoke before he could put his foot in his mouth. "Opinions vary, Alexa. In any case, a warrior can always benefit from the lessons of the battle-field."

Alexa grinned broadly. "Put very diplomatically, Lita. Are you afraid to openly criticize your commanding officer? Or have you forgotten the way of the Clans in your dotage?"

Immediately, Lita stood up from her chair, which tumbled halfway across the room as she confronted the much shorter Alexa. She stared down at her, but did not raise her voice above a low growl. "What I am and am not afraid of is none of your concern, cub. If you have a problem with me, you can challenge me or be done with it. If you have a problem with Jake Kabrinski, take it up with him."

Taken by surprise, Alexa backed down slightly. "Look, all I am saying is that we have a self-fulfilling prophecy here. It is no secret that the star colonel has doubts about

Jake's combined-arms abilities. Am I to think it is a mere coincidence when things fall apart the first time we face a true combined-arms force in battle?"

By now, the whole room had become deathly quiet. All eyes were on Alexa and Lita. Umbriel slowly sat straight up, and Ben opened his mouth to speak, but stopped when the door to the room began to open.

"Star Captain on deck!" a voice from the back of the room called out.

Immediately, all the warriors in the room stood and snapped to attention as Jake ducked under the door frame and entered. Looking at him out of the corner of her eye, Lita saw immediately how changed he seemed. His eyes seemed more deep-set eyes than usual, and he seemed to walk with a stoop. Gilmour had apparently given Jake more than an ordinary chewing-out. Something was seriously wrong.

Jake walked to the front of the room, then stood there with his hands clasped behind his back. "At ease, people," he said finally. "I have an announcement to make."

He looked around at the warriors standing here and there throughout the room. "I have just met with Star Colonel Gilmour, and he has given me new orders. We will see the battle here on Luzerne to completion, but after that we—"

Lita winced as Jake's voice caught mid-sentence. She dreaded hearing what came next.

Jake cleared his throat. "After that, we are reassigned to Predlitz for rest and refit."

The room was completely silent, except for the word "refit," which hung in the air like a shroud. The moment stretched out as the reality of the orders sank in.

Alexa pointed her finger at Jake. "This is *your* fault, Jake Kabrinski! I knew it all along. You are unfit for command, and I challenge you to a Trial of Grievance!"

Jake's expression remained neutral, but his voice sounded faint and haunted, as if it came from very far away. "Challenge accepted, Star Commander Alexa," he said. "Once Luzerne is secured, we will fight, and you will have your satisfaction."

With a quick nod, Alexa turned and hurried from the

room. The other four members of her Star quickly followed her out.

Jake seemed unfazed by her blatant breach of protocol. "Star Colonel Gilmour anticipates completion of this campaign by the end of the week," he continued, as though nothing had happened. "See to it that your techs prepare your 'Mechs for departure. That is all."

He turned and walked calmly from the room, but loud conversation exploded in every direction the instant the door closed behind him. Dodging the rain of angry shouts, Lita quickly ran after him into the hall.

She reached out and grabbed his shoulder, not caring if her touch was rough. His face was ashen as he turned to look at her.

Lita felt the words catch in her throat, but she pushed on. "You know I would never argue with you in front of the troops, Jake. So tell me now: what the *hell* was that?"

He seemed to look right through her, and spoke as though reciting a script from memory. "Gamma took heavy casualties out there. We need the rest and refit. It is standard operating pro—"

"Standard nothing, dammit! Gilmour is banishing you back to the Dominion, and you are dragging the rest of us with you."

Jake shook his head slowly. "The Trinary needs this break. It is for the best, believe me."

Lita stared directly into his eyes. "You want to know what I believe? I believe that DEST woman cut your balls off with her *katana*."

That got a rise out of him. The color was returning to his face, but he still seemed numb. "Perhaps Alexa was right, after all," she went on. "I hope she knocks some sense into you—hell, I hope she *beats you,* for all our sakes."

That did it. A snarl tore its way across Jake's face. Lita nearly jumped out of her skin when his fist slammed past her into the plasterboard wall, gouging out a head-sized hole and sending plaster chunks tumbling to the ground. Still without speaking a single word, Jake turned and stormed down the hall toward the Elemental barracks.

Lita looked down at the plaster fragments scattered over

the floor. Almost without realizing what she was doing, she crouched down and picked up some of the fragments. She wished she could feel some satisfaction in what she had done.

Lifting her head, she could see the form of Jake Kabrinski retreating down the hall. She crumbled the plaster pieces in her hand, letting the white dust drift through her fingers to the floor.

22

Nadir Jump Point, Courchevel
Pesht Military District
Draconis Combine
15 August 3063

"Jump procedure complete. Arrival in Courchevel system confirmed. All stations, maintain alert status."

The smooth, even sound of the duty officer's voice did little to soothe Jake's nerves, or his stomach. And he was one of the lucky ones. Many warriors suffered from Transit Disorientation Syndrome. For those unfortunates, every hyperspace jump threatened to turn their insides out, or at least so it felt. Even for those not afflicted, the rather unnatural process of vaulting thirty light years in the blink of an eye left the body queasy for a few minutes.

Val was seated across from him in the Elemental readyroom, always more anxious than he was in these situations. "My favorite part of a jump," she said, trying to be flip, "the '*blind time.*'"

Jake tried to reassure her. "Look on the bright side, Val. We are halfway to Predlitz, which means only two more jumps. Besides, the jump will only disrupt the ship's sensors for a few seconds."

"Yes, but in the meantime, we are sitting ducks."

"True enough, but any vessel within two thousand meters

of us would be in no shape to do anything about it after suffering through our emergence wave." The *Burning Paw* was docked to the JumpShip *November Wind* as it emerged at the nadir jump point of the Courcheval system.

Val tugged on the cross-straps holding her into her crash chair. "It is not that I worry about being attacked. The sensor blindness bothers me because it means we cannot know what is—or is not—out there."

"Once the *November Wind*'s sensors are back on line, the captain will send me a status report on the system's defenses, if any."

"In the meantime, you can tell me again about how you defeated Alexa in that Trial of Grievance. I am sorry I missed it."

"I am not so proud of it, Val. She had great potential as a warrior, but she was hurting morale and poisoning her Star against the rest of the Trinary. Her death was a waste, but we are better off without her."

Jake looked away, thinking back to the events on Luzerne. It had been a week since his duel with Alexa, and he still had not sorted through all the conflicting feelings about it. He had a sick feeling in his gut that he could not entirely blame on minor jump sickness or even Alexa's death. He had been feeling this way ever since Marcus Gilmour had sentenced his unit to their new duty. With or without Alexa, his Trinary's morale was suffering and he felt powerless to do anything about it.

His communicator beeped, and he tapped the line open. "Star Captain, you had better come up to the bridge," said the eternally calm voice of Ian, the *November Wind*'s captain.

Val raised an eyebrow and began to unbuckle herself from the crash seat. "I take it the sensors are back on line?"

Jake's pulse quickened as he shook free of his own harness. "It would seem so. Val, go round up Lita and Maxwell and meet me on the bridge."

Standing up, Val snapped Jake a quick salute. An excited smile tugged at the corners of her mouth. "On the double, sir!"

*   *   *

Ian pointed to a small red point of light on the monitor. "There it is."

Jake looked at the image, then back at the captain. Though he and the ship's captain were equal in rank, the man was so nondescript that he could have been a tech. "I have to admit, it looks inconsequential enough from this far away."

"Aye, but there is nothing inconsequential about that sensor contact. Our computer analysis tags it as a heavy cruiser. Most likely a *Kirishima*-class WarShip."

Jake's eyes widened. "Kurita, then?"

"Considering the type of vessel—and our location—absolutely."

The bridge doors hissed open, and Jake turned to see Lita, Val, and Maxwell arrive. Lita, as usual, was the first to speak. "I can tell from the glint in your eye that we might see some action, Jake. What is it?"

Jake smiled as a plan began to form in his mind. Waving his hand grandly toward the monitor, he said, "What we have here is a Combine WarShip attempting to sneak into the Courchevel system and retake it from Clan Ghost Bear."

Val frowned. "How very unClanlike."

Star Commander Maxwell stroked his red goatee in thought. "They are not Clan . . ."

"Which is precisely why we must do something decidedly unClanlike ourselves." Jake mentally ran through the details of his plan while his officers exchanged confused looks. He knew it was a bold move, but only boldness would make the rest of the Clan sit up and take notice of his disgraced unit. He had to prove Marcus Gilmour wrong in banishing Jake from the front lines.

"Before you all panic," he said, "I want you to know I have not forgotten the way of the Clan. We are Ghost Bears, but we are now of the Inner Sphere. I have seen much that I do not understand—and may never understand—but I have also learned some new lessons about war with this new enemy. Marcus Gilmour said it himself on Luzerne: 'The time has come to dispense with formalities and get on with the business of victory.' Well, we managed to achieve victory on Luzerne—"

Jake could not help but think it was no thanks to Gilmour. "—and we can achieve victory here, too. Besides, if we do nothing about that cruiser, it will either spearhead an invasion of Courchevel or jump after us anyway. What say you, captain?"

Ian nodded. "Our data indicates that they are operating on a lithium-fusion battery, so they could easily double-jump and chase after us."

Lita sat down in a nearby chair as though suddenly tired. She was shaking her head in disbelief. "You are not thinking what I think you are thinking. Are you?"

Val clapped Jake on the shoulder, grinning broadly. "I certainly hope you are!"

Maxwell walked over to take a closer look at the monitor. "I mean no disrespect, but our orders are to proceed directly to Predlitz . . ."

Jake suppressed a growl. Did the man ever finish a statement without trailing off? "No disrespect taken, Star Commander. I understand our orders, but this is an unforeseen emergency that demands immediate action."

Lita nodded agreement. "We could continue on with only a report so another Bear unit could take care of it, but it could take days—or weeks—for another unit to arrive. In the meantime, Courchevel could fall to the Combine."

"How could we call ourselves true Clan warriors if we let an opportunity like this pass us by?" Val put in.

Maxwell spread his arms in mute surrender.

Jake stabbed his finger at the red light representing the *Kirishima*. "We will prepare our Elemental suits for EVA immediately, then board and capture that WarShip. With one swoop of our claws, we will defend Ghost Bear possession of Courchevel *and* claim a new WarShip for our Clan!"

23

DropShip **Burning Paw**
Nadir Jump Point, Courchevel
Pesht Military District
Draconis Combine
15 August 3063

With no time to lose, Jake called his troops together in the *Burning Paw*'s main launch bay. The forty-nine Elementals of the Battle and Assault Novas were gathered around him in the large, C-shaped room. Attending each one was a tech, making the necessary adjustments to prepare the Elemental battle suits for space combat. Jake stood at the head of the room, while his own tech, Sara, knelt at his feet bolting on tanks of reaction mass that his jump jets would use as fuel in the airless void.

With his suit half on and half off, he could barely move, let alone reach over to the portable holoprojector standing on a wheeled table beside him. He looked down at Sara. "If it would not be too much trouble . . . ," he said.

Sara looked up and raised an eyebrow. "I am very busy here, you know." She was an excellent tech, even if she did have too much freebirth attitude at times.

Jake matched her expression with his own. "At your earliest convenience, then. I would not want those to come loose, after all."

Sara gave her wrench one last turn, then stood up, and went to help him with the projector. "You certainly would not. No fuel means no propulsion, and I would hate to see you drift off into the void . . ."

At the touch of Sara's finger, the lenses on the front of the holoprojector lit up, casting a large, slowly rotating image of the heavy cruiser on the wall behind Jake. He craned his neck to look at it, then turned back to his command, hoping he could inspire enthusiasm in them for his plan. If it worked, this operation would lift the gloom that had hung over the whole unit in the weeks since leaving Luzerne. Or, so he hoped.

"This is our target," he said. "A *Kirishima*-class cruiser, massing 790,000 tons and carrying enough weapons to turn the *November Wind* and all her DropShips to scrap in seconds.

"Our Trinary is not currently deployed for combat, as you all know, so we are not traveling with enough shuttles to mount a standard boarding assault. That could work to our advantage, however. The *Kirishima*'s capital weapons would make short work of the shuttles before we ever got close enough to clamp on to the hull. Instead, we will approach individually, using EVA gear and our jump jets."

Scattered murmurs ran through the room, and Jake understood their concern. "A WarShip's main guns are designed to fight other WarShips, and sometimes DropShips, but they have difficulty targeting small, fast-moving objects like fighters—or Elementals. When we get up close, there will be anti-fighter weapons to contend with, but they are no different from the 'Mech-mounted weapons we deal with on the ground."

Sara stepped away from his suit, giving a pat to the bulky thruster pack replacing the usual SRM launcher. "Be sure to jettison this before boarding, or you will be too bulky to move through the ship's corridors."

Jake nodded, then turned back to the assembled troops, who had quieted down. He backed up a few steps toward the projected image of the WarShip, his massive, steel-clad feet clanking loudly on the deck. Reaching up with his left-arm claw, he pointed to an external pressure door just aft of the bridge.

"This is the access point closest to the bridge. It will likely be well guarded by the time we arrive, but we cannot afford a long hike through the whole length of the ship. With this as our target, we can approach the *Kirishima* from the nose and avoid its heavily armed broadsides for most of the way. You will be issued demolition charges. Using those and your support lasers, the first to arrive should be able to cut through the door in thirty seconds."

At a signal from Jake, Sara adjusted the controls on the holoprojector, shifting the image to a cut-away view showing interior corridors.

"Mind you," Jake went on, "this is only an approximation of the interior—our Clan has yet to see the inside of a *Kirishima*—but it is based on a thorough analysis of similar vessels. This route should get us to the bridge, and I do not need to tell you that control of the bridge means control of the vessel.

"Once the bridge is secured, teams will move through the rest of the ship, directly disabling the DropShip docking collars and the engine room before the ship's techs can override the bridge controls and take independent action."

Jake looked around at his troops. Most of the techs had left the room by now. "Well, that about covers it. Are there any questions?"

More murmurs, then the usual long pause while everyone waited for someone else to speak first. A hand finally went up in the back of the room. It was Mark, one of Assault Nova's point commanders. Jake nodded for him to speak.

"Fifty Elementals against a WarShip? Those sound like tall odds to me, sir."

A fair question, and one that Jake had also been forced to confront. The operation was daring and dangerous, but he believed it could work if he and the others could set aside their doubts.

"I am not ordering any of us to directly assault the *Kirishima*, Point Commander," he said. "That would be a meaningless waste. Instead, we will approach the ship from its weakest side and board her there, sparing both the *November Wind* and ourselves the worst of her firepower."

Jake let his gaze travel around the whole room, trying to catch the eyes of each warrior in turn. "Make no mistake: nothing about this operation will be standard. That is precisely why it will succeed. They will not see it coming, and they will be unable to react until it is too late."

Much to Jake's relief, the gathered Elementals began to nod in agreement. He had won them over in the same way he had come up with the plan. By this deed, they would all have a chance to prove themselves true Clan warriors. They would live or die gloriously in defense of their Clan.

The lights next to each of the room's doors changed from yellow to flashing red, the alert that the moment had come to begin the attack. As his troops began lowering their helmets to the closed position, Jake saluted them. "Your courage makes me proud. We will be *remembered* for this."

The assembled warriors saluted in return, uttering as one the single word "seyla" through the external microphones on their battle armor suits. The word was sacred to the Clans, spoken since their earliest times to bind themselves in unity and purpose.

Jake's heart swelled with pride as he lowered his own helmet and turned toward the bay doors, which slowly opened onto a huge, star-filled nothingness. This leap into the blackness of space was an all-or-nothing gamble. He would defend his Clan and win back the honor he had lost since Alshain—or die trying!

If not for the chronometer glowing in the corner of his HUD, Jake would have sworn that the trip to the *Kirishima* took forever. When they started out, the cruiser was not even visible to the eye, and when it did come into view, their approach seemed so slow that Jake at times thought he was actually moving *away* from the ship. Again, a periodic check of the HUD's range-finder confirmed that he was indeed closing in on the target, although he could feel nothing since he'd stopped accelerating mere minutes into the trip.

"You there, Jake?" asked Val, her voice coming through

loud and clear in a laser transmission undetectable by the enemy. Jake could not see her, but he knew she was hurtling through space somewhere below him and to his right.

"I am, Val. Go ahead."

"This trip is mind-numbing. Perhaps your voice can keep me sane. Explain to me again why the *Kirishima* has not already blasted the *November Wind* into space dust?"

It was the same question that he had posed to Star Captain Ian earlier on. "The Kuritas probably know that *Invader*-class JumpShips like ours are used mainly for merchant transport among the Clans, especially when WarShips are available for combat duty. The *Kirishima* almost certainly detected the *November Wind*'s emergence wave when it jumped in, but there is a good chance her crew would have identified it as a civilian transport and ignored it. Besides, what harm can an unarmed JumpShip do to a WarShip?"

"So that explains why we immediately unfurled the jump sail upon arrival," Val said. "They probably think the *Wind* is merely recharging her jump drive and will leave the system as soon as possible. But a cautious commander would investigate an unexpected arrival, *quiaff*?"

"Perhaps, but Lita tells me Combine warriors can be incredibly stubborn and proud—"

"Like Clanners?" Val cut in slyly.

Jake chuckled. "Touché. But seriously, dealing with such a ship might be considered beneath the captain's station. Or, he might be watching for another ship to arrive, signaling an actual invasion force. He has tried to contact the *Wind* by radio, but we have not responded. He may be sending a boarding party to investigate, which is fine with me. The other fifteen Elementals of Gamma that we left behind should be able to deal with anything these Spheroids can muster."

"And if they send a boarding party, that means less marines on board the *Kirishima*."

"Precisely. So, have I answered your question?"

Val laughed. "Yes, and several others I did not realize I had. I think we passed the time rather productively."

Val was right. The *Kirishima* had more than doubled in

apparent size since they had begun talking, and Jake could see the muzzle-flashes of weapons beginning to fire in their direction.

"We had better continue this another time," he said.

"See you on the inside, Jake."

Their conversation was cut short when Jake was momentarily blinded by the flash of a capital-grade laser beam spearing past him. Its sheer size stunned him. Though he had no way to determine how close he was to the beam, it was at least as wide as he was.

Freebirth! he cursed silently. One of those hits me, and it is all over.

As he continued drifting toward the WarShip, its weapons continued firing. Jake knew intellectually that sound could not travel through space, but the total silence of such a massive barrage of fire surprised him. He switched his transmitter from laser to radio so he could broadcast to his entire force.

"All right, people," he said. "They know we are here and that we are close enough for their guns to hit us. See you on the inside. Begin evasive action!"

With that, Jake braced himself and looked at his HUD for a new control icon. He spotted it, a symbol made of arrows pointing in many directions. Focusing on it for a moment, he triggered the evasive-action sequence Sara had programmed into the thruster pack. It would send him on an erratic series of maneuvers designed to accomplish three goals. One and two were to avoid enemy fire and to prevent collisions with his own troops. The third was to make sure he ended up with the same heading and velocity as when he began, so that he would end up boarding the *Kirishima* and not hurtling out into interstellar space.

After a few seconds' delay, his thrusters blasted to life, pressing Jake down into the suit's feet as he rapidly accelerated. Before his body could become accustomed to the Gs, the thrusters changed trajectory, slamming him backward and then suddenly down again.

All he could do was hope his movements were as disorienting to the *Kirishima*'s gunners as they were to him. So far, it looked like they were. Shots from antifighter weapons raked the space all around him, but none scored hits. During one extended period between accelerations, Jake did see one of his Elementals take a direct hit from an autocannon. He cursed himself for not being able to tell who it was. In an instant, the warrior was gone, and Jake was accelerating again. It was becoming a supreme effort to maintain focus and consciousness.

And then it was over.

Jake realized that the evasive sequence was complete, and he was drifting again. The *Kirishima* loomed before him, filling his entire field of vision. He could see the stacked pair of wide bridge windows on the ship's nose, and above them the Kurita dragon emblazoned proudly in red and green. His Elementals—those that had survived the trip—would make contact with the vessel in less than a minute.

Jake needed a head count. "Status report. Sound off!"

Per standard procedure, the members of each point would sound off in reverse numerical order to their point commanders. The point commanders would then give the numbers to their star commanders, who would report to Jake. Immediately, the members of Jake's own point began sounding off:

"Five . . ."

"Four . . ."

". . . Two"

Then Jake said, "One."

The gap between Four and Two could only mean one thing—they had lost Lewis. They were probably lucky they had not lost more, considering the massive barrage of weapons fire.

The transmissions from the point commanders began immediately.

Dominic reported first. "Epsilon, three."

An unfamiliar voice followed. "Delta, two—I think. Sorry, sir. We lost Point Commander Kris."

Jake winced at the loss as John reported next. "Gamma, five."

Val's Beta Point was next. He breathed a sigh of relief when he heard her say, "Beta, three."

As he reported his own "Alpha, four," Jake mentally tallied seventeen out of twenty-five for his star. He did not have to wait long for the report from the Assault Nova. "Assault Nova, ten. I hope your star fared better, sir."

Stravag! Jake thought. They had lost too many, but he told himself that did not matter. They were Elementals. Nothing on board the *Kirishima* could hope to stop them.

"Aff," he replied. "We have seventeen. I will take command from here on. Over."

The voice on the other end sounded relieved. The star's commander must have been killed on the approach. "Roger that, Star Captain."

The *Kirishima* continued to grow in his view, becoming less a discernable ship than a massive wall pockmarked with windows and weapons. With a blast from his thruster pack, Jake angled to the right, veering away from the ship's nose and toward the port side. Several other Elementals followed.

Another thruster blast sent him hurtling directly toward the WarShip. Now he could finally see the target point: a hatch four meters tall and three wide. A quick adjustment to his jump jets and thruster pack turned him so that his feet pointed "down" toward the ship. Jake braced for contact.

He expected a noisy crash, but thanks to vacuum, the only sounds were the reverberations within his suit. Despite its myomer musculature, he could feel the jarring impact through his whole body.

After pausing to recover his breath—and receiving an automatic injection of stimulant from his armor's Life Support Sustaining Unit—Jake proceeded to plant his demolition charge on the hatch. He felt a shudder as another Elemental landed nearby, and he looked up. The newcomer approached with an unusually slow gait, his split-toed metal feet gripping the ship's hull with powerful magnets. They slowed his stride but kept him from floating off into space.

Immediately, Jake regretted looking up. The WarShip's hull offered some semblance of "down" for him to orient to, but the chaotic panorama before him now threatened to break his already tenuous grasp on consciousness. He could see more Elementals raining down from above, and several of them were turned around the wrong way.

Jake winced. Those landings would not be pleasant.

In addition, several Combine fighters had been scrambled in defense. They were flying in every conceivable direction: up, down, right, left, and sideways. Witnessing strafing runs over the hull from impossible angles did not help Jake pull himself together.

A tap on the shoulder from the newly arrived Elemental did. Kneeling beside Jake over the hatch, the other warrior pulled his demolition pack from the holster on his armored thigh and planted it next to the one Jake had placed there moments before.

As the rest of the Elementals touched down on the hull, Jake and his companion stepped away from the hatch, waving off the others. Banishing his anxiety, Jake opened a channel. "Charges ready. Detonate on my mark."

He checked the hatch area for stray Elementals. Seeing none, he used his suit's claw to press the button on the hand-held detonator.

A silent explosion was one of space combat's more unusual experiences. One did not realize how integral sound was to the entire concept of explosions until he or she witnessed one of these firsthand. In space there was, of course, no oxygen to fuel combustion. The explosives in each charge contained their own oxygen supplies, but still the explosion little resembled what ground-bound observers were used to.

The results, however, were the same. The metal surface of the hatch buckled inward severely, blackened and weakened by the explosion, but not destroyed. Jake and the others took care of that with their support lasers, heating the metal until it melted and dripped off into space in white-hot gobbets.

Jake waved for the others to enter. They had to open the interior door before they could gain access to the inside of the ship. Val's welcome voice came through on the radio as Jake waited for the next set of demolition packs to be set.

"The next hatch ought to put on more of a show, *quiaff*?" she said.

"Aff. Explosive decompression will blow it out into space, along with a healthy volume of air from inside the ship. They must have closed their emergency bulkheads by now, but we will probably flush several crew members and marines out anyway."

Elementals climbing back out onto the hull indicated that the charges were set. Point Commander John led them, and he held his detonator up. "Charges ready. Detonate on my mark," he said.

This time, Jake braced. The hull shook as the charges tore through the internal hatch. As promised, the difference in pressure between the inside of the ship and space resulted in explosive decompression. Flames leapt up from the tear in the hull, fueled by the air streaming out, then were quickly snuffed out. As the smoke cleared, Jake counted at least six bodies floating out into space.

Anticipation was replaced with adrenaline as he looked down through the jagged opening in the hull. Leading the way, he dove down into the ship and toward redemption.

The door to the *Kirishima*'s bridge melted into slag under the relentless punishment of half a dozen support lasers. Shotgun blasts filled the air as the ship's marines desperately tried to repel the advancing Elementals. When outfitted for shipboard combat, marines were equipped with weapons specifically chosen to avoid blasting accidental holes through the hull: shotguns, sonic stunners, and all manner of melee weapons. Unfortunately for them, those weapons had about as much chance of penetrating Elemental battle armor as they did the hull of a ship.

With his squad lying dead around him, the leader of the marines stepped forward. The telltale hum of the *katana* he brandished identified it as a vibroweapon. Jake stepped forward to accept the silent challenge. As the marine advanced, Jake's head began to swim with images of shadowy figures wielding swords.

Not now! he thought. Not when he was so close to victory.

Before the marine could come within sword's reach, Jake lifted his left arm and unleashed a blast from the shotgun slung under his claw. The shot took the marine square in the chest, dropping him where he stood. The vibrokatana clattered to the ground, its white-hot blade gouging the floor before the weapon fell silent.

Jake labored to control his breathing, and he looked around the bridge. All around him, among overturned chairs and scorched control panels, unarmed crewmembers raised their hands in surrender. Nodding in satisfaction, he opened a channel to the rest of his force. "Bridge secured. Docking collar team, status report."

The vast amounts of metal in the ship's structure created a hiss in Point Commander Dominic's response. "All but one DropShip locked down, sir."

"All but one?"

"Not to worry, Star Captain. We blasted two of its drives on the way out. There is no way it will make planetfall."

"Good work, Dominic. Engine room team, status report."

John responded, another loud hiss confirming his position in the bowels of the WarShip. "Engine room secured, Star Captain. Full pressure restored to all intact decks. Good thing we got here when we did, too."

"Oh?"

"They were all set to self-destruct. You better get a team of techs down here right away to make sure we did not miss any fail-safes."

"Copy that. My compliments to your team, John. The ship appears to be ours."

Jake's last moments on the *Kirishima*'s bridge melded into one dreamlike impression of colors, sounds, and sensations. Although time would later confirm what happened next, in that moment Jake could not tell whether it was dream, reality, or some horrible mix of the two.

He was looking out into space through the observation window, feeling as though a tremendous weight had been lifted from his shoulders. He felt satisfied, complete. And for the first time in his life, totally at ease aboard a spacecraft.

His heart lifted even more when he heard Val's voice from behind him. He smiled as he turned around. She was coming through the blasted remains of the bridge door, with the two surviving members of her point following close behind. She held her suit's helmet in her left-arm claw, and she was smiling as she spoke. Jake could not make out her words.

He was just about to say so when he caught something out the corner of his eye. A shape behind an overturned chair, moving ever so slowly in the shadows. Was that the muzzle of a rifle?

He opened his mouth to shout out a warning to Val, but it was too late. Had he lost his voice or she her hearing? It made no difference.

The rifle flashed even as Jake raised his own weapon. Blood blossomed on Val's forehead as she fell backward. Jake fired, too, but the assassin was gone.

Too late.

Rushing to Val's side, he tore at the clasps holding his helmet in place. As the hiss of the seal opened, he pushed the faceplate up and leaned down to Val's blood-spattered face.

She looked up at him, the light fading from her steel-gray eyes, and smiled. Her voice was faint, so faint he could have sworn his own thoughts were louder, but he would never forget her last words.

"You did it, Jake."

24

Cruiser *Urizen II*
Nadir Jump Point, Courchevel
Pesht Military District
Draconis Combine
16 August 3063

Jake gave his gray uniform jacket one more tug in a vain attempt to expunge every wrinkle before stepping up on the crate to stand before his troops. Behind him, on a raised platform, were arrayed twenty-six simple metal urns. He looked around at the assembled warriors of Gamma Trinary, rank upon rank of gray-clad men and women gathered in the WarShip's cavernous fighter launch bay. They stood at firm attention, solemn respect etched on every face.

He took a moment to appreciate the silence, but also to collect his thoughts. Less than twenty-four hours ago, he had held Val in his arms as she died, and it had cast a pall over his spirit.

He cleared his throat and began to speak. "Welcome, fellow Ghost Bears. As most of you know, I am a man of few words, so I will not weary you with a long speech today.

"As warriors, it is our duty and privilege to fight and die for the greater good of our Clan. These twenty-six have fulfilled their duty and more. The fact that we now stand on the deck of this WarShip is testament to their brave deeds.

Though not one among the fallen had earned a Bloodname, each one is deserving of our highest respect and admiration. They were our comrades. Our *trothkin*. Our friends."

Unbidden, an image of Val came to Jake's mind as he spoke the last word. She seemed to nod at him in satisfaction, as if to say her life was complete while his own was just beginning. In a flood of feeling, he realized how much he had counted on her presence through all the ups and downs of warrior existence. They had been together their entire lives. But now, it was time for Jake to go forward on his own. These strange thoughts made him deviate somewhat from his prepared speech.

"Friends . . . it might seem strange that I would choose that word to describe our fellow warriors. After all, true friendship can be a hindrance to peak combat-performance. The success of a mission might be jeopardized if a warrior allowed friendship to cloud his judgement, *quiaff*?"

Jake saw some nods of agreement in the crowd, and continued.

"All of you know the story of our Clan's founders, Hans Jorgensson and Sandra Tseng. Though the concept is now foreign—even repugnant—to most in the warrior caste, they were 'married' to each other, the closest of friends and lovers combined.

"Both were highly skilled warriors and able leaders, totally loyal to Nicholas Kerensky and devoted to his vision of a new society. Rather than focusing so much talent in a single Clan, Nicholas chose to appoint them to two separate Clans, thus maintaining balance and strength among all the Clans. That was a prudent strategic move on his part, of course."

Jake smiled to see more nods from his listeners. Good. They could see where he was going with this.

"But the Founder had not counted on the bonds of friendship. When forced to choose between their orders and each other, the pair chose the latter, fleeing into Strana Mechty's arctic wastes to die in each other's arms rather than be separated.

"There the story might have ended, if not for the intervention of the ghost bears. Huddled in a remote cave, Tseng and Jorgensson were nursed back to health by a family of bears, who were previously thought to be solitary hunters. Regaining their strength, our founders returned to find Kerensky. After telling him all that had happened, they pleaded with him to allow them to found Clan Ghost Bear together, in keeping with the true spirit of their totem. Kerensky saw the wisdom in their words, and granted their request.

"Since the very beginning, our Clan has valued friendship highly, sometimes above all other things. And although it sometimes creates weakness, it also forges immeasurable strength in loyalty, camaraderie, and esprit de corps. It is these strengths that have carried the Ghost Bears through our darkest hours and allowed us to become the strongest of all the Clans.

"So, today, we say goodbye to our departed friends and comrades. They held true in our darkest hour, and because of their loyalty, we prevailed. Let us never forget them, and let us never squander the victory they helped us achieve."

His heart heavy, Jake turned to face the urns. He brought his right fist to his chest, then extended it in salute. The assembled warriors of his command did the same. Joining their voices, they all spoke the solemn oath as one, "*Seyla.*"

Painting in microgravity was a skill Jake had worked many years to master. He had discovered early on that traditional paint pots and brushes simply did not work. Even if you could keep the paint from floating all over the room, the brush did not flow the way you expected it to. Although this sometimes resulted in interesting results, it was not what Jake had in mind for this particular piece.

There were several effective methods to choose from, but Jake had settled on thick, cream-like paints and tiny sponge applicators in place of brushes. Using such an applicator, he leaned in close to the canvas and added dabs of red to the cheeks of a weeping woman standing amid flames and sharp cliffs.

A soft tone signaled that someone was at the door of his quarters aboard the *Burning Paw*. Without taking his eyes off the canvas, he called out for whomever it was to enter.

The canvas was huge, nearly two meters tall and so wide that he had to roll up the sides so that he could work on individual sections.

"My apologies, Jake. I did not mean to interrupt," he heard Lita say.

Jake dabbed one last touch of rouge on the woman's image, then set the applicator down on a nearby palette. He turned to Lita. "Not at all. I was nearly finished with that section."

Lita came closer, and the automatic door hissed shut behind her. She took a moment to study Jake's work. "Very impressive, if I may say so."

"You may." Jake allowed himself that bit of pride.

"So this is your Great Work, then. Have you been working on it since your first Trial?"

"Yes, I have been at it more than three years now, although I have not touched it since Alshain. So much has happened since then, and it has given me a whole new perspective on what I had done so far."

He turned to look at the canvas. "It seems to evolve as time passes. There is always something more I can add or something I can change."

Lita sat on the edge of Jake's bunk. "And with such a broad topic—ancient Greek myth, *quiaff*?—you will not soon run out of subject matter. I imagine it reflects your experiences and feelings as you work on it. When it is finished, I am certain it will be a fitting memorial."

Jake nodded, looking down at the newest part, an image of Persephone living in the underworld. He wondered why he had chosen that part of the montage to work on this day, rather than the scene of Bellerophon and Pegasus destroying the Chimera or any of the dozen other images scattered across the canvas. It shocked him when he realized he had unconsciously changed the face of Persephone ever so slightly to resemble Val's.

Lost in thought, he barely heard Lita's next comment. "I mean no disrespect, but I never would have figured you for a Great Work."

"Why do you say that, Lita?"

"Not every Ghost Bear chooses to embark on such an

'endless expression of dedication to a long-term goal.' Take me, for example."

Jake looked over at her. "Really? I just assumed you had something going."

Lita shrugged and grinned. "I suppose I just never got started. At this point, I doubt I ever will."

Jake frowned. "You speak as though your career is nearly over." He could see that he had struck a nerve, for her face darkened. There was a distant look in her eyes as she spoke.

"Did you know that I was captured during Operation Revival, Jake?"

"I had not heard that. Were you taken by the Combine?"

"Neg, by Rasalhague. They took my unit in a surprise attack and carried many of us as bondsmen off-planet, behind friendly lines. They said they were going to ransom us, but I never believed it."

Jake nodded. "Most armies refuse ransoms, especially the Clans. They would have known that."

"Aff. I still do not really understand why they took us at all, but I ended up in a 'prison camp' among an . . . interesting variety of fellow prisoners. There were some other Clansmen there, but the majority were Rasalhagian criminals. Some were military, but most were civilians being kept out of the way while the war was waged."

"Perhaps they just wanted you Clanners out of the way, too?"

"Hmm, yes," Lita said. "Perhaps. I may never know."

She stood up and began to pace slowly up and down the room. "At first, I hated being held like that. They did not treat me like a proper bondsman at all. I could see there was no way I would be accepted into their warrior caste; they simply had no such procedure. All seemed hopeless, and I sank into depression. I felt as though my capture represented my final, greatest failure. One that I would pay for the rest of my life."

Lita stopped pacing and looked at Jake. "But after a few months, my attitude changed. A few of the—inmates, they called them—befriended me. Not that I made it easy for them, mind you."

Jake chuckled, and Lita's expression softened a bit. She

sat back down on the bunk and continued. "Most days, there was nothing to do except for the work they assigned us. Gradually, I relented and got to know the Inner Sphere people around me. You can imagine how strange it was. Up till then, the only time I had ever seen a Spheroid was through my targeting reticule.

"Many of them were not worth my time. They were criminals, scum. I am proud to say more than a few died at my hand, which the prison guards did not seem to mind. But there were a few who either claimed innocence or who were truly repentant. They had been there for many years and were trying to make the best of their incarceration. I learned a great deal about the Inner Sphere from them, and in turn, I am sure they learned much about the Clans from me."

Jake was mesmerized by her words. This was a side of Lita that he had never suspected. It explained her knowledge of the Inner Sphere, as well as her lapses into unClanlike behavior. "Go on, Lita," he said.

"After what seemed like years, but was really only months, the Ghost Bears reached the planet where I was being held and liberated me from the camp. I was allowed to re-test and become a warrior again."

"So that is why a warrior of your skill and age is only a star commander," Jake said, without thinking.

Lita nodded, a brief look of shame crossing her face. "Yes."

"I meant no disrespect, Lita. By all rights, you should be in command of a cluster by now."

She smiled gratefully. "That is kind of you to say, Jake." She looked toward the door, then back at him, then got up to leave. "I really have taken up too much of your time."

"No, Lita, your visits are never an intrusion, but I do have some things to attend to. By the time our ships' jump drives are recharged, a prize crew will have arrived from Courchevel to take control of this captured WarShip. Everything must be in order for them."

Lita smiled again and walked to the door. "I have often wanted to tell you these things since Idlewind. I thought it would help. Remember this: after my capture, I thought the world had ended. The truth is that it had only begun to open up for me."

As the door slid shut behind her, he turned to look at his painting. The image of Persephone gazed back at him, tears in her eyes at her cruel imprisonment.

Sitting down heavily on his bunk, Jake struggled to make sense of the thoughts and feelings that swirled through his being. With her last breath, Val had simultaneously accused him of causing her death and congratulated his victory.

Through the cabin's small porthole window, Jake could see Courchevel's distant sun. He kept turning over in his mind what Lita had said. He wished he had her hindsight. If only he knew whether Val's death was the end of his world . . . or the beginning . . .

25

As Jake stepped off the hover transport to report for duty, his boots immediately kicked up clouds of dust from the parched ground. The noonday sun cast a bright white light over Predlitz, Gamma Trinary's new home. Headquarters was a simple, prefabricated two-story building. It resembled so many others Jake had seen both here and back in Clan space that, for a moment, he almost thought he was home. The illusion was strangely enhanced when he saw who emerged from the front door to greet him.

Jake was stunned. Star Captain Carl? What was he doing here?

By the time Carl walked over, Lita, Maxwell, and Reese had also disembarked and formed a line behind Jake. The hover transport sped away, kicking up another dust cloud as it returned to the spaceport.

Carl raised his fist in salute. "Star Commander Carl reporting, Star Captain. And may I add that it is a pleasure to see you again."

His head swimming, Jake returned the salute and mumbled something vaguely affirmative.

"I am the garrison commander here in New Denver," Carl continued. "Of course, I will defer to you for the duration of your stay on Predlitz. You are now the superior Clan officer on-planet."

Jake nodded slowly, wondering if Gilmour had planned this as part of his punishment.

His three companions were equally surprised to see their former commander.

Lita was quick to step forward. "What a surprise to see you here, Carl."

"Aye," Maxwell added. "What are the odds?"

Carl smiled as he shook Lita's hand, then turned to shake Maxwell's. "I would have said the odds were zero until a few days ago. I thought you were on the front lines—you even captured a Kurita WarShip, *quiaff*?"

"Aff," said Reese. "But we met with some . . . difficulties earlier in the campaign. We have been reassigned here for rest and refit."

Carl smiled and nodded slowly. "*Star Commander* Reese, is it now? What happened to our charming Alexa?"

"Her ambition got the better of her," Lita said. "She challenged Jake and lost."

Carl's eyes widened, accentuating the deep furrows on his brow. "So she was demoted, then?"

"Neg. She was killed."

"Oh, I see." Carl squinted up at the sky. "Well, it is a scorcher today, *quineg*? I had better get you out of the sun and into your new quarters."

Jake nodded for the other three to go on ahead. Carl led them away toward the building, leaving Jake standing there. Running into Carl here on Predlitz was like seeing a ghost.

He looked down the hill toward the distant spaceport, where he could see the *Burning Paw* sitting on the tarmac refueling. At this distance, the techs working on the hulking DropShip looked like ants scurrying around their anthill, carrying out endless duties for their queen.

The image suddenly struck Jake as humorous, and he laughed.

"Something funny, Star Captain?" Lita asked, dropping back to wait for Jake.

Jake turned and walked toward her. "Yes, but I am not sure why."

Lita smiled. "Whatever it is, you seem to have snapped out of your trance. Seeing Carl seems to have affected you, *quiaff*?"

Jake shrugged. "Not just seeing him. I am surprised that he seems to harbor no negative feelings toward me. After all, I took his rank and his command away from him. He should be bitter. Resentful. *Something*."

Lita held the door open, and Jake walked into the building. "Take it from someone who worked with the man for years," she said. "You can never be sure what to expect from old Carl."

Jake stopped and looked down at Lita. "Take it from someone who he molded into a warrior. That man *never* forgets."

The building was cool compared to the heat of the day, but Jake barely noticed. Lita had already moved past him and was proceeding down the hall. For now, he shelved his concerns and followed her into his new home.

Jake stood at the observation window on the bridge of the *Urizen II*, flush with victory and feeling as though a tremendous weight had been lifted from his shoulders.

His heart lifted even more when he heard Val's voice. He smiled and turned to see her coming through the blasted remains of the bridge door. She was dressed in flowing white robes, and behind her he could see the corridor enveloped in flames.

She reached out toward him and pleaded, but her words were indistinct. Jake asked her to repeat what she said, but she did not respond.

Out of the corner of his eye, Jake saw something move. A shape behind an overturned chair, dressed head-to-toe in black.

He opened his mouth to call to Val, to warn her, but it was too late. Had he lost his voice, or she her hearing? It made no difference. She looked over her shoulder at the flames behind her, but did not see the assassin.

The DEST woman, clearly visible now, raised a rifle to her shoulder, aiming squarely at Val's head. But she did not pull the trigger.

Instead, she reached up and pulled the black hood from her head, revealing the delicate features of a lovely Japanese woman. Shaking her long black hair free, she looked at Jake and smiled.

On any other face, her expression might have been provocative, even arousing. On hers, it made Jake's blood run cold.

She frowned at his reaction, then raised her rifle and sighted Val through its scope. She pulled the trigger, a look of scorn and anger on her face.

As the rifle flashed, Jake raised his right hand to fire his laser, but the weapon was not there. Instead of a laser, his unarmored hand was holding a paintbrush. Then he realized that his other hand was holding his palette. Dropping the useless implements, he rushed to Val's side.

Lita came running to join him from the flaming corridor. Jake tried to wave her away. *You are not supposed to be here!*

The DEST woman was still there, too. Her rifle tilted to find a new target: Lita.

Dropping to her knees beside Val, Lita began to weep. Jake felt his pulse quickening, and the bridge around him began to fade. He wanted to shout at Lita, to save her from Val's fate, but the words would not come. *Why are you here? Why can you not see the assassin? You must leave here now!*

The DEST woman winked at Jake, then pulled the trigger.

The weapon fired, waking Jake from his dream. He could still hear the crack of the rifle ringing in his ears.

Disoriented, he sat up quickly. Through the port window he could see the twin moons of Predlitz shining down. They hung together in the night sky like a pair of eyes staring back at him.

Jake told himself that that was a crazy idea. He was only dreaming. He lay back down and closed his eyes, determined to go back to sleep, but sleep would not come. The whole night long, all he could see—eyes open or closed—was the image of Val's shattered, dying face looking up and accusing him.

You did it, Jake.
You did it.

26

New Denver Market
New Denver, Predlitz
Ghost Bear Dominion
15 October 3063

"There are so many people here, sir . . ."

Carl laughed at the young warrior's wide-eyed amazement. "Of course there are. After five weeks of training on that base with no break, I had to get your ass out of there and into the *real* New Denver. This market—with all the dirt, noise, and crowds—is definitely it. And please, cut the 'sir' stuff out here. Carl will do while we're off duty."

Ben nodded absently as he gawked at his surroundings. "Yes, sir—I mean, Carl."

"There you go, cub. You're catching on."

Normally, the vulgar use of contractions would have disturbed Ben, but this morning his senses were simply too overloaded to notice. It was a relief to get away from the base, too. The endless drills were eating away at the unit's morale. Many were complaining that they had been dumped on this rock and forgotten. Ben was starting to wonder if maybe they were right.

Leading the way, Carl edged through the throng toward an outdoor café. They hurried to capture one of the few empty tables. Carl waved to a waiter. "The crowd's getting to me too," he said. "We can wait out the worst of it here and still be right in the middle of things."

Ben nodded. "And take in a drink or two?"

The old warrior laughed again, a barking sound that was as unpleasant as ever despite Carl's recent mellowing. "I like you, cub. I have to admit that I did not much notice you when I was still your trinary commander, but now . . ."

That got Ben's attention. "Now, what?"

Carl shifted uncomfortably. "Let's just say you have done a lot of growing up over the last year. When you arrived here on Predlitz, I almost didn't recognize you."

"I barely recognized you, either, what with all the contractions you use . . ."

As a waiter approached, Carl dropped his voice almost to a whisper. "Sorry about the foul language. Helps to blend in. Not every Dominion citizen is jumping out of his skin to thank the Bears for moving in, you know."

A moment later, the waiter arrived, so Ben held his tongue. Carl ordered for them both, and the waiter hustled off to fetch their two coffees.

Ben picked up the thread of the conversation. "Blend in? Why? Are you ashamed of your Clan? Ashamed of what we have accomplished here in the last ten years?"

"Not at all, Ben. That isn't—is not—the point. By and large, Spheroids want to live their lives on their own terms. Unlike the Jade Falcons and the Wolves, the Ghost Bears have not tried to change the people of the Dominion into Clansmen. Khan Jorgenssen's 'hands-off' governmental policies made life business as usual for most of them. Sure, they know who is in charge, but they do not like to be reminded of it every day. Strutting around like the proud Clan warriors we are sets them on edge."

The waiter quickly wove his way through the maze of tables, then placed two steaming mugs on the table. Carl pressed a few coins into the young man's hand, and he was off again.

Ben looked at Carl, shaking his head.

"I cannot agree with you, Carl," he said. "If they forget who is in charge, they might forget more: our laws, our customs, our traditions. And there, the money you just handed that waiter. Clan warriors had no need for money until we came to the Inner Sphere."

Carl sighed. "It is not really so different from the work credits we used back in Clan space. Besides, you cannot expect dozens of worlds to completely change the way they handle trade overnight."

"I suppose not, but a decade is hardly overnight. I am no expert in economics—"

"My point is this, Ben. I have to live among these people. Neither the Clan nor I benefit from making them uncomfortable, so I do my best to blend in when among them. In uniform and on duty, it is a different story, of course."

Ben still did not understand entirely, but he saw no point in continuing the argument now. He pulled one of the steaming mugs over and took a sip.

"Ouch! That's hot," he said, not mentioning that he would probably never get used to the Inner Sphere version of the brew. He glanced around, looking for a change of topic. "This is a wonderful square. Is that a famous warrior?"

Carl followed Ben's pointing finger to a stone and bronze fountain that rose above the square. The imposing statue sat atop a fountain. It was the likeness of a man wearing fatigues and gesturing forward, as if urging his troops into battle.

Carl shook his head and smiled. "Neg, Ben. The Spheroids are different about their statues. In Clan space, all our statues honor our greatest warriors, but this represents an explorer. I believe he is the man who led the original settlement of New Denver."

Ben took another cautious sip of his beverage. "This is kaf, *quiaff*?"

"Not exactly," Carl said. "It is a bit more potent, but less bitter. The kind they serve here, at any rate. I am told there are more than a million varieties."

Ben leaned back in his chair, enjoying the sun's warmth before it turned hot in the afternoon. Out of the corner of his eye, he thought he recognized a face in the crowd.

"Hey, is that Lita over there?" he said.

Carl set his mug down and looked in the direction Ben indicated. "I doubt it. Not in this part of town."

"What do you mean, 'this part of town'?"

"Make no mistake, Ben. The main streets here are safe enough, but do not stray from them. And by all means, avoid this area at night—unless you *want* a fight."

That comment set Ben off. "I do want a fight, Carl. Just not the kind you mean. Any idea how long the trinary's assignment here might last?"

The old warrior laughed again. "Getting tired of me already? But seriously, I have no idea. The supplies you need to repair and re-arm your 'Mechs have only just arrived. Between that and the training you all need . . ."

Carl's voice trailed off as he got lost in his mental calculations. Quickly losing interest in the logistics, Ben scanned the crowd for Lita and thought he saw her again. He called out, but she did not hear him over the crowd noise.

He tugged at Carl's sleeve. "That has to be her," he said. "I am going to catch up with her."

Carl gave a long-suffering sigh as Ben got up to leave. "Have it your way, cub. I am having it mine: another cup of coffee. Don't get lost on me, now!"

Ben barely heard him as he jostled his way through the crowd.

Following Lita proved to be more difficult than Ben had anticipated. His whole existence had consisted of rural sibko training and field assignments on backwater and sparsely populated worlds. The Inner Sphere was his first contact with large cities—or large crowds. He had heard stories of the busy main square on the Clan homeworld of Strana Mechty, but he had never been there. He decided that if the Clan capitol was anything like this, he did not mind that he might never see it.

Just when he was ready to give up, Ben caught sight of Lita again. He was about to call out to her, but he saw something that made him hold his tongue.

Lita was standing a few steps into an alley off the main street. It looked like she was talking to someone, but Ben could not see who it was. Once, she scanned the people passing by, as if checking whether someone was watching.

Ashamed, Ben turned away quickly, letting the crowd carry him away. Skulking about like this was unClanlike, but he could not help the rush of adrenaline through his system. If that were true, then what was Lita up to?

He looked back once more, and this time he got a good look at the person she was talking to. Instantly, he understood why Carl had cautioned him about this place. Ben had never met an actual criminal, but the man leaning in to speak into Lita's ear matched perfectly anything he had ever imagined. Dressed in dark and cheap clothes, the man looked as though he had never taken a bath in his life. He also held a small object in one hand, and he clutched it to his chest like it was worth more than life itself.

Ben's mind raced. What to do? Lita glanced his way again, and he decided to get out of there. Retracing his steps, he hurried toward the café.

Jake was surprised to see Ben burst unannounced into his office, but the tale he told was equally surprising. Ben left out one important detail, however.

"You still have not explained to me why you were *spying* on Star Commander Lita in the first place," Jake said.

Ben grimaced at the accusation. "I was not spying on her, Star Captain. At least, not intentionally. I spotted her in the market, and I just wanted to say hello . . ."

"Yes, yes," Jake said. "You told me all that before." He leaned back in his chair and sighed heavily. "Then what do you think she was doing there, Ben?"

It took a moment for the young warrior to answer. He looked torn. "I do not know, sir. I could not hear what she and the man were saying, but he was holding something."

"Did he give it to Lita?" Jake asked.

"No, I did not see that, but I left while they were still talking, so he could have . . ."

"Did you tell Carl about this?" Jake asked.

Ben shook his head, then stiffened at the sudden breach of etiquette. "No, Star Captain. I came straight to you."

"Good. For now, I ask that you speak to no one about

this. Thank you for bringing this to my attention, Ben. You are dismissed."

The young MechWarrior saluted, looking relieved as he turned and left the office.

Jake walked over to the window. The hot sun of Predlitz was setting, and one of the planet's moons was already visible in the sky.

He leaned against the window frame and wondered what, if anything, he should do with the information Ben had brought him. He could not abide the idea of spying on a fellow warrior, especially Lita, but Ben's tale seemed too important to ignore. Lita had told him of living among criminals during her captivity, but how much more of her past did Jake still not know?

Perhaps the whole incident was nothing more than an innocent encounter, but Jake had to be sure. He would watch Lita closely from now on. If the whole thing turned out to be smoke and no fire, so much the better. If it was something more sinister, Jake did not want to be taken by surprise.

By now, the second moon had begun to creep up over the horizon.

He thought of Lita, hoping this would all turn out to be a big misunderstanding. The two moons stared down at him like a pair of evil eyes.

Jake turned away from the window, but he could not shake off his dark mood.

27

Jake stood at the head of twenty-five Elementals arrayed on the parade grounds, each one attended by a tech prepping his battle armor for combat. Next to him stood his own tech, Sara, tapping the keys of a handheld noteputer connected to his armor by a thin cable. She unplugged the cable and gave Jake a thumbs-up.

"You are all set, Star Captain," Sara said. "Give 'em simulated hell."

Jake nodded and waved his four point commanders forward. They were John, Dominic, Kris—only recently recovered from injuries suffered during the boarding action—and a new arrival, Taris. He had arrived with the other reinforcements from the Third Claw, which was stationed on the western continent.

Jake spoke first to Taris "Welcome to Gamma Trinary, Point Commander. We are glad to have you and the others from the Third. Perhaps you did not know that I, too, once served in a Claw Galaxy."

The warrior seemed unimpressed. "Neg, I had no idea, sir."

Jake was well aware that his unit morale had declined to dangerous levels. They had done nothing but drill incessantly for six weeks, and apparently the gloom was contagious.

Jake did not know what to make of Taris. He was thin for an Elemental, with a rough mane of brown hair that gave him a sloppy appearance. The serious expression on his face served to dispel that image somewhat, but Jake could not help thinking that Taris seemed a poor replacement for Val.

"Yes, well, good to have you," he repeated. "As you all know, today's exercise serves two purposes. First, we must train to bring the new arrivals from the Third Claw into the unit. Today will be the first in a series of daily exercises that will familiarize the new arrivals with the way we operate."

Jake thought he detected a flash of scorn in Taris's eyes, but he ignored it. "Second, we have not had a chance to perform this particular kind of exercise since arriving on Predlitz. As the resident 'Mech unit, we have the responsibility of defending the planet, should the need arise—"

He paused as his four officers had a good laugh. Predlitz was clear on the far side of the Dominion from the Draconis Combine. Invasion was inconceivable.

Jake looked at them sternly, then continued. "Should the need arise, the responsibility is ours. We must familiarize ourselves with our surroundings. The kinds of terrain we might have to fight in, the various routes through woods and mountains, and so on. We have seen the maps, but there is no substitute for the real thing."

The assembled warriors nodded in agreement, with the notable exception of Taris, who simply reached up to close the faceplate of his helmet. With a sigh to himself, Jake closed his own helmet and keyed the radio. "All right then. Let us go teach the MechWarriors of Gamma Trinary who the true 'kings of the battlefield' really are!"

With her *Mad Dog* perched high on a ridge, Lita had an excellent view of the approach to the valley they were guarding. She looked out the left side of her cockpit at the

Nova standing on the far side of the valley, and keyed her radio. "In position, Ben?"

The reply came after a significant pause. "Aye, Star Commander. I have no enemy contact."

"Are you all right, Ben? You have not been your usual eager self for a week or so now."

The response was quicker this time. "I am fine. At your suggestion, I saw the base medtech last week, and she gave me a clean bill of health."

"That is not what I mean, and you know it. Is there something going on that I should know about? I bet it has something to do with Carl, that cranky old—"

"No, no. Carl is fine. I am fine. Really. I think it is this new assignment. Maybe the shame of it all is finally sinking in. We are missing the war, you know."

Lita knew. She couldn't stop thinking about it on some days, but she hid her feelings better than poor Ben. "I know, but this planet is important, too. We must not allow what we *cannot* do to interfere with what we *can* do."

After another long pause, Ben said, "Yes, you are right." Then, nothing. With a shrug, Lita checked her sensor panel again.

"Point Alpha, I have sensor contact. Three 'Mechs in sector One-Four Bravo, over."

It was Point Commander John, the excitement evident in his normally blasé voice. It was obvious that being pulled from the front was affecting all of Gamma's warriors. Jake was itching for action, too. He was glad even for these practice sessions. "Excellent, Point Gamma. Hold your position while we anchor on you."

Jake switched to the command channel. "Point Gamma has contact with the bulk of the enemy force. They are in the valley, as I had anticipated. Point Beta, continue your sweep to the north and come around behind them. Point Epsilon, move straight in and join forces with Point Beta. Point Delta, stay with me."

A chorus of "rogers" set the Elementals in motion. It was all coming together. Soon, the three OmniMechs would be surrounded and outnumbered.

*   *   *

Petra was the first to spot the approaching battle armor. Without hesitation, she slammed her throttle backward and opened fire with her *Stormcrow*'s arm-mounted lasers. "Two points, right in front of me!" she called to the rest of her star.

She immediately began walking the *Stormcrow* backward, away from the onrushing Elementals, faster than they could keep up. They began firing their missiles, trying to slow her down. Caught in a deadly rain of SRMs, nothing happened to her 'Mech.

Nothing real, at any rate. These missiles were designed for field training, each one armed with a transmitter that impacted harmlessly on the target. The target received the missile's signal and registered every hit, inflicting a corresponding loss of capability to account for the effects of the damage had the ammunition been live. Petra's battle computer registered ten hits, scattered across her entire 'Mech.

"Ouch! I hope that did not hurt too much," said Mech-Warrior Willa, the new member of her star. Willa had replaced Reese after he earned command of the Striker Nova. She was a seasoned veteran who had proven herself to be a worthy addition to the star.

Like Reese, Willa piloted a *Hellbringer*, which came bursting from the woods to add its PPC fire to Petra's lasers. Between them, they knocked out three Elementals in less than a minute, their powered-down energy weapons registering kills in the target's suits and inflicting temporary paralysis. All the while, the two continued back-pedaling toward the east end of the valley.

They were soon joined by Umbriel in her *Viper*. She emerged from tree cover pursued by a third point of Elementals. Her voice came in loud and clear over Petra's radio. "A little help here?"

Petra rotated her 'Mech's torso and scored hits with both arm-mounted large lasers. The blast stunned two Elementals, but did not register enough damage to take them out for good.

"Keep moving, people," she said. "My radar shows the rest of them closing in."

Sure enough, another ten Elementals came bounding out of the woods on jump jets, weapons firing.

Willa's voice was filled with static, her computer simulating radio damage. "Are you sure about this plan, Petra?"

Petra was amused, but she kept her voice neutral. "Absolutely. This is an old favorite of Lita's."

Jake's satisfaction grew as he fired his laser at the *Hellbringer* again. They had formed the noose, and all that was left was to close it around their prey. "Close it up, people. They are running out of valley."

And out of time.

Behind the fleeing OmniMechs, the valley narrowed to meet a sheer cliff face with exits too narrrow for Battle-Mechs to fit through. Once their quarry backed into that wall, they would be trapped.

Suddenly, Umbriel's *Viper* lit up its jump jets and hurtled over the entire force of Elementals. Jake turned to keep her in view, and saw the *Viper* twist in mid-flight to land facing him. He fired his laser, but the *Viper* was out of range. "Where is *she* going? Point Alpha, follow me and keep that *Viper* in view."

Before his troops could react to the order, one hundred-twenty long-range missiles began to pour down on them.

"What the hell is that?" demanded Kris.

Jake checked his sensors, then looked up at the surrounding cliffs. Sure enough, there was Lita's *Mad Dog*, its arm and shoulder pods bristling with LRM launchers. Too late, he realized his error. The three retreating 'Mechs had successfully baited his entire Elemental force out into the open under the guns of Lita and Ben, who had configured their OmniMechs will full loads of LRMs. Umbriel completed the trap by circling behind them. Instead of Jake's Elementals completing the noose around the 'Mechs, the 'Mechs had turned the tables and closed the noose on *them*.

Everyone seemed to be shouting back and forth at once over the radio, but Jake could not hear them. He was back on Luzerne, his force overwhelmed on all sides . . .

That brief gap in attention was all the *Hellbringer* needed to walk over and tag him with a point-blank PPC shot. The warning buzzer from Jake's computer snapped him out of it in time to hear MechWarrior Willa's voice over the open channel. "Bang. You are dead, sir."

Jake's heart was thumping. His voice came out cracked and hoarse. "Congratulations, Willa. Welcome to Gamma Trinary."

Welcome, indeed. It was all Jake could do to drag himself back to headquarters to ponder his latest defeat.

28

New Denver Market
New Denver, Predlitz
Ghost Bear Dominion
31 October 3063

Flickering torches cast long shadows down the twisting alleyways running among the streets of the New Denver market. The heavy foot traffic at this late hour, combined with the black and orange banners, made Jake think he was in the middle of some local festival.

Lita was not far ahead of Jake, and he was sure she did not know he was following her. This was the third time she had ventured out from the base in the two weeks since Ben had warned him of her unusual activities, and the third time he had followed her. So far, none of his covert operations had netted any useful information; she seemed to do nothing but window-shop when she left the base. If tonight was another bust, he would dismiss the whole thing as a fluke and try to forget about it.

In his efforts to remain undetected, Jake paused and allowed Lita to get farther ahead. Based on her previous trips through the market, he projected her likely route and decided to take a shortcut through the alleys to beat her to her probable destination: a café near the center of the market.

By now, Jake had learned the winding streets of the mar-

ket fairly well, but the alleys could be challenging even to a
New Denver native. Confident that he was headed in the
right direction, he accelerated to a jog so he would not miss
Lita as she entered the café.

"What's the big hurry, pal?"

The voice, that of a boy who had not quite finished the
transition to manhood, came from behind Jake. He glanced
over his shoulder to see who was speaking, but no one
seemed to be there. Looking forward once again, he caught
himself and stopped just short of slamming into a pair of
figures blocking the alley in front of him. They were
dressed all in black, with the pattern of a skeletal structure
painted on their clothes in white. Skull-like masks covered
their faces, but Jake could tell they were teenagers by their
voices.

One of them stepped back, holding his hands up defensively. "Whoa, watch where you're going, man."

The second one, shorter and smaller than the first, played
the part of yes-man. "Yeah, watch where you're going.
Don't you know this is *our* turf?"

The boys' merciless use of contractions grated on Jake's
ears, but he maintained his composure. He did not have
time for this. "Pardon me," he said in a calm, deep voice. "I
am just passing through."

The voice from behind came again, this time closer. "No
one 'just passes through' around here, buddy. Not tonight.
And especially not Clan freaks like you. You must pay a
toll."

Turning halfway around so as to keep the first two boys
in view, Jake saw the speaker approaching around a corner.
Following him were two more boys, all of them dressed
like skeletons. The speaker, clearly their leader, had ram's
horns adorning his skull mask. He held a length of pipe in
one hand, which he slapping rhythmically against his other
hand.

The yes-man piped up again, a giggle in his voice born
of equal parts adrenaline and alcohol. "A toll. Yeah, like,
trick or treat, right?"

Jake took a moment to carefully scan the area while the
group moved to encircle him. He quickly concluded that

there were no more than the five of them. Jake could see where this was going, and decided to change his tactics. "If it is money you are seeking, I carry none. On the other hand, if it is a fight you are seeking, I can give you one you will not soon forget."

The leader laughed, twirling the pipe easily in one hand. He half-crouched into a fighting stance.

"Before you attack, be aware that I am a Bloodnamed Elemental of Clan Ghost Bear. Are you sure you want this?"

In response, the gang charged Jake as one. Although their technique was rough, they were well-practiced in working together as a team. As Jake anticipated, the leader led the attack, swinging the pipe high over his head for a crushing blow to Jake's left shoulder. Jake easily dodged to the right, throwing a stiff-armed punch with his left arm at another approaching boy, who collapsed under the impact.

He continued moving right in one fluid motion, and grabbed hold of the leader's pipe. "Never bring a weapon to a fight if you do not know how to use it," he said, easily tearing it from the leader's grasp and sending it smashing into another boy moving in to attack. As adrenaline rushed through his system, Jake realized how long it had been since he had engaged in a real bout of hand-to-hand combat. It was just what he needed.

Deprived of his favorite weapon, the leader reached into his belt and pulled out a butterfly knife, opening the blade with a skillful twirl of the weapon's two-part metal handle. "Point taken, giant," he sneered. "How's this?"

Jake feigned an impressed look. One of the other boys tried to capitalize on the distraction by rushing at him from behind with a garbage can lid, but Jake sensed it coming and braced himself. He took the noisy but ineffectual blow to his back without flinching, ignoring that attacker in favor of the knife-wielding leader.

It was a wise choice. The leader immediately lunged at him with the knife, tip-first. Jake grabbed his knife-arm at the wrist, picking him up off the ground and whirling him through the air to smash into the garbage can lid-wielding boy standing behind him. The two of them crumpled into a heap on the cobblestone ground.

Yes, indeed, thought Jake, exactly what I needed.

Straightening up to his full height, he turned to the last remaining skeleton-boy: the diminutive yes-man. The sight of his fellow gang-members being wiped out in a matter of seconds, and the fact that Jake had not even broken a sweat, was enough to convince him to find an easier target. Jake let the coward turn tail and run. Although the exercise was refreshing, he had wasted enough time here. Now he had to move quickly to catch up with Lita.

After taking a few wrong turns, Jake finally emerged from the alley into the main square. Glowing, pumpkin-shaped lanterns hung from the balconies of the buildings ringing the square, giving a strange orange hue to the faces of the crowd.

Approaching the café, Jake was thankful that many of the people around him were dressed in bizarre costumes, which allowed him to blend in a bit more easily than usual. It did not take long for him to spot Lita, seated at an outdoor table across from a rather ordinary-looking man wearing a feathered mask that concealed his eyes and nose. Seeing the two leaning in close as they talked, Jake thought he had finally caught on to something. Edging his way through the party crowd and into the café area, he found a table behind Lita and the man, far enough away not to be noticed but—he hoped—close enough to overhear their conversation.

Eavesdropping proved to be more difficult than Jake anticipated because of the noise of the festive crowd. Glancing up from his coffee occasionally to read the masked-man's lips, he could fill in some of the blanks. What he managed to hear painted a bleak picture.

"Yes, but does your organization have any information . . . security at . . . spaceport or . . . planetary sensor grid?" Lita asked.

The man smiled. "—more than . . . get through official . . . my friend. However, it is true that . . . off-planet party interested in this . . . Of course, they know . . . I cannot . . . precisely what information they . . ."

Jake could see Lita nod her head in the affirmative.

"—the need for secrecy . . . an invasion of Predlitz, you will . . . alongside us. Believe me, the . . . are preferable masters to . . . right now."

The masked man shrugged. "These details . . . none of my concern. I can . . . in contact with the anti-Clan resistance . . . take this up directly with them . . ."

Lita nodded her head again, and Jake saw her shoulder move as though she was sliding something across the table to the man. "That will . . . Your help is appreciated."

The masked man nodded and stood up, pulling his hand from his pocket as though he had just deposited something there. From this position, Jake could finally hear his words clearly. "It is nothing. This meeting never took place."

Lita lingered at the table a few minutes while the masked man disappeared into the crowd, then she left, too. Jake did not follow, temporarily in shock. It was almost inconceivable, but there was no denying what he had heard.

At first, he thought he should confront Lita directly. Accuse her and see what she had to say for herself. Perhaps even a Trial of Grievance would be in order. The more Jake thought about it, the less that course of action appealed to him. To his shame, he was not sure whether he could bring himself to make such an accusation to Lita's face after all they had been through.

A more powerful reason occurred to him that absolved at least some of his shame. Now that he was aware of her plans, he had the upper hand. By continuing to keep an eye on Lita, he could be forewarned of her plans, and have the advantage against her when the time came to stop her.

Saddened and resigned to this distasteful course of action, Jake stood up and took a deep breath of night air as he looked around at the strange decorations and costumes one more time. Whatever this macabre festival was, Jake decided he did not like it. Not one bit.

29

Jake's eagerness to attain high rank had blinded him to the less glamorous duties associated with high station. As the senior officer on Predlitz, it fell to him to complete additional daily, weekly, and monthly reports covering everything from combat readiness to equipment requisitions. Lately, though, he almost welcomed the tasks. They tended to distract him from the thoughts of Lita's treachery that had dominated his consciousness for the past two weeks. He and Ben had both been keeping close tabs on her, but nothing new had surfaced.

This evening, like so many others, these thoughts of Lita invaded the tedium of filling out requisitions. Unable to concentrate on either task sufficiently, Jake decided to take a break and get some fresh air.

New Denver, nestled among high mountains, offered wonderful scenic views, and was said to be named after one of Terra's major cities. On this night, Jake was treated to a spectacular sunset between the mountain peaks to the west, with thin stratus clouds striating the brilliant orange sky with strips of purple.

The peace of the moment was interrupted by the sounds of a fistfight taking place behind the main MechWarrior barracks. Intrigued, Jake walked in that direction.

Rounding the corner, he saw that it was no impromptu tussle, but rather an organized session of unarmed combat practice. Two MechWarriors of the Assault Nova were facing off within a five-meter-diameter circle traced into the dirt. Other MechWarriors stood on the sidelines, cheering for one combatant or the other, and at the head of the group—presumably serving as referee—was Star Commander Lita.

Reflexively, Jake averted his gaze from her. He had been uncomfortably following her activities for weeks now, but he suddenly realized he had been avoiding any other contact with her. Jake was far from an expert on subterfuge, but it occurred to him that such a habit might alert Lita to his suspicions. Resolved to maintain appearances, he looked straight at her and approached, circling around the combatants to avoid interfering with their sparring.

Jake could not tell if she was avoiding his gaze or simply watching the match intently, but he did not get her attention right away. Not exactly anxious to talk to her, he stopped a few steps away, waiting and watching the fight.

After some long minutes of uncomfortable silence, she spoke to him first, without looking away from the combatants. "They fight well, *quiaff?*"

Jake would have welcomed the small talk if not for the cloud of unanswered questions buzzing in his head. As it was, he had to struggle to maintain an even tone. "Aff. The taller one is MechWarrior Edmund, *quiaff*? He seems to be winning this match."

Lita shook her head. "You have not had the time with them I have had, Jake. Ferris is using his greater agility—and cleverness—to lull his opponent into a false sense of security. Then, when he least expects it . . ."

As if on cue, the smaller of the two fighters seized an opening and ducked under the other's wild right hook. Once inside his opponent's defenses, Ferris sprung up with a powerful uppercut, followed quickly by a quick series of jabs to the gut. The lightning-fast combination sent Edmund sprawling to the ground, kicking up a cloud that covered many of the onlookers with dust.

Lita stepped into the circle and helped Edmund up. Still dazed, the tall MechWarrior looked unsteady on his feet. She spoke to him, but in a voice clearly intended for the entire gathering. "I take it you have an idea why Ferris beat you?"

Edmund nodded. "Aff. I underestimated him early on. I realize now that he let me score some hits, and acted as though they were more damaging than they really were."

Turning to address the rest of the group, Lita continued the analysis. "This is a lesson that bears repeating. Never underestimate your opponent. If he appears to be weak, do not assume the appearance is accurate. And even if it is, the weakness is not likely to be all-encompassing. Seek his remaining strengths and counter them."

Lita stepped out of the circle, followed by Ferris and Edmund. She pointed at two others. They entered the ring and clasped hands before squaring off to fight.

Jake took this opportunity to continue his conversation with Lita. "I must keep a closer eye on that Ferris. He is a sharp one."

Lita turned and looked right at Jake. It was the first time in many days that they had been eye to eye, and it rattled him. "Aye," she said. "He is a valuable warrior and definitely has command potential."

Squirming under Lita's sharp gaze, Jake abruptly blurted out his next words without thinking. "It occurred to me the other day that I have never checked the status of the planetary sensors since we came to Predlitz."

Now it was Lita's turn to look uncomfortable. She seemed about to speak, but then turned to watch the two MechWarriors currently wrestling in the dirt. Jake was sure she was hiding something.

"According to Star Commander Carl," she said at last, "the planet's sensor grid is a bit primitive by Clan standards, but in perfect working order."

Jake nodded and also turned toward the fight. Standing next to her, he became more uncomfortable by the minute. "Well, I suppose this is enough fun for one night," he said after a few minutes. "Those reports will not fill themselves out."

Lita laughed softly, and Jake was surprised at her apparent light mood. Or was it relief that he was leaving? "Aye, self-completing reports are one technology our scientist caste has yet to perfect. Good evening to you, then."

"And to you." Jake turned and headed back toward the headquarters building.

Once he was out of sight, he detoured toward the nearest guard at the back of the barracks. The trooper, who was leaning heavily on his elbow immediately sprang to attention and snapped off a salute when Jake approached.

Jake returned the salute. "At ease. This is not an inspection. Do you know where I might find Star Commander Carl this evening?"

The trooper looked relieved and nodded. "Yes, sir, Star Captain. In fact, I saw him heading toward the main bay a few minutes ago."

Jake thanked the trooper and sprinted toward the boxy structure that served as a battle armor repair and maintenance bay.

"Planetary sensor grid?" Carl asked. "Don't tell me you're worried about an invasion?" He laughed so hard he nearly fell off the repair platform where he was standing while his tech worked over his battle armor.

Carl's laugh grated on Jake's nerves as much as ever, reminding him of their last battle. "Neg, but one can never be too careful. Lita said you told her everything was in order."

Carl leapt to the ground from the three-meter-tall platform. With only the barest sign of strain from the mildly acrobatic move, he straightened to face Jake. "That is what the reports say."

Jake could see his Sara working on his own armor nearby. She absently waved a wrench at him without looking up from her task. He turned back to Carl. "The reports . . . ?"

Carl scratched his head and sat down on a nearby bench. "Yes, the technicians perform routine checks on the sensor stations, then file their reports. Last time I checked on that—must have been a week ago now—everything was in good shape. Accompanied an inspection team myself once, before you all arrived—"

"When was the last time the entire grid was checked?" Jake interrupted, sitting down next to Carl.

Carl laughed again. "All at once? You must be kidding. The grid consists of dozens of monitoring stations scattered across the planet. Some of them are so remote they can only be reached by orbital drop. To check them all at the same time—hell, to check them all within a single week would be impossible. We simply do not have the staff—or the equipment—for that scale of operation."

The gruff old warrior was shaking his head. "Besides, a full-grid check is not really necessary. The monitoring stations are in virtually constant communication with each other and the handful of communications satellites orbiting the planet. If any one of them fails—and they do from time to time—the rest of the grid picks up on the problem and we are alerted automatically."

Jake sighed and rested his head in his hands. If all this were true, then sabotage would be impossible. What the hell could Lita be discussing with the stranger, then?

Sara's voice jolted him upright again. "In theory, you are right, Star Commander," she said to Carl. "That is how the system works under normal circumstances. On this planet, anyway. If I may be so bold?"

She came around the bench and stood looking at the two Elementals. Carl looked annoyed at being corrected by a lower-caste worker, but Jake nodded permission for her to speak. Sara was often brash for a tech, but he knew she would not interrupt unless it was important.

She fished a rag out of her pocket to mop her sweaty brow as she spoke. "Given enough prep time and a thorough knowledge of the sensor grid, it would, theoretically, be possible to set up a dummy transceiver that received the messages from the rest of the grid and sent the appropriate 'everything is fine' message for that station. Once that device was in place, you could disable the station and no one would be the wiser—unless the tech monitoring the boards was really sharp, and looking for a problem, that is."

Carl seemed bored and uninterested, but Jake asked her to continue. "How so, Sara?"

"Well, there would be a sort of blind spot on the radar, I suspect. The operator normally sees junk on the screens: passing birds, commercial aircraft, and so on. With the station knocked out, there would be no signals at all in its area. This is not my area of specialty, you understand."

Jake decided to ask her point-blank what he wanted to know, or he might never get beyond her hedging. "But given what you *do* know, Sara, could that kind of sabotage be used to land an invasion force?"

Sara tucked the rag back into her pocket. "I suppose so, if you knocked out enough stations. The whole area would lose the ability to detect incoming JumpShips and Drop-Ships, since Predlitz has a single grid that handles all space-detection tasks. The invaders could come in totally undetected, but like I said before, they would need very accurate information about our sensor grid to pull it off."

Jake was thinking it would require exactly the kind of information that Lita could access and pass on to the local anti-Clan resistance. "If you knocked out all the sensors around a city—let us say New Denver—that sensor blind spot you mentioned would be very noticeable, *quiaff*?"

"Neg," Carl put in. "Not if it was done during a time of low activity."

Realization dawned on Jake as Sara spoke. "Like tonight . . ."

"Carl, have Star Commander Lita detained immediately," Jake said, and Carl's jaw dropped in amazement.

"There is no time to explain, Carl. Just do it. I saw her outside the MechWarrior barracks about an hour ago. But do not raise the general alarm just yet. We do not want to alert any potential saboteurs. Once that is done, await further instructions from me—and me alone."

Carl took off at a run while Jake turned to Sara. "Load my armor onto a hover transport and meet me at the main gate."

"What is it, sir?" she asked, suddenly formal.

Jake had a sense of impending doom. "I could be wrong,

but it is possible that someone has blinded our sensor grid to allow an invasion force in."

"*Invasion*? By who?"

"I do not know. Whoever it is, they are well-prepared and willing to go to any lengths to get past our guard. We have no time to waste."

Sara nodded, then she too dashed away toward Jake's partially assembled suit, barking orders for some lesser techs to fetch a transport on the double.

Jake went to the door of the repair bay, and stepped out into the rapidly cooling night air. Looking up into the sky, all he saw were stars. He was not sure what else he expected to see, but the familiar sight reassured him—just a bit.

He hoped he was wrong. Wrong about the sensor grid, wrong about the invasion, and most of all wrong about Lita. Because if he was right, Jake dreaded what he would have to do about it.

30

"I am glad that is finally over," Ben said from the reclining chair he had set up on the barracks roof.

Stretched out on her own chair, Umbriel chuckled. "Oh? I thought you *liked* unarmed combat training."

Ben leaned over to look at her. "Do not get me wrong. It is valuable and necessary, but I would much rather be in the cockpit of a 'Mech."

"Or off-duty entirely?" Umbriel teased.

"Yes. Or off-duty."

Ben watched the sky, which had turned black, revealing the first stars of the evening. He pointed up toward a cross-like arrangement of six bright stars. "See those? I call that constellation the Big Cross."

"*You* call it? What is its official name?"

Ben shrugged. "I do not know. I think it is more fun to name them myself."

Umbriel laughed, a sound Ben had grown rather fond of. "If you are going to name them yourself, you could try more creative names than 'The Big Cross.' *Please*."

Ben shrugged. "I am starting small and working my way

up. The reason I call it that is to tell it from that other one over there. I call that the Little Cross. See how the tail of the Big Cross points to it?"

Umbriel squinted and tried to follow his pointing finger. "I think so. Those seven stars there, right?"

"No, it should be six, just like the Big Cross."

Umbriel sat up. "The Big Cross has seven, too." She paused and squinted again. "No, maybe eight. If we had a telescope, I could be sure."

Out of nowhere, Ben recalled her earlier jibe and also sat up straight. "Hey, what is wrong with off-duty?" he asked.

Umbriel smiled. "Nothing, but you used to be so formal and fixated on combat duty and training. I think Lita's attitude has rubbed off on you."

She reached over and patted his hand "Do not worry: it suits you. Besides, the relaxation gives us time to enjoy the stars and recover from all of Lita's yelling and cursing."

Ben laughed incredulously. "Oh, she is not that bad. I would take her over cranky old Carl any day."

"I heard that!"

Umbriel and Ben looked at each other with horrified expressions. It was Carl himself, calling up from the ground below. Ben froze, not sure how well the "kinder and gentler" Carl would take this kind of ribbing. Umbriel was equally silent.

Carl shouted up again. "Come on, you two. I will not hold it against you. There are more pressing matters to attend to."

Ben and Umbriel got up and walked over to peer over the roof ledge. Carl stood looking up at them, accompanied by two armed garrison troopers. Ben recognized the urgency on the old Elemental's face.

"Have either of you seen Star Commander Lita?"

Ben was startled by Carl's question. Had he discovered Lita's activities too? Or had Jake confided in Carl without telling him?

"No, sir," Umbriel said. "She is off duty. She wrapped up our training about thirty minutes ago. I think she was headed into town."

"Is there a problem?" Ben asked warily.

"There might be. Look, Star Captain Jake told me not to raise the alarm yet. To be on the safe side, why don't you two get your 'Mechs warmed up. Just don't make a lot of noise until you hear from me, okay?"

Umbriel and Ben nodded, then looked at each other with the same confused expressions as Carl walked toward the compound's main gates. Umbriel began to climb down the side of the building, and Ben followed. He looked up at the sky for a moment, remembering what Umbriel had said about the extra stars in his constellations. Right now, he thought he saw them, too. But he could not be sure without a telescope . . .

Sara took the wheel of the hover transport that would take her and Jake to the nearest monitoring station. She drove so fast that Jake had to hold on for his life during a few of the sharper turns, but to her credit, they got where they were going in record time. They could be back in town in an hour if need be.

As the vehicle came to a gliding halt, Jake saw that the station was a simple outpost consisting of a satellite dish, a radio-transmitting tower, and an outhouse-sized bunker with a single door. The entire facility was surrounded by a five-meter-high fence topped with razor-wire and adorned with garish signs that warned of electric-shock hazard.

Jake and Sara dismounted and approached the gate. Jake took a noteputer from his pocket, aimed its infrared transmitter at the lock, and entered the security override code Carl had given him when the trinary first arrived on Predlitz. A satisfying click told him that the gate was open, and the telltale hum of the electrified fence fell silent. He gestured for Sara to follow him.

The noteputer had unlocked the control bunker's door as well, which she opened to reveal a huge bank of switches, wires, and indicator lights that completely bewildered Jake. "This may take a few minutes," she said. "Not my area of specialty, remember?"

Jake walked back to the door. "Just do it as quickly as you can. I will stand guard."

Shifting nervously from one foot to the other, he hated

feeling so helpless while Sara worked. He looked toward the lights of New Denver, which looked strangely festive from this distance, then up at the satellite dish. It was small, only about a meter in diameter, but apparently it was big enough to do the job. The radio tower was much larger, a metal lattice standing at least twenty meters tall.

Then he saw it. Jake reached into the utility compartment of the transport for his electronic binoculars and took a closer look at the protuberance he spotted about halfway up the tower. Zooming in, he saw what looked like a small box mounting its own antenna and tiny satellite dish connected to the tower by clamps and wires ending in alligator clips. He was no expert, but a device looking that jury-rigged clearly did not belong on the tower!

"Sara, take a look at this!"

She came over, looking frustrated by her lack of success in the control room, and took the binoculars. She scanned the tower while he pointed to the device he had noticed.

"Do you see it?" he asked. "Does *that* belong there?"

She did not answer right away, then she found the spot. "Absolutely not," Sara said.

She lowered the binoculars and looked up at Jake. "Nice work, sir. We will make a tech out of you yet." She handed back the binoculars and went over to climb the ladder mounted on the side of the antenna.

While she worked on the mysterious device clamped to the antenna, Jake looked through the binoculars toward the base. Intervening hills and trees blocked his view of all but the tallest buildings, but everything seemed normal.

He panned over to the city proper then, and the twinkling lights of a vibrant city at night still showed nothing out of the ordinary.

Sara yelled down to Jake from the tower. "It is a repeater box, all right. Simple enough to deactivate, and there appears to be no booby-trap. Hang on."

Thank Kerensky for small favors, thought Jake as he continued to pan the binoculars over the scene. Seeing nothing on the far side of the city, he panned up to the sky above New Denver, where the usual riot of stars lit the heavens.

Then he saw something unusual that could have been a satellite or a meteorite. As he turned the zoom dial for a closer look, Sara shouted, "Here we go!"

As alarms began to sound from all over the monitoring station, Jake now saw that those moving points of light were no meteorites. They were DropShips coming in at full combat speed, the friction of atmospheric entry heating their hulls until they glowed more brightly than the stars around them.

Sara slid down the ladder in a matter of seconds. Holding her hands over her ears, she jogged over to Jake's side. She had to yell to be heard over the noise. "What the *hell* is that all about?"

Jake continued staring through the binoculars, turning the zoom dial until it hit maximum magnification, and what he saw made him shudder. He slowly shook his head as he handed the binoculars to her again. "Hell is right, Sara. Those are DropShips—Hell's Horses DropShips. And they are headed straight for New Denver."

Ben had just begun the power-up sequence for his *Nova* OmniMech when klaxons began to blare throughout the 'Mech bay.

"What in the name of Kerensky is that?" Umbriel yelled from the open cockpit of her *Viper*.

Before he could respond, the incoming transmission light flashed on Ben's console. He closed the canopy to shut out the alarms and hit the Receive button. "MechWarrior Ben here, over."

It was Jake. "Ben, already in your 'Mech, I see."

"Carl figured better safe than sorry. The alarms are going crazy. What is going on, sir?"

"Ben, you were right about Lita. The sensors were sabotaged, and now there are seven Hell's Horses DropShips inbound."

"Damn, I thought those stars looked wrong!" Ben said. Then the reality of the situation hit him. "Clan Hell's Horses? Here? But why would they risk the reprisals?" He had a million questions, and hardly knew which to ask first.

Another light flashed on his console. "Hold on, sir. I

have an open-channel transmission incoming. I will patch it over to you." Chills ran down his spine as Ben immediately recognized the inhumanly metallic voice.

"Defenders of Predlitz, this is not a batchall. This is your death sentence."

The speaker paused, as if to let his words sink in fully.

"The filth called the Ghost Bears will be purged from this planet. Their foulness will be cleansed by the flames of the way of the Crusaders.

"For all the indignities heaped on us by the Ghost Bears, for all the times they have scoffed at Clan ways and traditions, for their ultimate betrayal in leaving the Kerensky Cluster for good, I deny you the honor of a batchall."

Ben could scarcely believe what he was hearing, but he continued to power up as fast as his fingers could flip switches.

The ominous metallic voice resumed, startling Ben. He shuddered as the prospect of a full-scale invasion finally sank into his young warrior's mind.

"I, Khan Malavai Fletcher of Clan Hell's Horses, hereby declare war on Clan Ghost Bear, following the Inner Sphere tradition you have so brazenly chosen to embrace. No quarter will be asked, and none will be given. Our time is at hand, and we will not be denied. *Seyla*."

31

The sounds of weapons fire echoed through the alleys below as Jake bounded from rooftop to rooftop on jets of superheated plasma, followed by the other two dozen Elementals of the Battle Nova. It had taken him nearly two hours to return to the base, round up his troops, and lead them into the center of Hell's Horses activity: the New Denver Market. Now that he was finally there, he almost wished he was not.

Scattered fires raged through the once-bustling commercial district, and the wreckage of toppled buildings were witness to the violent passage of BattleMechs. He saw no 'Mechs, but he knew that the huge war machines were difficult to spot on radar in the girder-strewn confines of a major city.

Point Commander John was the first to break the radio silence they had maintained since leaving the base. "Point Alpha, this is Point Gamma. Enemy sighted ahead. One 'Mech and at least two points of battle armor. Stand by for visual confirmation."

Jake's heart began to race in anticipation of battle. It was an unfamiliar sensation, though. Jake wondered if it might not be anticipation after all, but something far more dangerous: fear.

Mercifully, another message from John cut short Jake's train of thought. "Alpha, I can confirm five Elementals, three Salamanders, and one *Timber Wolf* of unknown configuration."

Seeing the lights of the main square ahead, he engaged his jump jets and flicked the safety off his SRM launcher. He also issued a quick radio message. "Star One, all Elementals advance on the main square. We have a *Timber Wolf* there that needs to go down quick."

When Jake reached the edge of the last rooftop before the drop-off into the square, Jake caught sight of the battle armor John had reported, but no 'Mech. The enemy troopers were moving from building to building, indiscriminately blasting the storefronts with their weapons.

Among the standard Hell's Horses battle armor were the hunched-over forms of Salamander suits. Though still fairly new, they were immediately recognizable by their oversized and wickedly clawed feet designed for more effective grasping in anti-'Mech attacks. Mounting one inferno missile and a heavy flamer slung under each arm, the troopers were setting fire to every building within range.

John landed next to Jake. He pointed his armored claw toward the Salamanders and spoke over the command channel. "I thought Salamander suits were Clan Fire Mandrill gear. What are the Horses doing with them?"

"I doubt they obtained them directly from the Mandrills," Jake said. "But where is that *Timber Wolf* you mentioned?"

"It was in the square a minute ago, but then it disappeared behind those buildings over there, and I have not been able to re-obtain it."

Jake opened the channel to the entire star. "Point Gamma, continue your search for the *Timber Wolf*. The rest of you, follow me into the square!"

It did not take long for the Horses to notice twenty Elementals pouncing on them from above, and they exchanged vandalism for true combat. Anxious to engage the new Salamanders, Jake singled one out and opened fire with his support laser. Judging by the silver pentagon emblazoned on one shoulder, the warrior was a point commander.

The ungainly beast surprised Jake with its agility. Jake's attack hit just below his now-jumping target, scorching and melting the pole of a café umbrella.

Two could play that game, Jake thought as he fired his own jump jets. Arcing slightly higher than the airborne Salamander, he passed directly over it and fired his laser straight down, scoring a hit on the shoulder-mounted missile.

Under the laser's intense heat, the inferno missile's payload of highly explosive, flammable gel exploded in a glorious fireball, briefly lighting up the entire square. The Salamander appeared to survive the initial explosion, but the shockwave sent him hurtling head-first to the pavement below. The mangled heap that was once a trooper did not move after the impact, freeing Jake to choose another target.

Finishing his jump, he turned toward the center of the square and radioed John for an update. The reply came quickly. "Still no sign of the *Timber Wolf*, sir. Shall we keep searching?"

Before Jake could answer, a huge shadow fell over the fountain that dominated the square. An oval cockpit swiveled atop a pair of birdlike legs, and arms sprouted from boxy, missile-launcher shoulders, each ending in a reinforced laser housing with a hexagonal aperture.

"Do not bother, John. He has found us." Jake switched to the open channel again. "All Elementals, the *Timber Wolf* has come out of hiding. Converge on the fountain at once!"

Jake triggered his SRMs as the OmniMech strode confidently into the square. Corkscrewing toward the 'Mech on trails of white smoke, the missiles found their mark, leaving only the barest hint of a dent after exploding on its right leg.

Reacting quickly to Jake's orders, his Elementals began pouring in from every direction. Many became entangled with the enemy battle armor, but a handful of additional missile salvoes did make it toward the 'Mech. From the way it moved, the pilot at the controls did not bother about the insignificant damage as he continued toward the fountain.

Before the first Bear could close within support-laser range, the *Timber Wolf* raised one of its arms, leveling it at the nearest Elemental. The weapon took a few seconds longer than a standard large laser to charge up, generating an eerie yellow glow from the end of the barrel. It also seemed to produce a tremendous amount of heat: the 'Mech's entire forearm took on a warm, orange glow just before the weapon fired.

The blast was so bright and hot that it nearly blinded Jake through his protective visor. An amber beam a meter wide sliced the air between the *Timber Wolf*'s outstretched arm and Point Commander Dominic. In an instant, the intense heat burned through his breastplate, his torso, and out the other side. Jake watched in horror as the heat continued to melt and cook its target even after it had been discharged. Before Dominic could crumple dead to the ground, the ammunition in his backpack exploded, reducing what was left of him to a pile of ashes amid twisted fragments of metal.

John bounded back into the square from behind the *Timber Wolf* as it raised its other arm to fire again. "What the *hell* was that?" he called to Jake.

"I am not certain, John, but I think this *Timber Wolf* has a pair of Clan Star Adder's heavy lasers."

John sounded exasperated. "The Horses must have called in all their marks for this offensive, *quiaff*?"

"Aff," Jake said, his mind working through a plan to take out the 'Mech as quickly as possible. "Let us make sure that they wasted the effort. Get your point in close, and whatever you do, stay out of the way of those arms!"

John laughed, though he sounded tense and nervous. "You do not have to tell me twice. Poor Dominic. What a way to go."

Switching to Delta Point's channel, Jake tried not to think about it. "Kris, take charge of the rest of Epsilon Point."

"Roger that, Jake. What is your plan?"

"Those heavy lasers are going to wipe us out one by one,

but they run very hot. My guess is that the 'Mech cannot handle the heat of sustained fire, which is why the pilot is headed for the fountain."

Kris always caught on quickly. "We take out the fountain, and no more free cool-down, *quiaff*?"

"Aff, but hit it low and to the sides. Let us avoid destroying the statue if we can."

"I got it. Over and out."

Jake paused a moment to take stock of the situation. Beta Point was already in close, slowing down the *Timber Wolf*. Delta and Epsilon were moving into position to attack the fountain. That left his Alpha Point to deal with the remaining Horse battle armor. The other two Salamanders had returned to committing arson after the 'Mech arrived, and Jake jumped over to them.

They were only too happy to fire their flamers at him, but moving quickly as he was, their first attacks went wide, igniting a nearby awning instead. To keep them off balance, he immediately jumped again, this time aiming to land behind the closest Salamander. Reaching down with his left-arm claw, Jake crushed the jump-jet exhaust port on the back of the enemy's left leg.

The second Salamander engaged his own jump jets to close in.

As the first Salamander began to turn around, Jake shifted position to stay behind him. He kicked in the exhaust port on its right leg, smashing it and leaving the warrior unable to jump—at least not very far or very accurately. By now, the other Salamander had landed next to his mate, which was Jake's cue to get moving. Gripping number one under the shoulders with both arms, Jake engaged his jump jets just in time to avoid the flamer attack from the other one.

His plan was coming together nicely. As he sped toward the *Timber Wolf* with an enemy Salamander in tow, Jake called to John. "I am approaching from the north. Do what you can to keep the 'Mech's attention focused the other way. And keep him firing those heavy lasers."

"Not to worry, Star Captain. He has been firing non-stop. We have lost two more men, but he is running hot."

Exactly as Jake had planned. One more jump and he would be in back of the *Timber Wolf*. "He is about to run a whole lot hotter. Hang on."

The other Salamander was following close behind, and Jake's cargo was getting increasingly difficult to hold on to. He would get only one chance to pull this off. Firing his jump jets at full output, he set his arc to take him over the *Timber Wolf*'s boxy left shoulder, which housed a twenty-rack of long-range missiles—along with its volatile ammunition.

Just before reaching the apex of his jump, Jake released his captive and issued a single command to his Elementals. "Scatter!"

The Salamander sailed directly toward the *Timber Wolf*. Leading with the missile sprouting from his right shoulder, the trooper inside could do nothing to stop his impact. As Ghost Bear battle armor dashed away in every direction, the Salamander collided with the OmniMech, detonating the inferno missile and splashing burning gel all over the already-overheated missile launcher.

Jake finished his jump and turned to face the *Timber Wolf*, ready to react to its continued attacks. Fortunately, that was not necessary. The MechWarrior inside had panicked after the inferno impact. As the crushed Salamander fell smoking to the ground, the 'Mech took three ungainly steps to turn around and then ran ponderously for the fountain. The fire continued to rage on its shoulder, the inferno gel dripping down its left arm and over the cockpit window.

As the 'Mech reached the fountain's base, the rest of Star One blasted the fountain walls, letting all the water leak out into the streets. Denied the cooling sanctuary of liquid, the inferno gel skyrocketed the 'Mech's heat well beyond safety limits. Continuing its haphazard run, the *Timber Wolf* smashed into the statue topping the fountain, sending the proud figure tumbling end over end to add its rubble to the street.

Just after the 'Mech crashed into statue, its canopy blew off on explosive bolts. The MechWarrior rocketed out mere moments before the ammunition in the LRM launcher exploded in a fireball that brought virtual daylight to the market square. An ammo explosion would not normally cripple a *Timber Wolf*, equipped as it was with cellular ammunition storage equipment. In this case, the 'Mech's heat was entirely too high, triggering secondary explosions inside the torso and setting off the ammunition in the other LRM pod.

Turning away from the fireworks, Jake saw that the Salamander chasing him had been intercepted by John's Gamma Point. That gave him a few moments to check in with the rest of his forces; he had been ignoring the incoming transmission light for several minutes now.

"This is Alpha Point," he said. "Go ahead."

It was Carl, who had stayed back to defend the base and to coordinate communications among the various parts of the trinary scattered over the city. "I was starting to think you were dead, Star Captain," Carl said, sounding more gruff than usual. "I have new data on the Hell's Horses force composition. Although our sensor data cannot be completely trusted, I counted enough DropShips for a full cluster, maybe more."

"Any idea which units?"

"Aside from Malavai Fletcher, the bulk of the force seems to consist of elements of their Twenty-first Mechanized Assault Cluster."

Jake remembered the unit's flaming-horse insignia on the *Timber Wolf*'s fuselage. "They certainly pulled out all the stops this time. That is one of the best units in their Alpha Galaxy. The patrol we hit here had only one 'Mech. Any indication if this was a vanguard or a rear-guard? Are they headed into the city, or out?"

There was a brief pause as Carl checked his data. "Your bunch seems to be outriders or possibly vanguard. Reports from Striker Nova on the far side of the city indicate that the bulk of the force is heading out of town, toward us here at the base."

Jake knew what had to be done, and it would not be easy. "Then our first priority is to get them out of the city: I have seen more than enough collateral damage this day. After that, we will keep wearing them down until reinforcements arrive. Speaking of reinforcements, any news from the Third Claw?"

Another pause as Carl consulted his information. "They will arrive in force tomorrow morning."

"Damn. I was hoping they could get here sooner. Without their support, I do not know how long we can hold out."

"We sent our DropShips to help transport them, but they *are* on the far side of the planet, after all."

Even with so few options, Jake did not intend to give up. "Contact Ben and have his star use hit-and-fade to draw the Horses out of the city and away from the base, if possible. Have Striker Nova act as a sheep-dog on that one. Between them, they should be able to corral the larger force. At least for a while."

"Should I send Assault Nova out to help, too?" Carl asked.

"Neg. They do not have the speed to keep up on that kind of operation. Besides, if the Horses break through, you will need them to hold down the base."

"You are putting a lot of stock in the cub, Jake. Do you think he can handle it?"

Jake looked back at the crumbling remains of the fountain, the face of the once-majestic statue shattered into dozens of unrecognizable fragments.

"He can handle it, Carl." Jake just hoped Ben realized that himself.

"We do not have Lita any more, so he *has* to handle it," Carl said. "I wonder where she is right now?"

Jake wished Carl had not brought up her name. He could imagine her behind enemy lines, triumphantly counting her bribe money.

"I do not care," he said, "unless she has the courage to stand against me in battle, that is. Then we shall see if her treachery was worth the price."

32

New Denver, Predlitz
Ghost Bear Dominion
18 November 3063

If one thing was becoming increasingly clear to Ben, it was that mobility was an effective counter to firepower only in the short term. Sooner or later, if you wanted to achieve your objective, you had to put up or shut up. With every passing minute, shutting up was looking more and more like a viable alternative to cat-and-mouse.

For the better part of the morning, he had been trading pot-shots with a Hell's Horses *Supernova*, so named because it was, for all intents and purposes, a bigger and more powerful version of the *Nova*. Its major weakness against its smaller cousin was speed. Ben's *Nova* was sixty percent faster, and he could move in, strike, and pull back with relative ease. The game was becoming wearisome, though. Because his quarry out-ranged Ben with extended-range large lasers against Ben's mediums, it was difficult for him to draw the *Supernova* anywhere it did not want to go.

The rest of his star, also armed with short-range weapons, was having similar difficulties fighting a pair of Epona hovertanks. One of them was armed with LRMs to support its pulse-laser equipped partner.

For the third time this hour, Umbriel called. "I am finally in the clear, Ben. You only need to move another two kilometers back to join my position."

Finally, she had found a route out of the city, and most likely the Eponas were hot on her tail. "Great news, Point Kappa. I should be able to pull this *Supernova* out there before the New Year at this rate."

Ben looked up from his monitors just in time to see the *Supernova* leaning out from behind a building some five blocks away. It fired the three large lasers at the end of his left arm, the brilliant red beams stabbing out at the speed of light. Two of them hit the *Nova*'s right leg, despite Ben slamming the control stick to the left in a quick evasive move. Before his opponent could line up another shot, Ben engaged his jump jets. He headed for Umbriel's position, leaping over three buildings, only to come crashing down on a pickup truck parked next to a vidphone booth.

Ben struggled to recover from the clumsy landing, all the while cursing himself for the blunder. His neurohelmet tapped into his brain's electrical impulses to give the *Nova* its sense of balance. That, combined with Ben's skillful manipulation of the control stick and jump-jet foot pedals, allowed him to keep the 'Mech upright while trying to disengage one of its feet from a two-ton motor vehicle.

"Nice landing, Star Commander pro-tem," he heard Taris say. His point happened to be paralleling Ben's movement one block over, and they were converging on his position. He chose to diplomatically ignore the insult in favor of checking his instruments again. Something was not quite right.

Taris confirmed Ben's concern as his Elementals reached the *Nova*'s feet. "Did you feel that?" he asked. "It was like your rough landing had an aftershock."

The laser hits had not damaged the internal workings of the 'Mech's leg, and the landing had caused only minor scratches. "There it is again," Ben said. "What is that? Do you have an assault 'Mech on your scanners?"

"No, but in this mess of steel and stone, I would not be

surprised if a *Dire Wolf* popped out from around the corner."

The ground shook again under another ponderous footfall, then the side of a nearby building cracked, crumbled, and collapsed toward Ben's *Nova*. Ben began backpedaling as another footfall brought the front of the 'Mech into view. It had a massive pair of trunk-like legs, each taller than his entire *Nova*. It sprouted the enormous muzzle of an assault autocannon where a head should have been and lacked any arms at all.

Ben knew immediately what 'Mech this was, even though he had never seen one in person. The *Thunder Stallion*, a design unique to Clan Hell's Horses, was a four-legged weapons platform of monstrous proportions. As the back end of the 'Mech came into view, he saw the four LRM-15 launchers sprouting from its hind quarters that comprised the remainder of its arsenal.

Lacking a waist with which to torso-twist, the *Thunder Stallion* had to pivot with its legs to bring the autocannon into firing position. That fact probably saved Ben's life, giving him enough time to trigger his jump jets and go sailing directly over the four-legger. Glancing left, Ben could see the *Supernova* rapidly approaching, tromping down the middle of the street, digging up divots of blacktop as it ran.

Before he landed, Ben heard the thunderous discharge of an assault-class autocannon behind him. Pivoting the *Nova* around, he saw the smoking remains of an Elemental spread across three lanes of the street.

"Go ahead and open up some holes with your lasers, Ben," Taris said, which told Ben he was not the Elemental that had bought it. "We will then swarm this beast and put it out of our misery."

Ben smiled in spite of himself. "Sounds like a plan. Then I can concentrate on that *Supernova* again."

The *Thunder Stallion* had just begun to shuffle its feet in an attempt to turn around and bring its weapons to bear on Ben. That presented Ben with an ideal broadside target, which he gladly attacked with ten of his twelve medium lasers. Five ruby beams shot from each of his 'Mech's arms into the flank of the behemoth, gouging scorched red and black trenches and sending more than four tons of melted armor bubbling to the pavement below.

Despite the massive damage, the assault 'Mech ignored the attack. It finished its about-face and unleashed sixty missiles in Ben's direction just as he fired his jump jets. He sailed through the air toward Umbriel's open field to a symphony of warning buzzers accompanied by a riot of angry, flashing lights. His computer was warning him of the *Nova's* seriously overtaxed heat sinks as well as the swarm of missiles closing in on him faster than his jump jets could carry him away. He braced for impact.

Considering the damage his 'Mech had already suffered, the missile salvo could easily have torn his *Nova* into shreds. This time, Ben was lucky. Fewer than half the LRMs found their marks, and those that hit spread evenly over his 'Mech, scorching armor but only penetrating the right leg previously softened up by the *Supernova*. Another warning siren added to the cacophony, telling him that he had lost control of the knee actuator in that leg. For the second time in as many seconds, Ben braced for impact.

His jump was knocked off-target by the impact of thirty missiles, but as luck would have it, he came crashing down on his 'Mech's good left leg. This offered him some chance of controlling the landing and keeping his *Nova* upright. This time, however, he simply could not beat gravity. All fifty tons of his 'Mech tumbled to the ground face-first, smashing his cockpit window into the dirt.

Severely shaken by the fall, Ben thought he would gladly lose consciousness at this point. Then he looked down at the cracked window, and saw soft, black soil. Not pavement.

He had made it out of the city!

As he wrestled with the control stick to get his 'Mech upright, he heard the welcome voice of Umbriel. "Glad to see you made it! Better get up fast, though. We have more company."

Ben felt and heard the whine of an overworked gyroscope under his seat as the *Nova* staggered to its feet, favoring its good left leg. Turning his 'Mech to face the city, he saw a tableau of good news and bad news.

The good news was the fireball climbing into the sky where the *Thunder Stallion* used to be. Apparently, Taris was as good as his word and had finished off the monster.

The bad news was the telltale flash and sonic boom of four gauss rifles firing from a parking lot roof at the edge of the city. With no time to dodge, Ben was relieved when the attacks missed, digging two huge trenches on either side of him instead. Increasing the magnification on his HUD, he could see that the attackers were a pair of Athena combat vehicles.

"Leave it to the Hell's Horses to sink two gauss rifles *and* an advanced targeting computer into a simple tank," Umbriel scoffed.

In his position, Ben could not so easily dismiss these new antagonists. "That means they will not miss me a second time. They are stuck on that roof, though. If we can make it to the tree line, they will be useless, despite their expensive armaments."

Umbriel's *Viper* came up alongside him, and Ben could see the *Stormcrow* and *Hellbringer* also finally emerging from the city, with no hovertanks in evidence. He keyed the Battle Nova's open channel. "Taris? If you are out there, get over to Petra's *Stormcrow* on the double! We are heading for the tree line *now.*"

Ben saw two Elementals emerging from an alley, with the *Supernova* in hot pursuit on its jump jets. Without waiting for an order from Ben, the four Ghost Bear 'Mechs turned their combined firepower on the *Supernova* just as it landed. Lasers stabbed at it from every direction, tearing at armor weakened by hours of fencing with Ben's *Nova.*

The coup de grace came from Willa's *Hellbringer.* The huge autocannon on its right shoulder, twin to the one on the late *Thunder Stallion,* hammered round after armor-piercing round into the chest of the *Supernova.* Holding the trigger down, Willa "walked" the burst up the target, carving a jagged line of holes all the way from the 'Mech's foot and torso on up into the cockpit.

For a brief second, all the weapons fire stopped. It seemed to Ben like the *Supernova* stood there, bereft of its head, for what seemed like an eternity. Then the huge machine crashed to the ground, and all hell broke loose. He hit his jump jets just in time to avoid the flash of the *Athena's* gauss rifles again. Looking at the rest of the 'Mechs in his star, his seemed to be in the best repair. That was not good. Checking his radar, he saw more Hell's Horses 'Mechs approaching from the city. That was even worse.

Ben was calm despite the reign of chaos all around him, and that surprised him. "All right, people. Reinforcements are on the way, so we need to make it to the woods to lick our wounds. And watch out for those Athenas."

Umbriel laughed. "Thanks, Ben. I was about to let them turn my 'Mech into scrap."

As if on cue, another storm of gauss rifle slugs screamed into the assembled 'Mechs. This time two of them impacted on the flank of Willa's *Hellbringer*, knocking it to the ground and adding urgency to Ben's last order.

Taris and the other surviving Elemental had managed to climb onto Petra's *Stormcrow*. "Speaking of reinforcements," Taris called to Ben, "where are ours?"

Ben was too focused on the combat to generate a half-truth. "Carl says they will be here first thing in the morning."

Petra groaned. "*Tomorrow* morning?"

"Where is the Petra I served with on Idlewind?" Ben asked. "Yes, tomorrow. None of us wants to keep up this hit-and-run battle, but we can certainly hold out until then if we do." Ben again surprised himself at how naturally the words came. He had never thought of himself as a leader, but now everything seemed to fall into place.

Willa's *Hellbringer* trotted up beside Ben's retreating *Nova* as another blast from the Athenas fell short. Ben was relieved that she had survived the last attack. His force was finally getting out of range as they entered the edge of the forest.

"Then what?" Willa asked.

Ben had to think about that. Even with help from the Third Claw regiment, they were still outnumbered more than three-to-one, according to Carl's estimates. He decided the best thing was to tell her what he was telling himself. "I am sure Jake has a plan. He pulled off a miracle at Courchevel, and he can pull off another one now."

He knew that a lot of wishful thinking went into that statement, but at least it quieted the grumbling. If only Lita were here, he thought. She would know what to do.

33

The sounds of purposeful activity filled the camp the Ghost Bears had pitched in a valley some fifteen kilometers from New Denver: the turn of a tech's socket wrench, the crackle of a welding torch re-attaching an armor plate, the low murmur of conversation. Beneath it all, the rhythmic thud of distant BattleMech footfalls provided a barely audible bass line.

In the midst of it, Jake Kabrinski and his officers were gathered around an overturned ammo crate for a strategy meeting. Spread out on the crate was a beat-up hardcopy map of the New Denver area. Holding it down against the wind were four steaming coffee cups.

Jake almost had to shout to be heard over the din. "I am not going to lie to you, people. Things are bad. We are on the run from New Denver, while Malavai Fletcher rapes the city unopposed. I did not want to withdraw last night, but we would never have survived otherwise. Even with Third Claw's Beta Trinary, we are still sorely outnumbered and out-gunned."

Jake looked over at Star Captain Enya, Beta's commander, nodding grateful acknowledgment for the arrival of her unit. She was a tall and lanky Elemental, a veteran warrior with a number of battle scars showing though her close-cropped blond hair.

Jake turned to Carl. "Have you got the status report?"

Carl looked down at the hand-held computer that now served as his field office. "We are in decent shape, all things considered. We have one hundred-twenty battle-ready Elementals, including Beta Trinary, with another fifteen in sick bay for at least a week. The 'Mechs of my garrison star were all destroyed, but twelve of Gamma's fifteen Omnis are operational. Two are salvageable and one is . . . missing in action."

Jake and Ben exchanged knowing glances. They knew that Carl was referring to Lita's *Mad Dog*. No one had seen her or her 'Mech since the invasion began.

"So, that is the good news," Carl went on. "On the minus side, we are facing a much larger force. We still lack complete information about the Horses' composition, but we know that Fletcher landed with at least a full cluster: four trinaries, possibly five."

Reese broke the momentary silence. "Not all of them are 'Mech trinaries, *quiaff*? My star encountered more tanks than BattleMechs in our patrols, and I think the same is true for the other stars."

He turned to Ben and Maxwell, who nodded agreement.

Jake did not think they could afford to overestimate the advantage. "They do have an inordinate number of conventional vehicles. These are the Hell's Horses, after all. But our best estimate still gives them—after the damage we took yesterday—at least thirty BattleMechs."

"Aye, and let us not forget their battle armor support," Carl said. "They are fielding at least as many Elementals as we are, plus Salamanders and possibly Gnomes, though we have yet to sight any Gnomes."

Jake thought that was good news. Gnomes were the heavy battle armor developed by the Hell's Horses to give them an edge over standard Elemental suits. Although ungainly, they could take a lot of punishment, and their enhanced weaponry could make short work of any other battle armor on the field.

"So, we are outnumbered more than two-to-one," Maxwell said, stroking his red goatee thoughtfully. "They hold both the city and our base. We are ready to return to battle, but to what end? We cannot expect reinforcements while our Clan is still at war with the Combine, so a decisive victory is impossible. We have been fighting a guerilla war for the last two days, but look where that has gotten us. It is not the Clan way."

"Max is right," Ben said. His face was flushed, and his eyes glittered with battle fever. "This hit-and-run will wear us down before it ever stops Fletcher. I say, let us strike at their heart and go down fighting, taking as many of them with us as we can!".

The other officers were nodding agreement with Ben's words. All except Enya, who spoke up at last. "I am the outsider here, but a suicide run is not our only option. It is best that we save this—enthusiasm—for the battlefield, *quiaff*?"

Jake was grateful for her level-headedness. By now, half the camp was listening in. "You are right that we must strike at the heart of the enemy, Ben. But we cannot do it only for the sake of glory. We still owe something to Predlitz and its people as well as to the greater good of our Clan.

"We do not know what Fletcher has planned. He might come after us, or he might leave Predlitz once his troops have had their fill of destruction. One way or the other, we have to stop him here and now before one more Dominion building falls to his troops!"

A ragged cheer went up among the officers, then grew to include the troopers who had stopped to listen. Looking around at his commanders, Jake saw that their expressions had shifted from frustrated resignation to grim determination. Not ideal, but it was something to work with. Leaning over the map, he began outlining a plan.

Ben squeezed the trigger on his control stick, sending two beams of coherent light stabbing across more than seven hundred meters of scrub plain and into the side of an unsuspecting enemy *Summoner*. Staggered momentarily by the loss of a ton of armor, his target pivoted toward Ben's *Nova*, hastily firing LRMs from the canister on its left shoulder.

Ben smiled with satisfaction as the missiles fell well short of his position. "All right, Gamma," he called to the rest of his star, "I think I got his attention. Get ready to hit them with everything we have."

Sure enough, flashing lights in the compound indicated that an alarm had been raised. The wounded *Summoner* bounded toward Ben on its jump jets, rushing to get its weapons into range. Behind it came the rest of a heavy star, and farther down the valley, Ben's radar picked up two more stars approaching.

Kicking down on both foot pedals, he lifted the *Nova* up and back on pillars of flame. At the apex of his jump, Ben triggered both large lasers again. "Does he not know that I can keep this up all day?" he called to Umbriel.

She laughed. "Perhaps he is new at piloting a *Summoner*; perhaps he thinks he will eventually catch up somehow."

"How? My *Nova* can jump backward as fast as he can jump forward. Unless he breaks into a full run, I will pick him to pieces with my large lasers without a return shot being fired."

"Maybe he is hanging back to allow the rest of his star to catch up," Umbriel said.

As if to prove her point, four more OmniMechs were rapidly catching up with the *Summoner*. A *Mad Dog*, a *Timber Wolf*, and two *Hellbringer*s moved up on either flank of the seventy-ton 'Mech, which ceased its jumping and began to run as well.

Ben opened a channel to the entire trinary. "Now that they are all lined up for us, let us take them down quickly before the other two stars get their acts together. Gamma Trinary, engage! Fire at will!"

Shrugging off their tarps as they crashed through the trees, eleven Ghost Bear OmniMechs emerged from concealment and opened fire on the approaching wedge of five Hell's Horses 'Mechs. Ben closed in so he could fire the *Nova*'s full complement of weapons, adding the twenty LRMs in its left arm to the two large lasers in the right. A wave of heat washed through his cockpit as his barrage streaked downfield toward the *Summoner*, which was knocked off its feet and crashed to the ground.

The rest of the star did not take too kindly to the ambush. Though attacked from every direction, the pair of *Hellbringer*s moved forward to engage Ben's *Nova*. Each one triggered luminous blue fire from the double PPCs in their arms, filling the air with charged particles and the smell of ozone. Fortunately for Ben, only one shot found its mark, hammering into his 'Mech's torso and sending it staggering back a few steps. Wrestling with the control stick to stay upright, Ben shuddered to think what would have happened if the entire fusillade had scored.

The rest of the Battle Nova quickly moved in to distract the *Hellbringer*s. Umbriel's *Viper* leapt up on jump jets, all the while raining pulse-laser fire down on the left one, while Petra charged forward at top speed and blasted the one on the right. A single burst from her *Stormcrow*'s massive autocannon tore the 'Mech's stubby head off its shoulders and sent it crashing to the ground.

A cheer went up on the open channel as Assault Nova closed in from the left and Striker Nova came in on the right. For now, while they held the advantage, the Bears had the upper hand. Checking his radar, Ben saw ten more 'Mechs approaching from the base. He quickly radioed to the others. "We need to finish this quickly. Reinforcements are on the way."

Petra snorted in mock-contempt. "Any faster than that last kill and I would have to pick them off as they left the assembly line."

Ben triggered two more large laser shots at the *Summoner*, which was struggling to get back on its feet. "That was good work, Petra, but this is still a diversionary raid. We cannot hang around all night. Our job is to do enough damage that they have to send reinforcements out this way."

"And to make it seem like all of our forces are concentrated here," added Umbriel.

Ben switched to their private channel, concern creeping into his voice as he watched the *Summoner* fall again. "This diversion had better work. If Jake's Elementals encounter too much resistance in the city, they will not be able to take out the Horses' headquarters, even if they do find it."

"Not to worry, Ben. The Horses are so hungry for a fight, Jake's plan will work. But that is not what is on your mind, is it?"

He hated to admit it, but she was right. "No, it is . . ."

"Lita?"

"Yes. If she were here, we would have the upper hand for sure."

"She may be a better MechWarrior than you or I, but never forget that she betrayed us all, Ben. We should consider ourselves lucky that she did not stick around to sabotage us on the battlefield, too."

"Aye," Ben conceded. He knew Umbriel was right, but he still could not believe that Lita was a traitor. Not after all they had been through together.

Seeing that the *Summoner* was not getting up, Ben jumped his *Nova* onto a small hill to get a better look at the battlefield. His warriors were pulling back, away from the two advancing stars, as the last of the first Horse star fell in combat. Scanning the horizon, he saw no additional enemy reinforcements on the way yet.

Wait a minute, he thought. What was that? "Umbriel, do you pick up a 'Mech on the edge of sensor range, directly to the west?"

Her *Viper* jumped while pouring pulse-laser fire into a falling *Timber Wolf*, but she answered once she was on her feet again. "Nothing, Ben."

"That's it, then. Let's pack it in."

He didn't tell Umbriel what he thought he saw. Far off to the west and silhouetted in the moonlight was the unmistakable profile of a lone 'Mech standing on a ridge, as if looking down on the battle. It was gone by the time he looked down to check his radar and glanced up again, but Ben could have sworn it was Lita's *Mad Dog*.

34

Downtown New Denver
Predlitz
Ghost Bear Dominion
20 November 3063

As a rule, the Clans abhorred waste. Enormous amounts of Clan ritual had evolved from the need to conserve resources while recovering from back-to-back civil wars. Collateral damage was viewed as particularly wasteful, and was traditionally avoided by staging combat Trials far from population centers. Traditionally avoided, but not always avoided, as Jake witnessed to his horror while leading his Elementals through the darkened streets of downtown New Denver.

In less than two days, the bustling metropolis had been reduced to virtual ruin. Fires spread unchecked through much of the city center, sending up columns of black smoke thick enough to blot out the twin full moons. Most of the civilian population had fled to the countryside. The few remaining sat on broken curbs or shambled along the streets, looking up at Jake as he passed with empty, accusing eyes.

It was painful. He tried to avoid their stares and stay focused on the mission at hand.

"All clear on the left flank, Star Captain," Taris radioed

in. "Only the odd infantry patrol. Your diversion seems to have worked."

At least for now, Jake thought. "Sooner or later they will catch on that there are no Elementals back there with the OmniMechs."

"Aye, and we will want some 'Mech support once we locate the command center."

Engaging his jump jets, Jake leaped up to the roof of a partially ruined store. "Widen your search pattern, Taris. We need to find Malavai Fletcher before morning, or this whole operation will have been for nothing."

"I will spread further out, but I will probably lose radio contact."

"Just find a way to check in every thirty minutes," Jake said. Looking out over the remains of the city, he spotted a solid-looking, six-story office building that was remarkably intact.

"Roger that," said Taris. "Over and out."

The rest of Jake's point joined him on the roof, and the structure groaned under the extra weight. Chunks of concrete tumbled down onto the street. He switched to Beta Trinary's frequency. "Enya, do you copy?"

"Aye, Star Captain. No activity worth mentioning on the right flank, and no sign of a possible command post. How about you?"

"I am going to take Star One and check out one possibility nearby, but it is no more likely to house the Hell's Horses Khan than the last half dozen. Maintain your patrol on the flank and check in every thirty minutes, whether you find anything or not."

Enya chuckled. "S.O.P. in other words? I am on it. Good hunting, Jake Kabrinski."

"Good hunting to you, Star Captain." Although they had met less than twenty hours ago, Jake already liked and respected this Enya. He decided that, if they both survived this battle, he would make a point of getting to know her better. She would certainly have war stories to tell!

But all that was for later.

Jake pointed with his battle claw toward the building he had noticed, and radioed his point commanders. "That structure to the north is suspiciously stable. John, take your point around back and secure any enemy retreat. The rest of you, follow me in."

A chorus of affirmatives came through as twenty Elementals sprang into action. Jake leaped off the roof, landed hard, then fired his jets again, hurtling toward the building as fast as possible while crossing the wide-open ruins between here and there. He was totally exposed—too easily seen, too easily fired upon.

To his right, Jake saw the five Elementals of Delta Point bounding alongside him. At their head was Point Commander Kris, her battle armor's chest-plate painted with a bright white bear wreathed in blue flames.

Turning away, Jake caught the flash of an explosion blossoming from Kris's chest. When he looked back again, a second missile impacted against her right leg, and a third sheared off the laser on her right arm. Still another warhead hit the ground next to Kris a split-second before one exploded directly against her faceplate, knocking her to the ground and almost certainly killing her instantly.

Jake followed the dissipating contrails of the missiles using his HUD's infrared filter, and quickly found the source of the attack. They were four troopers in battle armor painted black and red and trimmed in gold. Without a doubt, those were the Keshik's colors!

With a glance at the tiny magnifying glass icon on his HUD, Jake increased the magnification of his view. What had appeared to be ordinary Elementals from a distance were nothing of the sort, which explained the surgical accuracy of the missile strike against Kris. These were Gnome suits, armed with extended-range lasers, streak missiles, and half-again as much armor as Jake's suits.

Emblazoned on the shoulder of each suit was the Hell's Horses insignia over the Greek letter alpha. Jake's heart raced as he opened a channel to all units. "That is the Alpha Keshik, Fletcher's own unit. Ghost Bears, converge on my signal!"

This was it. Fletcher had to be somewhere nearby. For the moment, Jake focused on the targets he could see, using his one advantage: mobility. Triggering his jump jets, he launched to the left rather than directly toward the Gnomes, adding an extra blast of jet in mid-jump, altering his course to make himself a more difficult target.

A good move, as it turned out, for the next salvo of missiles was aimed at him. Only one of the SRMs hit, impacting against his right foot, but it did no real damage.

Back on his feet again, Jake ducked down to radio his commanders. "They are head-hunting! Point commanders, keep moving and let your troopers handle the offensive moves. That should keep them off-balance for at least a few minutes."

John responded immediately. "There is a rear-guard point back here, Jake. Gnomes. Should I engage or just keep them busy?"

Jake knew his troops could not hope to overcome Alpha Keshik's Elementals in an even match, especially when they had Gnome suits. But caution at the wrong time was what had cost him the battle on Luzerne . . .

He hit his jump jets before the Gnomes started firing their lasers. He was getting an incoming transmission, too, this time from Enya.

"Message received, Jake. We are closing in from the east, E.T.A. five minutes. Any sign of Fletcher?"

"Not yet, but he has to be here somewhere."

He called to John. "Gamma Point, we cannot hold back now. Engage the rear-guard at once!"

"With pleasure, Jake. With pleasure." Jake could almost hear John smiling.

Landing from his jump, Jake turned and fired his support laser at the nearest Gnome in the group of four. Why were there only four, though? Where was the fifth?

Jumping again, he happened to glance up at the edge of the roof. For the briefest moment, he thought he saw the outline of a Gnome suit silhouetted against one of the moons. Drifting smoke obscured his line of sight as he came down, firing once more at an approaching Gnome and melting the barrel of its laser. With no ranged weapons left, the enemy trooper was forced to charge toward Jake with only its razor-sharp battle claw as a weapon.

Jack jumped up to the roof just as the Gnome swung at

him, missing him by centimeters. There would be another time to fight that Elemental. Right now, he had to follow his hunch.

Alighting on the edge of the building, he took a quick look around the roof. It was covered with vent pipes and coolant towers, as well as a three-meter-tall satellite dish and a small structure that probably led to the roof-access stairway.

A satellite dish—perfect for orbital communications, Jake thought. This had to be where Fletcher had set up shop: the office of the local holovision station!

His hunch was confirmed when the fifth Gnome stepped from the shadow of the concave dish. The ornate golden decoration on the armor's shoulder, tracing the image of a Hell's Horse *en rampant* and wreathed in blood-red fire, sent his mind reeling back to that night two years ago on Talon Ridge. This was no ordinary Gnome trooper.

Khan Malavai Fletcher's voice came thundering through his armor's external speakers. "Do my eyes deceive me, or is that my old friend Jake I see standing before me? A star captain now. Very impressive."

Jake ignored the hammering of his heart, which felt like it would burst from his chest. He activated his own external speakers. "I am Star Captain Jake Kabrinski of Clan Ghost Bear. You and I have unfinished business, Malavai Fletcher."

"Unfinished business, indeed," Fletcher said, his tone scornful.

The Khan strode across the roof, keeping Jake in view. "Jake *Kabrinski*, is it now? Believe it or not, I once held your Clan in the deepest esteem. But anyone with eyes in his head can see that you Bears have gone soft since deserting the homeworlds for the Inner Sphere. Now it seems that the Ghost Bears will give *anyone* a Bloodname."

It took every ounce of Jake's self-control to hold back after that insult, but he forced himself to walk forward calmly, countering each move the Khan made. He did not intend to miss any weakness, or any opportunity. Let Fletcher say what he would, just as long as he kept talking.

It all came flooding back to Jake now: the maniacal

laughter, the bombs raining down from above, and Malavai Fletcher's departing promise.

"There are no Snow Ravens here this time, Jake." Fletcher gave a coarse, metallic laugh. "Precious few Ghost Bears, for that matter. Just you, and me, and our . . . unfinished business."

Jake and Fletcher were circling each other now, neither one willing to make the first move and open himself up to the other. Jake knew that Fletcher was more than twice his age, and that his dexterity would be hampered by the heavier Gnome suit. Speed was Jake's only ally.

The sounds of battle intensified from below. Jake wondered whether his forces were winning or losing and whether some of his BattleMechs had arrived by now. At the moment, he dared not take his eyes off Fletcher for even an instant to find out. The two continued a slow circle as flames leapt up all around the building, the smoke drifting between them at irregular intervals.

It was through just such a wisp of smoke that Fletcher finally sprang toward Jake, bellowing a fearsome roar of pent-up rage. He rocketed almost horizontally on his suit's jump jets, both arms extended in front of him.

The move took Jake by surprise. He dodged to the left, firing his support laser, but he only succeeded in melting armor off Fletcher's helmet. The Gnome suit's shoulder rammed into Jake's arm, denting the laser housing and knocking him off his feet. Pain lanced up and down his back as his spine twisted a bit too far to the right. The hiss of auto-injected medication rapidly dulled the pain, but he knew he would pay for that injury later, if he survived.

It was a good surprise first move, but it cost Fletcher a few moments as he rolled to a rough landing on the far side of the roof. As he got slowly to his feet, Jake turned and triggered his SRM launcher. Both missiles found their marks against a virtually stationery target, impacting on Fletcher's back and sending shreds of ferro-fibrous armor in every direction.

The Khan did not even pause. Finishing his slow but steady recovery, he raised his laser and fired. Jake was already lifting on his jump jets, but Fletcher must have anticipated the action, and adjusted his aim accordingly. The red laser beam sliced a trench in Jake's armor from head to toe as he jumped toward the top of the stairway housing. He recoiled in pain from the white heat of his suit's melting armor, ruining the trajectory of his jump. Instead of landing lightly on top of the structure as planned, he crashed headlong into it. The weight of his SRM launcher pack forced Jake to roll over onto his back after the fall, momentarily stranded like a flipped-over turtle.

A moment was all Fletcher needed. Closing the distance faster than seemed possible on his jump jets, he rammed his suit's claw into Jake's chest, penetrating the wound opened by the laser and digging into his flesh and ribs.

The pain was unimaginable.

Closing his claw around armor and bone both, Fletcher dragged Jake across the roof to the edge. With a sickening sound, he pulled the claw out of Jake's chest and held it in front of his expressionless faceplate, as though admiring the gore and HarJel dripping from his sharpened steel fingers.

His voice boomed out from his speakers again. "I have to hand it to you, cub. You have guts."

Metallic laughter erupted from the speakers as he thrust the blood-drenched claw in front of Jake's faceplate. "See? Here they are."

Jake had been hurt more times than he could count, and on several occasions the medtechs had thought he was near death. But this battle opened up whole new worlds of pain.

He did not know if it was the drugs or the approach of death, but the universe suddenly came sharply into focus after having been blurry forever. The first sight that greeted this new clarity was the leering face of Malavai Fletcher, the front of his helmet no longer in evidence.

The Khan leaned in close to Jake, reaching down with his claw to wrench open the helmet mechanism. Peeling the helmet away, he squinted with his one human eye into Jake's. "At last we meet, face to face. At last, I have my revenge for the little indignity you handed me on Bearclaw."

Jake tried to move, but could not. It might have been the massive knee of Fletcher's battle armor pressing into his gaping chest wound, or perhaps the stench of the man's foul breath that paralyzed him.

Droplets of spittle rained down on Jake's face. "You think you are pretty smart, *quiaff*?" Fletcher ranted. "Smarter than me, anyway. Old Malavai Fletcher is crazy, after all."

Jake thought he was losing it again. The man was not making any sense, and there appeared to be something moving in the flowing smoke behind him.

A flash of dry lightning streaked across the sky. It bathed the two Elementals in bright yellow light for the briefest of moments, giving Fletcher's disfigured face a strange, corpse-like cast. Again, he ground his knee into Jake's wounded chest. "They all think they are smarter than me. Especially that rat, James Cobb. But none of them—*not one of them*—holds the Hell's Horses in the palm of their hand like I do."

Malavai Fletcher stood up, taking in all of New Denver with an expansive gesture of his claw. "Crazy, eh? Could any of *them* gain the loyalty of an entire Clan? No. Could any of *them* muster the support needed for this crusade? No. Could any of them even *think* of destroying Clan Ghost Bear single-handedly? Absolutely not."

The sound of thunder rolled across the battlefield as Fletcher brought up his right arm, pointing the barrel of his laser directly at Jake's ruined chest. "And you, my young friend. You *clearly* think yourself smarter than me. You think your little diversion worked, *quiaff*?"

Jake's mind raced. How could he know? Did Lita tell him? But she had left before the plan was even hatched . . .

The shadows moved behind Fletcher again. Jake was certain of it this time. He could even make out a shape: it was a woman, brandishing a sword in both hands, raising it to strike.

No! Not here. Not now!

The Khan fixed Jake with his gruesome stare, and Jake thought his flesh-and-blood eye looked as lifeless as the artificial one. "Diversion, indeed. What if I told you that this was precisely what I wanted, all of it just to get you here. You will never know. Jake Kabrinski, you are not smarter than I am. Our battle was not over on Talon Ridge, but it is now. When I am through with you, there will not even be any dust left to send back to Strana Mechty."

"Not if I can help it!" a voice cried from the shadows.

That voice, thought Jake. Could it be?

He saw a silvery blur strike Fletcher upside the head. Blood spattered Jake as the Khan staggered a few steps under the force of the impact. Now his attacker was revealed.

Although Jake could scarcely believe his eyes, the voice did not lie: it was Lita.

She looked like she had literally fought her way through hell. Battered and bruised, with her cooling vest hanging in tatters from her shoulders. What Jake at first took to be a katana was, in fact, a length of steel pipe, which she hoisted again with both hands to lay into Fletcher a second time.

By then the Khan had recovered enough of his senses to raise his claw to parry. As the pipe slammed into the claw, sparks rained down onto the roof. Another fork of yellow lightning flashed across the sky. As smoke drifted past the combatants and filled Jake's eyes with tears, his mind once again reached crystal clarity. How could Lita be both a traitor and a selfless defender? Something did not add up.

While grasping her pipe with his claw, Fletcher swung his right arm over and into Lita's side, forcing a strangled gasp from her lungs as she struggled to pry her weapon free. Thunder shook the building as Malavai grinned at her. "What do we have here? Has the mother bear come to defend her cub?"

Jake's mind was staggered by how wrong he had been. Lita was not a traitor. Lita could *never* be a traitor, he saw that now. There was no proof of her misdeeds, no proof at all. He had simply filled in the blanks the quickest and easiest way he could, forgetting the most important part of the equation:

She was his friend.

Although Fletcher was still staggering from the head wound Lita had given him, there was no question that she was out-classed. She was less than half his size and unarmored. It was only a matter of time before the Elemental regained his balance and finished her off. Finally getting the right angle and leverage, Lita managed to pull the pipe from his grasp and dodged another swipe with his laser-arm. Fletcher took a few steps back, watching the pipe carefully to avoid another blow to the head.

Lita was watching his laser, which could easily end the fight with one blast. So far, whether by choice or lack of opportunity, Fletcher had chosen not to do so. As lightning once more flashed across the sky, Lita glanced down at Jake, and smiled.

In that moment, consciousness returned fully to Jake, despite his physical agony. Finally, all the introspection, all the unwanted advice, all the self-doubt, came down to this moment. Here Lita stood, a MechWarrior without a 'Mech, alone against a man who was arguably the finest Elemental in known space. She did not hesitate because she was smaller or weaker than her opponent. Just as Jake had not hesitated when facing down an *Atlas* on Alshain.

All of it seemed so obvious to Jake as the roar of thunder rumbled through him. Lita had spelled it out for him, but he had refused to listen. Losing to that DEST trooper held no shame.

The shame was in allowing the loss to become a defeat.

Fletcher was smiling now, beckoning to Lita with his claw as he stepped slowly back. "Come on. Give it your best shot. I will give you one more chance with that pipe, then my laser will finish this."

He was playing with her! Jake shut out all the pain, by sheer force of will sending feeling into his limbs. Feeling returned and, with it, came the pain. Excruciating and wonderful, for the pain meant that he was still alive. Levering himself up with one arm, Jake tilted his SRM pack so it pointed directly at Fletcher and fired.

The pair of missiles streaked past Lita and slammed into the Khan, one in the leg and one in the chest. The blast burned his exposed face and sent him staggering back toward the edge of the rooftop. The explosion knocked Lita down, too. She collapsed, immediately unconscious.

The spent missile launcher automatically dropped from Jake's back, lightening his load enough that he could stand fully. Words came unbidden to his lips as he charged at the stunned Khan. "I do not need to be smarter than you, Malavai Fletcher."

With the full force of a ton of myomer-enhanced armor behind him, Jake rammed his shoulder into Fletcher, sending him staggering back one, two, three steps until he dropped over the edge of the roof and out of sight. Jake dropped down heavily with his head poking out over the edge, narrowly missing a fall himself but enjoying the view. Hurtling toward the ground, the Khan of the Hell's Horses was trying in vain to right himself with his suit's jump jets as he tumbled head over heels into the billowing smoke and flames around him.

Consciousness was fading fast, but Jake was still awake enough to smile. With precious little air left in his lungs, his words hissed out in a whisper just before he passed out.

"I do not need to be smarter than you, Malavai Fletcher, because I *know* I can beat you."

35

140th Striker Cluster Headquarters
New Denver, Predlitz
Ghost Bear Dominion
22 November 3063

Jake was sure that the last year of his life must have been some sort of fevered dream, for when he opened his eyes he saw his old trainer Carl and Dr. Svensgaard standing on either side of his hospital bed.

The doctor, glancing up from his charts, was the first to notice that Jake was awake. "Star Captain," he said, looking over the tops of his spectacles, "we really must stop meeting this way."

Jake smiled, but the movement brought nothing but pain. "What a relief. I was just thinking this last year was all a dream."

Carl patted Jake's shoulder, which was one of the few places on his body not covered in bandages or casts. "Not a chance, Jake. Although I would welcome the chance for a rematch . . . when you are healed up, that is. It would not be a fair fight now."

Jake tried to sit up, but immediately regretted it. The dull ache throughout the length of his body instantly intensified into a firestorm of pain. It was all he could do to keep from crying out.

Dr. Svensgaard went quickly to check the I.V. connections. "Don't do that! You don't want to know how many tubes we have hooked up to you. Just relax. You'll be mobile in a few days."

Cautiously, Jake turned his head slightly toward the doctor. "What are you doing on Predlitz, anyway?" he asked. "I do not recall seeing your transfer paperwork."

"Nor would you," Carl interrupted. "He is lower caste, after all."

The doctor nodded, glaring at Jake over his glasses, which had slid halfway down his nose. "Hmm, yes. Beneath your notice, Star Captain, sir. But if you must know, I am here because I am an expert on tissue regeneration and organ replacement. I have been learning all the Clan techniques I possibly could and passing them on to hospitals across the Dominion. The New Denver hospital was recently . . . redecorated, so they sent me here to the military infirmary, where I found you."

Jake slowly rotated his head to face Carl. "Fletcher . . . Did they find his body?"

"Sorry, Jake," he heard Lita say as she entered the room. She looked tired, and her entire torso was wrapped in a pressure bandage, but otherwise she seemed well.

"Lita, I . . ."

She turned to Carl and the doctor. "Could we have a moment?"

Svensgaard hung his charts on a hook on the wall. "Of course. But no more than ten minutes. This warrior's lungs need plenty of rest."

Carl followed the doctor out of the room, letting the door swing shut behind him. Lita looked down, avoiding Jake's gaze as she went to sit in a cushioned chair opposite his bed. Pain greeted Jake again as he turned his head to look at her. "Please, stay in one place. All this head turning is killing my neck."

That made Lita smile, and their eyes met. "It was my fault—I should have—" they both blurted at the same time.

Jake tried not to laugh because it hurt too much. "Look," he said, "I was wrong about you. There is no excuse for what I said about you, for what I did—"

"No, Jake I—"

"Please, this is hard enough. Let me finish."

Lita crossed and uncrossed her legs nervously as Jake continued. "I should have confronted you directly about my suspicions. I failed in my duty as your superior officer, a fellow warrior, and most importantly, I failed you as a friend. For all that and more, I am sorry."

Looking relieved, she stood up and came over to his bed. "I *wanted* to tell you, but it was all so unClanlike—"

"Water under the bridge, Lita. So, tell me, what were you doing all those late nights in the market, anyway?"

She looked up at the lights on the ceiling as if searching for where to begin. After a moment, it came rushing out all at once. "Well, a few days after we arrived here, I ventured out into the market. You know, to get a look at the 'real' New Denver. I was shocked when I ran into Luther Dawson at the café. He was one of those 'good' inmates I told you about meeting in prison. He had befriended me despite my Clan origins, and stuck with me in a few fights. He was all right, and here he was on Predlitz."

The whole notion of Inner Sphere-style prison camps still baffled Jake, leaving him uncertain of how Lita and some filthy hardened criminal could ever learn to get along. He reminded himself that his days of doubting his friends were over and just listened.

"We hit it off right away, and after we got done talking about old times, I decided to do a little . . . research. I asked him if he knew anything about the local antiClan resistance. Remember, this guy was held in a Rasalhague prison camp. Hell, the Ghost Bears liberated him at the same time they freed me, so he sort of owed us one."

Jake still did not truly understand, but nodded for her to continue.

"Anyway, he said that he had heard some things. Just rumors really. He had heard that there was off-world support coming in for the local resistance: shipments of weapons and supplies piggy-backed with normal civilian cargo, that sort of thing. Naturally, I was interested to learn more, but he had no details. He wanted to help, so he put me in contact with an information broker."

Jake interrupted. "A what?"

"Information broker. He buys and sells information. More often than not, information not suited to public vidphones."

Jake nodded, a mildly painful effort. "I see. Illegal information."

Lita smiled. "Right. So, he sets up a meeting with this guy, but on the first meet he just wants some money. He will not give me such dangerous information without knowing whether I can be trusted. So he has me do a few courier runs for him. I carried a few small packages and so on. That took a few weeks, which is why I was off-base so much."

Jake smiled; another painful effort. "Yes, all that so-called 'window-shopping.' "

Surprisingly, she blushed. "Yes . . . Once he finally decided that he could trust me, he handed me all the data I needed. You now know about the plan to sabotage the sensor grid. Initially, the resistance was going to do it as a large-scale prank. Disrupting shipments, screwing up our schedules, and so on. They figured if they were lucky, it might crash a DropShip."

Once again Jake was baffled by these Inner Sphere people. Crashing a DropShip was a prank? Lita probably noticed the confusion on his face, and hurried to wrap up her story.

"But then the Hell's Horses came in to the picture. They kept a tight lid on their activities, of course, but they gave the resistance piles of weapons and other supplies in exchange for detailed information about Ghost Bear procedures and codes."

Jake thought he could see a hint of tears on her cheeks, but she kept on talking.

"I should have come to you directly with the data, but considering my methods of obtaining it, I decided to try and put a stop to the sabotage myself. As luck would have it, I took my *Mad Dog* out just as you discovered what was going on. By the time I destroyed their explosives and transports, the Hell's Horses invasion was already in full swing and I learned that you had put out a warrant for my arrest."

A twinge of guilt mixed with Jake's persistent pain. "Sorry about that."

Lita laid one hand gently on his shoulder. "Like you said, water under the bridge. Considering the circumstances, I thought the best course was to fight the Horses on my own until I could find you and clear my name in person. With your armor painted the way it is, and all those wonderful open-channel transmissions, you were not hard to locate."

Again, Jake smiled painfully. He realized he had seriously missed her, and it had hurt her more than he could have imagined to be accused of wrong-doing. She sat down again in the chair. "You pretty much know the rest. By the time I made it to Fletcher's headquarters, my 'Mech had been shot out from under me."

"Leaving you to attack a Gnome with a piece of plumbing," Jake said. "Very bold, Star Commander, but next time I advise a more substantial weapon. An I-beam, perhaps."

They both had a good laugh at that one, which trailed off to muffled coughs as they each clutched their injured ribs. "Next time, remind me to stay away from you when I am injured," Lita said. "All this laughing hurts too much."

"I will take that as a compliment."

"Take it however you like, Jake."

Despite his injuries and pain, Jake felt the pressure of the past weeks flowing from his body. It suddenly occurred to him that he had not asked about the fighting. "So, how goes the invasion?"

Lita laughed again, wincing and tearing up with pain. She could barely get the words out. "It is over."

"What?"

"Over. Finished. Complete."

"Since I am here and not on a DropShip somewhere, I take it we won?"

"Yes, sort of."

"Sort of?"

"Well, it depends on what you consider victory," Lita said. "We still control Predlitz, so, in that respect, we most certainly won. But the Horses caused major damage in New

Denver during the attack. Considering the fact that they packed up and retreated off-world of their own accord, I would say we scored a marginal victory at best."

"Retreated?" Jake tried to sit up again, and the chorus of pain reminded him of the doctor's stern advice. He fell back against the pillow. "For Kerensky's sake, why? They held a defensive position. They outnumbered us two-to-one. They had every advantage."

"Every advantage but one: a strong leader," Lita said. "Malavai Fletcher said it himself on the rooftop. Only he could lead this attack. It was his personal crusade, and without him, the enthusiasm for pressing what would surely have proved a losing battle evaporated instantly."

"You mean that once the war with the Combine was over, there would be no way the Horses could stand up to us. You say they lost Fletcher, but his body was not found?"

"He was gravely injured, worse than you, I think."

An image of the pipe slamming into the side of the Khan's head flashed in Jake's mind. "Remind me never to get on your bad side."

"His body was not found near the place where he fell, which leads us to believe the Horses retrieved him first. If we are lucky, he died in transit."

"Neg. I say we are lucky if he survives. A Clan with Malavai Fletcher as Khan is much less dangerous than one with cooler heads prevailing."

"Admit it, Jake. You are only saying that because you want one more re-match with him."

Jake feigned innocence, but it was true that he felt cheated by Fletcher's escape. "Hey, with no battle armor and equal footing, I could take him down."

"I am sure you could, Jake Kabrinski. I am sure you could. Now get some rest. We have a long journey to the jump point." Lita got up to leave.

"Jump point?"

"No one told you? Your bold defense of Predlitz—not to mention the capture of the *Urizen II*—have not gone unnoticed. We have been recalled to the front, on direct orders from Khan Jorgensson himself. Pack your bags, Star Captain. Our DropShip launches tomorrow."

Jake's heart swelled with pride as he raised his hand to stop her from leaving. "Promise me one thing. From now on, we will be totally open with each other about all our activities, no matter how unClanlike they may seem to us at the time."

Lita nodded. "It is a promise I will be proud to keep, Jake Kabrinski."

As the door swung closed behind her, Jake's mind turned to the exciting prospect of returning to front-line duty. To his surprise, the thought of battling Combine warriors—and possibly encountering the DEST woman again—did not hold the old sense of foreboding.

For the first time in a long while, strapped to a hospital bed and nearer to death than he had ever been, Jake felt truly alive.

36

Unity Palace
Imperial City, Luthien
Pesht Military District, Draconis Combine
20 December 3063

Flanked by stone-faced DEST commandos, Ninyu Kerai-Indrahar stepped through the double doors. This office, one of several in the palace, was more Spartan than the others, but its position offered a superb view without seriously compromising security. A hand-carved teak desk dominated the center of the room, its polished wood gleaming in the morning sun that streamed through the floor-to-ceiling windows that served as two of the room's walls.

The office was occupied by one person. Silhouetted against the sunlight, he stood looking out the eastern window, hands clasped behind his back. The man's sheer presence identified him instantly as Theodore Kurita, Coordinator of the Draconis Combine.

Ninyu waited patiently to be addressed by his lord, glancing at his hand-held noteputer for what seemed like the hundredth time today. Then he followed Theodore's gaze out the window.

"Winter has come late this year, Ninyu," Theodore said to the Director of the Internal Security Force without turning from the window. His voice was clear and strong, but Ninyu picked up a strange, melancholy note that was new.

"*Hai,* Kurita-*sama.* And like most late winters, it is cold and harsh. Speaking of winter, I bring news of the Ghost Bears."

At the mention of that most powerful Clan, Theodore turned suddenly and Ninyu was shocked at his appearance. The Coordinator was as tall and trim as ever, but he lacked his usual air of health and vitality. His expression sagged somehow, making his lined face look uncharacteristically tired. Recent events had given Theodore much to do and to think about, but until now, he had always seemed like a seemingly bottomless well of strength.

"The final battle has been arranged, then?" Theodore asked, and Ninyu saw the old spark flash in his eyes.

"*Hai.* Lances from every unit that has fought in the war are arriving on Courchevel now. The Ghost Bears are likewise sending representative stars to face them."

Theodore nodded and accepted the noteputer Ninyu extended toward him. His eyes narrowed as he examined the screen. "Yes, this is as it should be. A fresh start—and a clean end—to this whole affair."

Ninyu was moderately surprised by Theodore's directness, and took his cue from him. "If this battle ends as I predict it will, we will lose Courchevel to the Ghost Bears. The forces arrayed against ours will be too strong for a decisive victory."

"As it was in the beginning, on Alshain." The Coordinator's face took on a dark expression. The shame of the Avengers' renegade assault still troubled him.

"As you requested, *Tai-sho* Minamoto entered into a batchall with the Ghost Bear Khan," Ninyu continued. "We agreed to certain conditions if the Bears win the fight. All other planets captured in their campaign will be returned to Combine control, provided we return the few Dominion planets we seized."

Theodore nodded approval, then turned and walked back to the window. "I was concerned that he might have been too proud to bid as instructed. I am glad that he proved me wrong. Kiyomori Minamoto is a true son of the Combine. He will make a fine Warlord."

And so quickly after his last promotion, thought Ninyu. Minamoto had been content in the Sword of Light for so long, but now he was vaulting up the ranks at a record pace. Perhaps the old general was merely making up for lost time, but perhaps there was more . . .

Despite his misgivings, Ninyu knew better than to voice his concerns directly at this time. Theodore had made up his mind, and at this delicate moment the Dragon could ill afford unnecessary distractions. Ninyu resolved to keep an eye on Minamoto, but the issue at hand was more pressing than mere politics right now.

He risked further directness. "Forgive me for being blunt, my lord, but there are many within the Combine who believe that this battle is a sham."

Theodore gave the faintest hint of a sigh. "Perhaps," he said. "But there are many more who will see it for what it truly is: an honorable end to a dishonorable war."

Eventide Salt Flats, Courchevel
Pesht Military District
Draconis Combine
22 December 3063

With not a single terrain feature to impede its progress, the angry wind howled past the assembled armies. Battle-Mechs, armored vehicles, and battle-armored infantry faced off across a kilometer of parched, cracked land. The two armies stretched out in parallel battle lines, as far as the eye could see in each direction. Neither side made a move to attack the other, as if waiting for the signal to strike.

"I remember battles like this against the Combine, in the early days of Operation Revival," Lita said to Jake over her *Mad Dog*'s radio. "They would line up their forces on one side, and we would line up on the other. At the appointed time, the battle would be joined in a series of one-on-one duels. The Kurita warriors damn near followed the rules of *zellbrigen* back then."

While Lita reminisced, Jake watched the chronometer in the corner of his HUD ticking down the minutes toward the appointed time for this particular battle.

"It was glorious."

"So why do you think that all changed?" he asked.

The radio was silent for a moment as she considered her answer. "To be honest, I blame it all on the Smoke Jaguars. Those *surats* gave the Combine plenty of reasons to truly *hate* the Clans. Once the war was no longer about glory and conquest—but about vengeance—that is when it got ugly."

"This battle brings us full circle, then."

"What do you mean?" Lita asked.

"Why did we start this war?" Jake asked back, checking his chronometer again. In less than five minutes the battle would commence.

Lita sounded outraged. "We did not. The Draconis Combine did, when they attacked Alshain."

"Naked aggression, to be sure. But that was not a war; that was more a large-scale raid. The Ghost Bears responded with war. We wanted revenge for their brutal, all-out assault on our capital."

"So we started this war, then," Lita conceded. "What is your point?"

"The very basis of this war was vengeance, pure and simple. We counterattacked in response to the attack on Alshain. They struck back for those attacks. And so on." Jake's chronometer now showed four minutes to go. Anticipation of the coming battle quickened his heartbeat.

"Aye, it got ugly," Lita said.

"Exactly. I think that is why things bogged down, right before we were . . . reassigned to Predlitz. I think both sides lost their stomach for the war, but neither wanted to accept the loss of face that would come with admitting it."

Three minutes and counting.

Lita ignored Jake's open criticism of their Clan—or perhaps she agreed with it. "That brings us to this battle," he said, "which includes representative forces from every Ghost Bear and Draconis Combine unit that participated in the war. We are all here in spirit, and we can resolve this in true warrior fashion."

"Yes," she said. She was following him now, with two minutes to go. "The way it should have been right from the beginning. But that does not explain how this battle was arranged without loss of face."

"It was not. The Combine was willing to come to us and admit that they were wrong. It was they who sued for peace and suggested this final Trial. The way Gilmour explained it to me, their emissary said they had been 'too blinded by the demands of honor to see the way to duty.' There was also something about 'the Dragon's great time of loss, when honor must give way to duty, and hearts and minds must turn inward.' Something like that. I am not sure what it all means."

Lita chuckled. "The Kuritas are pretty tight-lipped with their press releases, but I think I get the point. It sounds like something big hit them, maybe from the Federated Commonwealth side?"

Jake wondered at the implications of a Federated Commonwealth attack on the Combine so soon after the war with the Ghost Bears, but Lita went on.

"Of course, when they say 'the Dragon,' sometimes they are talking about the Kurita ruling family and sometimes the Combine as a whole—their use of language can be frustratingly vague. If I recall correctly, 'the Dragon' most commonly refers to the person of the Coordinator himself. I wonder . . ."

Jake glanced at his chronometer again. Less than thirty seconds to go. "I am sure we can pick this up later," he cut in. "Right now we have a score to settle."

"Roger that, Star Captain. All points report in ready to go. Hold on tight. This ride could get bumpy."

The thunder of BattleMech footfalls shook the ground beneath Jake Kabrinski's armored feet as duels raged all around him. Missiles exploded gloriously, lasers melted armor, autocannons chattered their staccato rhythms. But to him, all the battlefield chaos was but dreams and ghosts.

Once again, he stood before the object of his fear and obsession for the last twelve months. She was clad in black-enameled Raiden armor, but he had no doubt he was face to face with the same DEST commando who had first defeated him on Idlewind.

He had played this scene in his dreams countless times, but now there was a difference: he was unafraid.

In fact, he felt a strange calm wash through his body as she bowed to him. This time, he followed her tradition and returned the bow.

As the battle raged around them, both stood motionless for a long moment. Jake knew better than to rush headlong into this opponent's clutches, and apparently she felt the same way. Then, when it seemed like the waiting would stretch on into the night, Jake spotted the barest hint of a move: the Raiden's right arm twitched.

He sprang into motion with such speed and fluid precision that he was not consciously aware of his own actions. Simultaneously triggering SRMs and jump jets, he rocketed into the air moments before she fired her laser, deftly avoiding the shot and forcing her to dodge the incoming missiles.

That gave him the time he needed to finish his maneuver. Landing behind and to her left—and thus out of reach of her main weapon—he fired his laser and then jumped again, this time directly over her head.

His shot scored a glancing blow to her left arm, but had the desired effect of keeping her off-balance. Or so it seemed. Turning in mid-air, Jake landed in front of her and fired his second missile salvo. She had already lit her own jump jets, and sailed easily over the attack.

Just as he expected she would.

As she passed over him in a predictable arc, he raised his support laser and fired. The ruby beam scoured armor from her right flank as she flew by, but did not knock her from the air as he had hoped. He turned to face her as she landed. There was a hiss and a pop as the spent missile launcher automatically separated from his back and crashed to the ground.

Jake could have kept up the pressure all afternoon, alternating jumps and attacks. But that would be what she expected him to do, and if he had learned anything from this enigmatic foe, it was *never* to do what your opponent expects.

Ever since he stood on the receiving end of the attack from Malavai Fletcher, Jake had practiced the move over and over in his head, and later in the simulator. Using the powerful myomer muscles in the legs of his suit, he launched into the air, then straightened his legs at a precisely measured angle. He fired his jump jets before he could crash to the ground, propelling himself like a cannon-ball directly at the black Raiden.

Her laser shot went high and wide moments before he impacted, proving that she had anticipated another high jump. Slamming into her at high speed, Jake was treated to the satisfying sound of crumpling armor and cracking bone as his momentum carried her forward until they both hit the hard ground and tumbled unceremoniously to a halt.

Staggering to his feet, Jake turned to face his handiwork. The helmet of her suit had been knocked free, and was just now ceasing its lazy spinning some ten meters to his right. She lay on the ground face-up and feet pointing away from him, but her mass of tangled black hair concealed her face from view. Worst of all, his jump jet-assisted impact had caved in her chest plate along the fault line carved by his laser.

Jake took a half-step forward, then stopped. After all this time, he was not sure he wanted to see what she looked like. As he stood there, her prone form stirred, and then convulsed as she was wracked by a coughing spasm.

He took another half-step forward, this time extending his claw to help her up. She lifted her own suit's claw to wave him off, rolling over onto her belly with a barely audible gasp of pain. Her hair was draped down over her face, caked with blood and dirt, as she slowly got up on one leg, and then the other.

Jake lifted the faceplate of his own helmet. He watched with apprehension as she brushed the hair away from her face with her armor's claw.

Seeing her in the flesh for the first time, Jake was surprised that she was nothing like the beautiful, horrible creature conjured by his nightmares. Blood and grime notwithstanding, she was remarkably . . . normal.

Then, despite the obvious pain it caused her, she bowed very deeply, and held the bow for several long seconds. When she at last straightened, Jake thought he saw—just for a moment—the faintest hint of a smile on her blood-flecked lips.

Only then did he realize that the sounds of battle around him had ceased. As the sun set on the Eventide Salt Flats, the war between Clan Ghost Bear and the Draconis Combine had ended.

And so too had Jake Kabrinski's personal war.

37

Jake tugged again at the corners of his uniform jacket, then resigned himself to live with the perpetual wrinkles. Lita, standing to his right, nudged him with her elbow and laughed. "Give it up, Jake. No one is going to notice your wrinkly uniform in this crowd anyway."

He had to admit she was right. Miraborg Plaza spread out from the planetary capitol in a wide oval, and today it was packed to capacity. They stood among a virtual sea of humanity, an intermingled mass of Ghost Bear military and Gunzburg civilians gathered to witness history in the making.

He looked at Ben, who was standing on his other side. Ben was buffing his Clan Wolf campaign ribbon with the cuff of his jacket. He was beaming with pride. "It was about time we taught those Wolves to mind their manners," he said. "Do you think it is true that they were behind the Hell's Horses attack?"

Jake smiled down at the newly promoted star commander. "We may never know the truth, but it really does not matter now. Without the Combine war to distract us, we were free to deal with our true enemies. Now, the Horses are headed back to Clan space, and the Wolves have a bloody nose to think about before they mess with the Dominion again."

The Combine war. Speaking the words turned Jake's thoughts back to the final battle on Courchevel five months before. It all seemed so very long ago, almost like a dream. One could almost call it a dream, since in the end neither side kept the worlds they had seized from the other. Even the *Urizen II* was returned to the Combine as a gesture of goodwill in response to House Kurita's willingness to bring the conflict to an honorable end.

Of course, it was no dream for those who died in the fighting. The final death tolls were still not in, but Jake knew that both sides had lost many clusters worth of fine troops. So many warriors lost . . .

"Gunzburg is much more than a bloody nose, Jake," Lita said, snapping him out of his momentary flashback. "This was one of Clan Wolf's most amazing victories, why—"

Jake interrupted, pointing up toward the capitol. "No time for a history lesson. Look."

A stage had been erected at the top of the capitol's stairs. Standing there, his face solemn and his body at rigid attention, was a man wearing the uniform of a Ghost Bear star colonel. He began to speak, but the public address system could not possibly compete with the cheering crowd.

Ben stood on tiptoe and strained to hear the speech. "What is he saying?" he said, turning to Jake.

"I know as much as you do, Ben. Did we miss a briefing?"

"I think this is for the masses," Lita said, "not so much for our benefit." She nodded toward the stage. "That man is Star Colonel Ragnar. They say he was ruler of the Free Rasalhague Republic in absentia before he became a bondsman of the Bears. He used to be known as Ragnar Magnussen."

As Lita spoke, Jake looked back toward the capitol, where a guard was pushing an old man in a wheelchair up a ramp onto the stage. The old man wore the uniform of a Rasalhague general, and the festoon of medals and ribbons on his chest indicated his once glorious career.

A quiet settled over the crowd. Bending slightly at the waist, Star Colonel Ragnar handed the old man a small object, spoke a few words, and then snapped to attention. He saluted, bending his arm and touching his flattened palm to his forehead in Inner Sphere style. The old man looked down at the object Ragnar had handed him, then held it up close to his face to inspect it.

Ben leaned across Jake to Lita. "Sunglasses?" Lita shrugged helplessly.

The old man carefully tucked the glasses into his breast pocket and returned the salute, then both turned toward the flagpole over the capitol. As everyone watched, two flags were being hoisted into position. One was familiar, a blue field emblazoned with a roaring white bear's head against a radiating star of six claws. The other displayed a blue shield bearing a gnarled, snake-like dragon.

Jake did not have Lita's knowledge of the Inner Sphere, but even he recognized it as the flag of the Free Rasalhague Republic.

Both men on the stage saluted, and Jake, Ben, and Lita obediently followed suit. To Jake's surprise, the flags were being raised simultaneously, and stopped at precisely the same height. A roar of approval thundered from the crowd, and fireworks exploded overhead while a pair of *Batu* fighters streaked by, adding sonic booms to the cheering.

Lita tapped Jake's arm. "That old man was the ruler of this planet before it was conquered by Clan Wolf," she shouted above the din. "Now that we have liberated it from the Wolves, it looks as though the Khan has returned him to power under our Dominion."

Ben looked completely baffled. "But what does it all mean?"

Jake looked over at him. "I think it means that nothing will ever be the same for Clan Ghost Bear."

All around him Jake saw happy faces, Ghost Bear and civilian alike. He realized that he was happy too, excited at the prospect of an unknown—but bright—future. And he owed it all to a certain tiny Kurita commando and his own test of vengeance.

Epilogue

Hell's Horses Council Chamber
Fort Gehenna, Niles
Kerensky Cluster, Clan Space
12 August 3064

Khan Malavai Fletcher stood alone at the center of the circular council chamber. All around him the Bloodnamed of
Clan Hell's Horses sat in solemn silence, a sea of black and
red uniforms and ashen faces. Although their lips said nothing, their cold eyes spoke volumes.

The heavy, iron-bound oak doors of the chamber
slammed shut behind saKhan Tanya DeLaurel as she strode
into the room to stand before her Khan. Tall for a Mech-
Warrior, she carried herself with an air of superiority that
was rightly earned through tactical brilliance, but that
Fletcher thought ill-suited to this occasion.

This farce would end now. Despite the rage in his heart,
he forced himself to speak calmly. "I, Malavai Fletcher, am
Khan of this Clan. How is it that *I* am summoned to appear
before *you*?"

Tanya speared him with her gray eyes, then her eyes
went cold. "You have been summoned here on a matter of
grave importance, Malavai Fletcher. A matter brought to the
attention of the Clan Council by Star Colonel James Cobb."

She nodded toward a tall, blond Elemental sitting in the

front row, and he stood up. "I call for a vote of no-confidence in Khan Malavai Fletcher," he said in a clear, almost musical voice.

A buzz of murmurs erupted throughout the chamber, echoing in the high-domed room as they built in intensity to an all-out shouting match. Fletcher thumped his prosthetic right leg against the floor, calling for order. When the noise died down, he turned to James Cobb, pointing his finger accusingly.

"No-confidence, indeed! I made this Clan what it is today, and you dare come here and try to rob me of my station by stabbing me in the back?"

Cobb took a step toward the wooden railing separating him from the council floor, then vaulted over it with ease. An Elemental himself, James Cobb stood nearly eye to eye with Fletcher as he spoke. "You certainly did make the Clan what it is today. Let us take a look at your accomplishments, *quiaff*?

"You did manage to contract with Clan Wolf to stake a claim in the Inner Sphere, then you squandered that foothold in an insane crusade against your personal nemesis, the Ghost Bears."

Fletcher could contain his anger no longer. He took a step toward Cobb. "Insane crusade?" he roared. "How *dare* you. Had I not taken over from that weakling Lair Seidman, the Hell's Horses would have been Absorbed years ago. Never forget that!"

Cobb folded his muscular arms defiantly across his chest. "How *can* I forget it? That is your only defense for actions that now threaten to destroy our Clan from within."

Fletcher met Cobb's defiance with a raised fist. "Coward! There will be no vote today. Or do you lack the spine to challenge me and be done with it?"

Cobb's blue eyes narrowed, but that was the only hint of emotion on his face. "So be it, Malavai Fletcher. I challenge you to a Trial of Possession for the rank of Khan, to be ratified by the Bloodnamed of this Clan after your death, in accordance with Clan law."

Fletcher let his fist drop to his side almost without realizing he did. His pulse thrummed so loudly in his ears that it almost blotted out all other sounds. He looked up into the stands, searching for and, at last, finding Alicia Ravenwater. For the briefest of moments, she held his gaze. Then her expression turned from admiration to fear, and she averted her eyes.

He could take no more.

Fletcher rushed toward Cobb, drawing the ceremonial sword at his hip and slashing down and to the right. "After my death! After *my* death?" he screamed, no longer in control of his words or actions.

Cobb dodged the wild swing easily. He pulled his own sword and slashed at Fletcher's leg as he came around from behind. His blade drew a line of blood as he stepped back and struck a fighting stance. Fletcher turned to face him.

"Admit it, Malavai," Cobb said, with a fleeting look in his eyes that might have been sadness. "You are mad and unfit for duty. You owe your Clan, at least."

Never! "I owe you nothing but *death*, James Cobb!"

As Fletcher lunged forward, Cobb slapped the blade aside with his wrist. The thrust drew blood, but opened the way for Cobb's riposte. Fletcher's momentum carried him forward as James Cobb sank the blade of his sword into his chest to the hilt.

Fletcher staggered a step back, then reached to pull the blade from his chest with a mighty effort of will. Blood poured from the wound. He looked down at his bloody uniform, and then up at the warriors surrounding him. His mouth opened, but no sound came out. The light began to fade as Fletcher sank to his knees, grasping his chest with both hands as though that would be enough to hold off his end.

He looked up at Cobb, who stared back with a look of pained resignation. Now, in his final moments, clarity came to Fletcher. With that clarity came strange, alien thoughts.

Perhaps he was meant to die that fateful day on Niles. Perhaps the radical surgery and prosthetics that kept him alive had kept his Clan from following its true destiny. He was dying, of that he was certain. So he would never know the truth of it.

As he drew his last breath, Malavai Fletcher spoke to his

executioner in a harsh whisper filled with blood and spittle. "Succeed where I have failed, Khan James Cobb . . . Punish the Wolves for using us . . . and punish the Ghost Bears for . . . using . . . me."

All around him now was blackness, but he was lifted on a wave of sound, a single word that began to carry him down a dark river. Around him, a hundred voices spoke as one. "*Seyla.*"

About the Author

BRYAN WILHELM NYSTUL was born in Chicago, Illinois, and has lived there his entire life (not counting a brief misadventure in Austin, Texas . . . but that's another story). His parents, fans of fantasy and science fiction literature, introduced him to *Dungeons & Dragons* at the tender age of seven, and countless other games of all types and genres followed, from *Cosmic Encounter* to *Champions* to Avalon Hill's *Civilization*. (There were even some games that did not start with the letter C!)

Not only did all this gaming *not* rot his developing brain, it gave him the skills and experience necessary to snag an editorial job at Mayfair Games, Inc. in 1992. After working on the *Underground, Role-Aids,* and *DC Heroes* lines, Bryan moved to FASA Corp. to become their BattleTech Developer in 1994. From then until the year 2000, he coordinated the BattleTech® universe across all of its many media, and was directly responsible for all BattleTech® "paper-gaming" products as well as the overall plot contained in books like the one you hold in your hands (his first novel, incidentally). Among his proudest professional achievements (so far) is the planning and coordination of the *Twilight of the Clans* series of novels.

With no spouse, offspring or pets to mention on this page (assuming invisible friends and dust bunnies don't count), Bryan felt compelled to tell you a little something about his personal interests. In his spare time, he is a computer game junkie, likes watching movies and listening to music, has an inexplicable fascination with historical and scientific reference books, enjoys hanging out with his niece Lauren and tickle-torturing his nephew Jim, misses his dear departed *Kids in the Hall* and *Mystery Science Theater 3000,* and can't get enough of *The Simpsons*.

Summoner

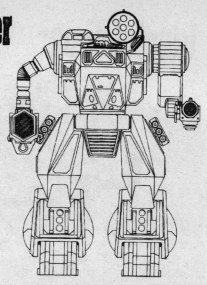

Nova

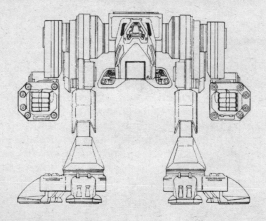

Black Lanner

Timber Wolf

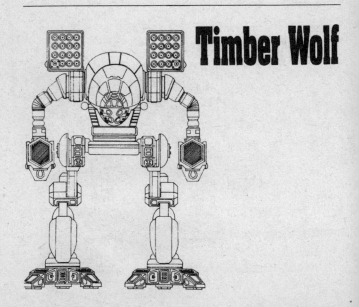

Elemental

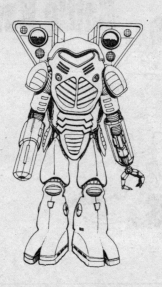

Shadow Cat

Battle Hawk

Salamander

(0451)

More Deep-Space Action & Intrigue From
BATTLETECH®

PATH OF GLORY *by Randall N. Bills*
(458079)
When the Nova Cat Clan is forced to ally with the Inner Sphere it forces two
MechWarriors from different worlds into a precarious friendship. For Zane
and Yoshio, the line between ally and enemy will be drawn in blood. . . .

ILLUSIONS OF VICTORY *by Loren L. Coleman*
(457900)
Solaris VII, home of the ultimate sporting event—war. Now, ancient
grudges have reached beyond the arena and given rise to a championship
match where the winner is the last man alive.

MEASURE OF A HERO *by Blaine Lee Pardoe*
(457943)
As the fires of rebellion burn on Thorin, a local militia leader holds the fate
of the world in his hands...

To order call: 1-800-788-6262